CW00495810

LIFE

Rob & Phil Edwards

www.lifedivine.co.uk

Rob & Phil Edwards

Decorum
Productions

www.decorumproductions.com

All rights reserved; no part of this publication may be
reproduced or transmitted by any means, electronic,
mechanical, photocopying, telepathically or otherwise
without the prior permission of the authors.

All characters are the sole property of the authors.
Copyright and trademark © Decorum Productions 2011

ISBN-13: 978-1460956588
ISBN-10: 1460956583

www.lifedivine.co.uk

Life Divine

A *Decorum* Book

LIFE DIVINE

Foreword:

Inspired by the many stories told and experienced over the years, set against the back drop of the brass band world we set about writing 'Life Divine'. A concept book due to its structure, and a story of family life where the reader need not have any experience of the brass band world. We have tried hard to ensure that those people 'in the know' feel rewarded and those who simply love a comedy, with elements of tragedy, feel they are accepted without a need for prior knowledge. Hopefully, the book will also teach people something about the music referred to as well, and may even inspire them to listen.

'Life Divine' is one of many 'test pieces' used to judge bands' performances at contests. Each chapter is named after a test piece whose title has some relevance to the story; adding to the readers knowledge of this world of brass bands.

Decorum semper

Rob & Phil Edwards 2011

Chapter 1

Music For A Common Man

(Kenneth Downie)

Perhaps it was because the cold, dark, cloudless January night sky stirred nostalgic, comforting feelings of childhood winters. Perhaps it was simply human nature to find contentment and familiarity in tradition. All Harry Jones knew, as he strode across the coach-park of Swansea's majestic Brangwyn Hall towards the coach waiting to whisk an elated Midtown Silver Band back home, was that he had seldom experienced the pride, the euphoria, and the sheer sense of triumph that now coursed through him.

A mere two hours earlier, the main auditorium, spectacularly decorated in the most imposing traditional style complete with huge oil-paintings and intricately ornate ceilings, almost had its roof raised as the final band to compete had concluded its awesome and resounding offering of this year's test-piece. Minutes later, the resulting applause, mixed with the echoing final bars, had been replaced by the longest, agonisingly tense silence imaginable as over 500 bandsmen, conductors and supporters waited for the formally-dressed officials on stage to announce the results of the contest. Nothing ever changed, year in year out. The ambient noise, the unique smell of the polished floors, the faces of the senior representatives of the brass-band organisation, all seemed to have been there forever. The silence had continued, the tension increasing in parallel. Everyone present knew that only the bands which achieved either 1st or 2nd place would qualify to appear at the coveted national finals in London, later in the year. As 4th, then 3rd place was announced, the cheering of the respective winners had given gave way to new heights of tantalizing expectation as silence once again reigned, the remaining bands not daring to breathe until the final, most crucial, two results had been revealed. Harry had stood at the back of the packed hall, knowing that Midtown had delivered a winning performance, but wondering if the adjudicator would agree. He'd looked around, spotting Midtown players dotted throughout the hall, transfixed, hands over mouths as though trying to contain outbursts of nervous emotion.

"And in 2nd place, going through to the national finals", the adjudicator had begun, "the band that played no.3; Midtown Silver!"

Harry had not heard the thunderous cheering straightaway.

A combination of senses had engulfed his entire body like a bolt of electricity passing through him. A wall of delighted, almost manic faces had rushed towards him, fists aloft, tears in eyes. He felt himself jolt forward as someone actually jumped on his back and shook his shoulders in an instinctive display of congratulation. And only then, did his brain catch up with the overload of information, and the almost deafening applause hit him like a sledgehammer.

Following the result, he had not yet had a chance to speak to the band as a whole. The last he'd seen of them was almost an hour ago as 20 Midtown players exited the bar in a conga-line led by percussionist Lawrence Ap Dafydd, all singing "We're on our way to Lon-don, we're on our way to Lon-don, the Al-bert Hall, the Al-bert Hall, yes!" And this was why Harry now made his way to the coach; he and his wife Mary had driven to Swansea by car, intending to "kill two birds with one stone" by staying with family for the remainder of the weekend, about 40 miles away in Cefngoed. However, Harry would not dream of leaving without a few valedictory words following the tremendous result. Amongst the rows of coaches, all preparing to commence their respective journeys home, the atmosphere in some ecstatic, others deflated, Harry could see the Midtown coach, instantly recognisable by its silver livery, the words "Wyn D. Day Travel", followed by their slogan "Travel with us, by coach not bus!" Even from 50 yards away, he could see the unmistakable silhouette of bass player Steve Pepper, standing next to the driver's seat, using the coach's public address microphone to lead the 40 occupants in a chorus of "Delilah", complete with ad-lib harmonies.

Harry walked around to the front left-hand door, and pulled the vertical handle. The door hissed open, and he alighted, walking slowly up the three steps to where Steve Pepper stood. Steve ceased singing, everyone else suddenly trailed off into expectant silence in response to Harry's appearance. Harry stood, lips tightly pursed, observing the 40 passengers.

"Our Father", Steve's solemn voice crackled out of the coach's speakers, "who art in Heaven..." 40 voices suddenly joined in, years of tradition dictating their role, "Harold be thy name!" followed by a prolonged cheer that literally rocked the coach. Harry's lips transformed into an impossibly broad grin, as he looked at the floor, head shaking slightly and palm aloft, modestly motioning everyone to calm down so he could speak. "Who wishes they'd stayed at home and watched Emmerdale Farm instead of coming to band practice now?"

he began, to be instantly answered with a round of applause and a series of whistles.

"Seriously though" he continued "we played the piece better than we've ever played it today, and win or lose you should all be proud of that. According to this, there was only 1 point between us and the band that came 1st"; Harry held up a copy of the adjudicator's synopsis of their performance, "so I don't want anyone dwelling on what we could have done better. The fact is, the band that beat us was excellent, they only beat us by one point, and we couldn't have played better than we did today." Another cheer filled the coach.

"Every one of you should feel very proud of yourself", Harry continued, "Particular congratulations, it says here, go to the 2nd and 3rd cornets during the staccato passage. Where's Mr. Lightfoot?"

About half way along the coach, a small boy stood up. Norman Lightfoot, youngest member of Midtown Band, lived in a council flat with his mum, never missed a practice, may not have the best trainers or latest video-games but in the Bandroom he felt like a king, and today more than ever he was a winner. He was one of the original members of Harry's learner-class, had been lent a battered cornet, which he treasured, and to him, the band boys and particularly Harry, were like family.

"We wouldn't be going to London in October if you hadn't played your best today", Harry factually stated, "and that goes for the two Dans as well. Where are they?" Two 2nd Cornet players also stood up. The three players, chests puffed up, grinned all over their faces.

"Now, let's have 3 cheers for these boys, and for all of you!" Three cheers followed, led by Steve Pepper, still on the microphone, and Harry concluded, "No practice next week, but remember, Rhyl's coming up so be thinking about that. But for now, have a good trip home. And Toby, for God's sake try and keep your trousers on!"

The band erupted into applause and laughter, cheering Harry once again as he waved and stepped off the coach. The engine fired into life, and a waving Harry, cutting a solitary figure in the swiftly emptying coach-park, disappeared from view as the band made their way onto the main road, and the 3-hour journey home.

Harry watched the red tail-lights disappear from view along the wide street-lit busy road, and could only speculate about the shenanigans that would ensue on the way back to Midtown. It was why he would encourage anyone to be involved with brass-bands. Yes, it was about the music of course, but it was also about the memories, the experiences, the friendships and the joy. To Harry, anyone who was not part of this world was missing out, and he truly couldn't understand why anyone would want to do that. He'd enjoyed his 45th birthday the previous year, and brass bands had been in his blood since one Christmas, when he was around 7 years old, having come downstairs in his flannel pyjamas to see the presents he had been given, laid out on the settee in the front room, only to discover, after tearing off the wrapping paper, a bottle of valve oil and a mute. It was a story he often told his children, James and Emily, both members of Midtown Silver Band, who had always thought he was joking.

The sound of footsteps walking across the coach-park caused Harry to turn around. Mary, love of his life, though he would never it admit to her or anyone else, stood in front of him. She was Harry's wife of 22 years, and a self-confessed "band widow".

"Better hit the road then love", she said grinning, "Bet you can't to wait to tell your Mam the result."

"I still can't believe it", said Harry, "Midtown Band are going to the Albert Hall!"

Mary put her arm through Harry's and they both started walking back towards the Brangwyn Hall, around the back of which their car was parked. The Hall now seemed strangely peaceful, as if it were enjoying the fact it could now relax after a hard day's work. Mary and Harry wandered leisurely around its perimeter in the chilly evening air, chatting about who they'd bumped into that day, which bands they'd heard, and of course Midtown's dazzling performance and superb result. As they reached the car and sat inside, Mary glanced at her watch.

"We might just make it to Cefngoed before A Fish Called Rhondda shuts"

"Lovely", said Harry rubbing his hands. He started the car, switched the lights on and turned the heater up.

Mary had one priority in life; the happiness of her family. She knew Harry was happy as long as he was living, eating and sleeping brass-bands. James was happy as long as he was dreaming about being somewhere else. Emily was happy as long as she was making plans, studying, and trying to map out her entire future. The family had always been a happy one. Mainly because everyone understood that band came first. Mary knew that on the rare occasions they went out with friends or had people over, Harry wouldn't be talking about the day they met or what James and Emily were doing now. He would be telling everyone how happy he was that time he was standing in line for the toilet at Treorchy Town Hall and Nick Childs, conductor of the legendary Black Dyke Mills Band, had said, "Excuse me" as he tried to get past. In reality Harry had just stood there of course, mouth wide open, but over the years embellishments to this event had reached the point where him and Nick had discussed for some time the intricacies of circular breathing, and Nick had gone away with Harry's advice on how best to play the last ten bars of Cavalleria Rusticana.

Of course, Mary knew Harry better than anyone, and she'd been there at the origins of this love, this passion, this obsession with banding.   Harry had been brought up in Cefngoed, a mining town in South Wales, where the terraced housing clung to the impossibly steep hillside and was overshadowed by the black coal heap mountain to the north of the town. During autumn and winter, the earthy smell of coal fires wafted through the mist, and the black mountain which dominated the town rose out of the swirling leaves. The roads in and out of the town-centre were steep, and in the bitter cold of winter, exposed on a mountainside, it felt merciless. Getting into the band-room and the chapel really had offered salvation! Dedication to the Salvation Army and its brass band were the cornerstones of life in the town. Harry's dad had played tenor horn in the band, while his mum played the organ in the Army hall. Harry had often proudly said, in response to Emily and James' exhaustive Christmas-present requests over the years, that he didn't have any toys when he was a boy just a home-made catapult, and a cornet. Emily, James, and even Mary never knew if this was altogether true, but knowing Harry, they had to consider it a possibility!

But what Mary knew to be absolutely true was that Harry had spent his childhood in band-rooms rather than playgrounds. When he had become a teenager, and he and his dad became more and more silent with each other, the only time he felt close to his dad was sitting next to him listening to the International Staff Band playing the Pines of Rome by Ottorino Respighi at St. David's Hall, Cardiff. As the music evoked the ceaseless marching Roman army looming towards them, and the tremendous crescendo had built to a point where the audience felt they may be crushed by the sound, Harry's dad had been overwhelmed enough by the occasion to lean over and whisper,

"You could have joined the staff band you know, you were good enough"

Harry had felt so proud he could have burst, and his applause at the end was as much for his own happiness as for the players on stage. So, to Harry, brass bands were not just part of life, they were life. They were an essential ingredient to who Harry was. If you cut him in half, like a stick of Porthcawl rock, he would have Midtown Silver Band written through him, because now, at the age of forty five, Harry was musical director, taking Midtown into a year of contests which would hopefully see them go into the first section of the brass-band league for the first time in the band's history. He had brought this band a long way since he took over, and this year was to be the culmination of that dedication. Of course in Harry's dreams, he may one day take them into the Championship Section.

Mary grinned as Harry drove the car towards Cefngoed, drumming the steering-wheel with his fingers, humming various snippets of the test-piece, and only pausing to recount the events of the day. Mary was happy to listen. She had to admit that even though there's a line to be drawn between passion and obsession, banding was infectious. There was always something going on, and life with Harry was never boring!

"Hey, tell you what Love", she said to Harry, "instead of getting chips, shall we see if we can get a nice meal at the Old Mill? We haven't done that for years".

"We could do", Harry deviated from his half-hummed, half-whistled rendition of the test-piece, "although I was hoping to pop in the Dragon. Some of the Cefngoed Band boys are bound to be in there tonight. You don't mind if I get out there, you can drive the car up to my Mam's house and pick the chips up on the way!"

"No, I don't mind", said Mary, "perhaps we'll see about going to the Old Mill for lunch tomorrow before heading back home."

"Yeah maybe Love, maybe", Harry automatically responded, his mind now once again captivated by the call-and-response section during the 2nd movement.

Mary knew there was little chance they'd be dining out this weekend. If she had suggested, however, they somehow get to Glasgow before midnight in order to attend a special concert by Brighouse & Rastrick, she suspected Harry would have inexplicably summoned up the resources to not only get them tickets, but also transport and accommodation within the next half-hour. And as they headed towards their childhood town this reflection was heightened as she remembered a more romantic and unpredictable side of Harry that she seemed to see less and less of with each year that passed.

As conductor and wife were sedately cruising into Cefngoed, the band coach meandered northwards, traversing the increasingly deserted roads with a surefooted dignity, while playing host to what could only be described as a mobile nightclub. Steve Pepper's CD of party anthems boomed through the stereo accompanied by the uninhibited tuneless bellowing of "Cel-e-brate good times, come on!" at propitious moments from half of the passengers. The other half were either eating, drinking, involved with the poker-school near the back seat, or attempting to relax; notable amongst whom was tired and disgruntled bass trombone player Carl Davis, struggling to get comfortable as he sat next to an ecstatic and animated Owain Owain's mum, also percussionist Ieuan Efans who was actually stretched out on the floor in the aisle, somehow managing to be fast asleep.

"Party at your house tonight then Jim?" shouted cornet player Michael Keys.

"No chance", replied James Jones, "they'd kill me if they found out!" He referred to his parents, Harry and Mary. James was 22, played Solo Euphonium, and had been left in charge of not only the house, but 17-year-old sister Emily who sat a few seats behind.

"Too right they will", interjected Emily, "plus it's me that would probably be cleaning up afterwards!"

"Yeah, actually it would be", James agreed, resulting in laughter from Michael, and a rolling of eyes from Emily.

"Bet your dad's over the moon though", continued Michael, "he put me in a headlock and rubbed the top of my head on the way out of the hall!"

"Yeah well, there'll be no parties at our house tonight", concluded Emily, "not by a long shot."

"Chalk!" a yet further irritated Carl suddenly shouted over from his seat.

"Uh?" Emily looked over at him quizzically as he stretched, scowled and generally exuded an air of tired impatience.

"I said Chalk!" Carl repeated in clipped, slightly lowered tones.

James nudged Roger, his fellow euphonium player who was sat next to him, "Why's Carl saying Chalk?", as though he was experiencing some kind of self-doubt, like some vital part of the conversation had gone over his head.

"Dunno mate", a well-oiled Roger muttered, peering through drunken half-closed eyes, throat slightly sore from singing for the last hour, "Carl, why you saying Chalk all the time 'butt?'', he enquired across the aisle.

"Because it's one of those things that annoys me, that's all", Carl shouted back over the melee of the coach.

"God, just one of the things that annoy him?" James said under his breath.

Roger, unable to completely comprehend what was being said, asked "Why does chalk annoy you? It's really useful. You can write stuff with it, you can...well you can write stuff with it..."

"It's not chalk that annoys me", Carl answered.

"Why say it does then?" an observing and confused Emily interjected, "and what's it got to do with a party at our house?"

"I didn't say chalk annoyed me", Carl snapped.

"You did", said Roger, "I heard you, just a minute ago. I don't know what you've got against chalk..."

A slightly high pitched voice pierced the din of music, multiple-conversations, singing, cheering and general bon viveur; "For the love of Peter, can you lot stop saying Chalk all the time? I'm trying to sleep. Do you mind?" Ron Titley, sitting a few seats in front of James was craning his head over the top of his seat, face scrunched into a pale, wrinkled, rudely-awakened grimace.

"No, we don't mind Ron", James replied, "you go ahead and sleep."

Roger sniggered childishly and obviously, Emily in the seat behind James also giggled out loud.

"Well just stop saying chalk then. It's going straight into my head like a drill", and with that Ron disappeared from view.

"What I said", continued Carl, "is that that the saying is *not by a long chalk*, not a long *shot*. That's all I'm saying. A long shot is something that's unlikely, sort of thing."

"Fascinating that is Carl", Roger replied.

"Yes, well it's like should *of* and could *of*, instead of should *have* and could *have*", Carl continued. "Why can't people talk properly?"

The members of Midtown Silver Band's bass section, who were all sat a few seats back, all seasoned drinkers and experienced in late-night tired coach journeys, could sense that the evening had reached the point where the initial euphoria would potentially give way to general irritability. Eric Trefelyn threw his playing cards onto the pile, slid 10 matches towards Terry Horner, who then stood up and shouted;

"Hey Drive, let's pull over at the next services shall we?" There was a clap of agreement from most of the other passengers, and the opening bars of "We Built This City On Rock And Roll" was briefly interrupted by the driver's voice as he announced "No problem, there's one in about 10 miles". Another round of applause followed.

Motorway services have an atmosphere and culture all of their own, particularly as it gets later into the night. An underclass of failed hospitality-industry employees carry out their endless, depressing tasks, as though even this provided some welcome distraction from the inconsequential drudgery and woe that represented their home lives. The band coach pulled into an almost empty car-park and drew to a halt. A brief announcement from Ron Titley instructed "Everyone back in 30 minutes, those that aren't get left behind. Thank you."
And with that the 40 passengers filed off the coach, the last of whom was Toby Stephens who had taken the opportunity to stand on his seat and retrieve his trousers which had been hanging out of the sunroof since Merthyr Tydfil. "Nobheads!" yelled Toby to the culprits, as they walked across to the main building of the Services.
James and Emily walked together, trying to decide whether they actually wanted anything. In any case it was a good opportunity to stretch their legs and take in some fresh air.

Emily decided she wanted to make a phone call, and went off in search of the public phones. James wondered if she was ringing this "mystery bloke" that she was apparently seeing, and about whom she'd been noticeably cagey to Harry, Mary and even her brother.

James decided to sit down and have a coffee, so caught up with Terry Horner who was making a determined bee-line for an area entitled "Munch a Mynd!", which was what looked like their own in-house burger-bar.

"One coffee please", James shouted optimistically in the direction of a disinterested-looking girl dressed in an overall which inaccurately displayed "I want to help!" Without a word, she walked over to the large chrome machine, extracted a cup of coffee from it, and placed it on the counter in front of James.

"How much is that please?" enquired a cheery James. The girl just pointed at the Drinks section of a menu on the counter top. James handed her £1.50. The girl took it and walked over to the cash-register. Again without a word.

"Thanks then!" shouted James sarcastically, as Terry stood; hand quizzically on chin, still trying to decide what to order.

"Right", he finally announced, "Oi, Miss Happy, can you take my order?"

The girl trudged back over, placed her hands on the counter top and raised an expectant eyebrow.

"I'll have two of those Pedwar Burgers"; he began, pointing at the pictures above the counter, "large chips, and a diet coke."

"It's not Coke", mumbled the girl, "it's Munch a Mynd Cola. Is that alright?"

"As long as it's diet", Terry confirmed, "as long as it's diet."

The other players were wandering round the Services, mostly visiting the toilets, using the phones, or in the small amusement arcade. Emily was standing at a phone, chatting in hushed tones, turning her head away if anyone walked past. The girls in the band suspected she was seeing someone, and a resulting rumour had circulated, however Emily had yet to confirm or deny the truth in it.

"I've got to be up at 8 tomorrow", Terry Horner chatted to James while simultaneously directing copious amounts of burger and chips into his mouth, "taking little Jack to a Cubs day out."

James was reminded of the time he had flirted with the idea of joining Cubs, many years ago. As a ten year old, he had come running into the lounge to find no-one there. He'd shouted for his dad and heard the muffled reply from the bathroom upstairs. Excitedly he'd ran up the stairs, and burst into the bathroom hitting his dad with the door,

"Watch what you're doing!", Harry had barked in his deep South Welsh accent and continued, not with washing or shaving, or other perceived bathroom activities, but to pull a cloth through the tubing of a deconstructed cornet lying in a bath filled with three or four inches of water, a tumble of springs, valves and slides surrounding it, looking to the untrained eye like nothing but an incomprehensible mess of brass tubing. James had been with his friends all morning and they had decided to ask their parents if they could all go to Cub Scouts together,

"Dad, can I go to Cubs with Carl and Tam?" James had asked.

"I suppose…when is it?" Harry had reached a particularly tricky intersection of pipes and was twisting the cloth to get right into it.

"It's on Monday nights", James had cautiously answered.

Harry had tutted, shook his head and briefly looked up from his cleaning,

"Well Monday night's Junior Band night 'innit? How's that going to work?"

And that was it. James had known there'd be no discussion. Harry had not actually said no, just made it seem obvious there'd only really be one inevitable outcome. That was it for James and Emily and anyone else in Harry's life. If it clashed with band practice forget it. Weddings, funerals, christenings, all had been missed if there was a concert or contest on the same day. And if it was Black Dyke band playing then you may as well put the world on hold, as Harry would put his "Black Dyke blinkers" on, seemingly not hear anything else, and proceed with tunnel vision to the concert hall. "Alright is he, little Jack?" James replied, as Terry polished off the last crumb of burger and chips.

"Yeah, he's right into it mate. Arkala this, and dib-dib that, I haven't got a clue what he's on about half the time. Right then, time for a quick fag then back to the bus". And with that, Terry stood up, let out a deep unashamed belch, punched his chest once, and loped off towards the exit. James gulped down the remainder of his coffee and headed for the gents' toilet, catching a glimpse of Emily as he walked past the public phones, still chatting away.

There seemed to be Midtown Silver Band players scattered all over the Services as Ron Titley appeared, striding through the main thoroughfare pointing at his watch. The younger lads hurriedly finished their arcade games, those standing outside stubbed out their cigarettes, and everyone else was already back on the coach or wandering back chatting. The break had managed to calm everyone's spirits a little, and although still enraptured with the day's finale, everyone was pleased to get back on the warm coach, their seats somehow seemed suddenly more comfortable and inviting; the windows provided a welcome cocoon from the blackness of the outside world as everyone settled down for the remainder of the journey home.

James closed his eyes, sat back in his seat, and looked forward to a relaxing Sunday. He had some work lined up for Monday. He'd been enjoying a "gap-year" for the last 4 years, much to his parents' annoyance who had big dreams of him going to university, was at the moment temping, for want of a better term, and seemed to be inadvertently carving out a career as a delivery driver with a local courier firm. He was saving up to go travelling, convinced there was more to life than Midtown, and was sure his biggest obstacle wouldn't so much be the financial aspect, more telling Harry that he wouldn't be in band for the duration! Emily reflected on the phone call she'd just made. Mam and Dad would certainly not approve. There was an age difference, not to mention the fact she was right in the middle of her A-level courses. Still, she was also looking forward to chilling out tomorrow. Although her brother would be at home, she would basically have the house to herself until Mary and Harry returned in the evening. Her dad had already registered his irritation at the fact that she'd missed some band engagements and rehearsals over the past few weeks, and a day without having to wonder if there'd be any more questions about it was just what the doctor ordered. She hoped that Harry and Mary would soon start treating her more as an adult. She knew it was unfortunate that her new boyfriend was usually only free on Band nights, which meant she would have to miss the inevitable practice, but she felt that she'd tried to keep this to a minimum, often at the expense of driving over to see him. Something her dad had said as a throwaway comment did keep niggling her though; "How come we never see him over here then? When will it be his turn to miss something and come and see you?" So Emily too closed her eyes and dozed, helped on her way by the subtle motion of the coach.

Many of the passengers were still asleep as the silver and blue monolith passed the outskirts of Midtown at around

1am, through the deserted town centre, and out the other side towards the factories, nestled amongst which was the Bandroom. A surreal sight greeted the 40 passengers as the coach rumbled to a halt and the door once again hissed open; around 100 people stood in the eerie half-light of the car-park, partially illuminated by the escaping beams of fluorescent strips through the open Bandroom doors. As the first tired players stepped off the coach, shivering as the cold air hit them, they were greeted by an enthusiastic cheer. A combination of parents and spouses waiting to collect their loved ones, and band supporters to whom the Midtown grapevine had spread following phone calls home from the Service station a couple of hours ago. News had already circulated that for the first time in the band's history, it would be competing at the Royal Albert Hall later in the year, and the diverse group of bleary-eyed, pasty faced players who now wanted nothing more than to crash out in their own beds were the heroes of the hour. Emily stepped out onto the gravel and was given a congratulatory cuddle by Steve Pepper's wife Gilly. As James's feet touched the car-park and he walked over to join Emily, he too was congratulated as the waiting crowd basked in the reflected glory. He somehow couldn't help considering, following his earlier conversation with Terry, that although he was the Solo Euphonium player in a band that would be appearing on stage at the Albert Hall, he still had no idea what a woggle was or how to tie a running bowline.

Chapter 2

Judges Of The Secret Court (Hector Berlioz)

On the outskirts of Midtown, on the site of the old dairy, stood The Bandroom. In the middle of a gravel car-park, accessible through what amounted to little more than a gap in the hedge alongside the main road, it was simply there. James had decided to walk to the meeting, enjoying a quick livener in The Castell Coch en-route, and fully intending to have another on the way home later. As the rows of shops and houses gave way to a more industrial domain, where factory roofs were just visible over the hedge tops, and the last of the streetlights bade farewell to visitors, James trudged along, hands in pockets, taking in the evening air and contemplating the question that seemed to dominate his every thought these days, "What if I just buggered off somewhere and left all this behind?" Between two small industrial parks a dropped-curb, a very faded wooden sign in the shape of an arrow literally pointed the way to "Midtown Silver Band". James turned into the car-park and noted the familiar array of vehicles ranging from Rachel Parry's brand new company- BMW, to Steve Pepper's ancient, bright yellow and omnipresent Volvo estate. James grinned as he walked past it. It was like

Steve had always owned that Volvo, and it had faithfully heaved Steve, and his bass, to most band functions since James could remember; a not particularly exclusive car, as much as a plodding workhorse. They say pets grow to resemble their owners, and James wondered if it was the same with cars, pausing only to consider the irony that Steve, probably the least religious person James knew, had never bothered to remove the "Honk If Jesus Saved You" sticker on the back window, obviously placed there by some previous owner, along with "I Love John O'Groats". There was also a car James didn't know; a newish dark blue Vauxhall Vectra whose registration ended with the letters "ANL". "Retentive?" thought James. His daydreams were concluded as he approached the front door of the Bandroom, light dimly penetrating the net-curtains and dust on every window, and two shadowy figures standing in the porch, resembling colluding Russians in a 1960's spy movie. Eric Trefelyn and Terry Horner, respectively hurrying a cigarette and the remains of a hot-dog procured from the whimsically but one-time-accurately named "Sam and Ella's" burger van located near the factories down the road.

"Jim-eee", sang Terry, his voice lowering in tone on the "eee" part.

"Alright butt?" gasped Eric, finishing his fag, dropping it on the gravel outside the porch and treading on it.

"Hiya boys," replied James, "what's happening?"

"Just about to start", said Eric, "Better get in I suppose".

"Right, settle down then, let's call this meeting to order", Ron Titley, as well as playing tenor horn in the band, was the band committee's secretary. A role he relished and guarded jealously, due to really wanting to be Chair but beaten to that position by Delmie Evans. Harbouring a deep resentment for Delmie and the knowledge that he would do a far better job as Chair, Ron often took on the role of 'quasi-chair' in a show of superiority to Delmie which everyone in the band thought was extremely funny rather than viewing Ron as anyone of any great importance. It was for this reason that various nicknames were bandied around; Mao Tse Ron, Rulebook Ron and quite simply The Gitley. It was a constant thorn in Ron's side that Delmie didn't give a forte about being Chair and was only voted in because on that particular night, there had been heavy snowfall, and only three people had turned up for the committee election; Delmie, Harry and James.

The crowd hubbub and general murmur did not abate despite another plea from Ron; "Come on now, come come, let's get some order here please". This was a very well attended meeting, with most of the band in attendance and many spouses and friends of the band as well, all squashed into Midtown Bandroom. Silence fell only after Harry resorted to a short vocal assault, "Shut up then! We're not getting any younger and there's important business tonight." Final chair adjustments were made, as James, Eric and Terry took their places, coats were taken off and the room fell silent. The gathered rows of people faced the long top-table where the committee were sat in office, along with one other person yet to be identified, who sat in a suit with the air of someone who had something grave to impart but who would ensure there was enough gravity before imparting it, so as to really emphasise the gravitas of the imparted! The reason for the large attendance tonight was made clear in Delmie's opening address.

"Good evening all. As you know we face a grave hour and it is my job as Chair, to lead the discussion tonight. I mean, I don't think there will be much discussion, unless anyone here wants the Bandroom flattened. No, thought not."

Ron rolled his eyes.

"So, anyway, that's what it's all about; The Bandroom, being flattened." Delmie finished to a perplexed and unsatisfied room. Harry felt he should step in. "Thanks Delmie, very uninformative." A chuckle ripple went round the room. "As you are all aware, we called this emergency meeting of the band, friends of the band and relatives after receiving some news from the planning department of Bedgwylam County Council."

Harry paused both for dramatic effect and to consider his next words carefully.
"Plans have been submitted for a development in Midtown which would mean that this Bandroom would be demolished, and we would have to find another home for Midtown band."

The room was coldly silent. Most people knew of the plans of course, that's why they were there, but hearing Harry say it out loud suddenly made the whole thing a lot more real and a lot scarier. There is good reason why this was such devastation to the band. Bandrooms are not just rooms where brass bands rehearse. They are the historic map of a band, told through the fading pictures on the walls of bands past; conductors past; and trophies won. They are the rooms where band discos are held and first kisses exchanged; where friends are made and jokes are shared; they are the band's spiritual home. To a musician, music is everything. It flows through their being with a need to be let out through fingers, breath, body, voice and soul. Listening to music can be uplifting and mesmerizing; playing music, that's something else altogether. Being part of a creative process which sends harmony and melody into the air around you is as close to spiritual fulfillment as anyone can get. Being part of a group of people which does that together, in symbiosis, with reliance on each other, in harmony with each other is, well, magical and can be miraculous. This miracle, this attainment of joyous celebration in music happens every night, of every week in Bandrooms up and down the land. And that's what a Bandroom is; a place where this collaboration is born and nurtured. The music is in the walls, in the ceiling, in the tiled floor and crumbling paint, in the roof beams and squeaking toilet door. The room is held together by music in the very fabric of its being.

And this is where the people sat now, contemplating its destruction.

Now, if walls could talk, of course that romantic picture lovingly crafted, may not be as truthful as it should be. The Bandroom has borne witness to many incidents of, how best to describe it, musical manslaughter? Many times Harry has stood in despair as Rachel Parry tried desperately to play a top D, only to push out a reluctant indiscriminate squeak reminiscent of a rudely-interrupted hamster. Many times Harry had thrown his baton down and shouted to the third cornets, "It's B flat! It's bloody B flat!" and once (in living memory anyway) the trombone section actually came to blows during 'Chivalry' by Martin Ellerby. This however, again demonstrates the importance of this place. It is a place of human emotion; A place of honesty. And, under Harry's rule, it is a place of equality.

In the years before Harry took over, or as they are affectionately known 'Pre-Harry', Midtown Silver Band had been a different place. Many potential players were put off by some of the pomposity of ex-military men, retired bank managers and Rotary nobs. The Bandroom was more a gentlemens' club than a band, with a few outings to the town fete, the odd fundraiser concert but generally a retiring band for retiring people. Oh, and there was strictly no women allowed. No women allowed in the Bandroom unless for an event where they could make the tea and serve some buns; also no children. No children allowed in the Bandroom. Unaccompanied and indeed accompanied children should be kept to a minimum. Rehearsals had comprised fifteen to twenty men talking and smoking, with a break for a quick practice, more talking and smoking and then maybe someone would have brought along a bottle of malt, to raise a toast to the Queen at the end of the night.

Then Harry moved to Midtown.

The family had moved to Midtown following work. South Wales offered little prospects due to the far reaching and devastating effects of the Thatcher political machine, chewing up the working class and spitting out dole-hangers, unintentional criminals and a bewildered once proud workforce. The resulting underclass straining the NHS, police, DWP, judicial system, tax inspectors, watchdogs, homeless shelters, environmental health and protection, community police, community workers, social workers, doctors, A&E, once caring parents, teachers, classroom assistants, drug and alcohol workers, local shopkeepers sick of shoplifters, smashed windows and distant memories of customers who, like Harry, had moved out of the town leaving boarded up shops, charity shops and vacant windows; a result of those treacherous, ill conceived and morally bankrupt policies emanating from, in James's Nan's words, "That woman". Harry always insisted that the knife that pierced the heart of so many communities from South Wales, through the Midlands, up to Lancashire, across to Yorkshire and up the A19 to Teasdale, Middlesbrough, Sunderland and Newcastle, prompting the trickle of life-blood that seeped out and slowly killed them; was held by one woman. And she will be held responsible.

Harry had moved the family up to Midtown where new factories were being built, ironically by the private sector, to meet increased demand globally from the aerospace industries for technology, parts and rubber seals. Yes, one may look at a plane and see the engine and the fuselage, but deep in the joints, between the nuts, bolts and rivets are hundreds and hundreds of rubber washers. Many from the factories in Midtown, many produced under the watchful eye of Harry Jones, Charge-hand.

Harry had been brought up playing with some of the best musicians in South Wales at the time. Many famous names went from the Salvation Army band, and other bands he played in, to make names for themselves in the brass band world. When Harry walked into Midtown Bandroom that first night and was asked, not what his favourite piece of music was, not how long he had been playing, not who he had played with but; "And what do you do for living?", Harry had got the measure of those men instantly, and had began turning the wheel of change.

Within the first year, he had made himself conductor. Not really *that* difficult as the last conductor, Granville Dent, had borderline obsessive compulsive disorder and had to wipe the baton thirty two times before each piece, only really liked playing four pieces, one of which was the theme tune from The Thirty Nine Steps and was very rarely there due to his Freemason commitments. When Harry had approached him to take over as conductor, Granville tried to affect a persona of strength, puffed himself up and said; "Well, why should I go? Hmm? Well, why should I?" He was notably worried, and with good reason. In his eyes, being band conductor was good for his standing at the Rotary. Harry had been willing to offer a compromise of being deputy conductor and working 'together' on improving the band, but when faced with this front from Granville, decided that honesty was the best policy. And in the spirit of un-ambiguity, Harry had answered, "Because you're crap Granville."

Within the second year, Harry had established a youth band and a beginner's class, leading all of them himself initially, to ensure that the band always had a feed of new young talent coming through.

Within the third year Harry made it known in the town, to anyone he spoke to and at the growing number of events the band now played at, that anyone and everyone was welcome from whatever background, regardless of race, religion, colour or gender. The first night that Denise Lewis, ex-Hymac Rhymney Works band player, turned up with her trombone, three of the stalwarts still hanging on to the old band order addressed Harry about it, their first mistake; doing it in front of everyone, their second;

"Excuse me Mr Jones but this is just not correct. We have established a place where we are free of female interruption or distraction and where we can relax. We all have wives at home and we all come here for a release. I, and Henry and George have all accepted your changes to our band with little fuss and can see sense in some of the changes, but this goes against a long tradition in banding. We don't mean to offend this good lady who has appeared here tonight, we just don't want to upset older and more long serving members for the sake of, how would one put it these days, good PR?"

"Hear, hear", George had added needlessly.

Harry had looked at the band. The vibrant and optimistic faces of recently-joined players and learners had greeted him, amongst them the youngsters he'd brought in and who he had given a purpose to, at least twice a week anyway. Being a conductor is more than the music. For some of these people he was their only adult guide outside of school. For some, although he did not fully realise it, he was a father figure. He'd turned to Denise, who was standing nervous and embarrassed.

"Hymac, Rhymney. Great band. Watched them play many times. Sit down there next to Paul love, and welcome to the band."

Denise smiled.

Gordon, the ex-police inspector had raised his voice angrily;
"I must protest! You have blatantly ignored the wishes of three of the oldest members of this institution. Myself,

Henry and George will be forced to leave this band if she stays!"

Harry paused, not for effect, but more to contain his anger at the complete lack of protocol, form, and actual manners that had been adopted in order to put their point across. The fact that the pause did create an eerie moment had been entirely incidental. When he did reply, it was coldly simple. "Good." he'd said. Predictably the hot air emanating from the pseudo-aggrieved members dispersed as quickly and pointlessly as it had appeared. No-one left the band, at least not that night, and an understanding was cemented into the unwritten constitution; meetings were for raising points of order; rehearsals were about the music, and only the music.

Denise had sat down next to Paul Harris, Lead Trombone, "Does it bother you that I'm a woman then?" she asked defensively.

Paul had replied in his low Welsh drawl, "I don't care if you're a one-armed hermaphrodite, as long as you can reach seventh position".

She relaxed a little, "Wouldn't that be quite difficult if I only had one arm?"

Paul leaned in conspiratorially, "Harry would still expect
you to try."

And after that, the band had seemed to flourish. They were
asked to play at more events in the town, their junior band
started bringing good young players through, the band went
on a run of fundraising events and bought new uniforms,
new stand banners, got the Bandroom painted and tidied
up. Harry dedicated rehearsal time into how the band filed
onto stage, section by section, and remained standing until
he walked on and gestured to them to sit. They had
marching practice in the car park, sectional rehearsals,
Harry called in favours from old friends to come and lead
rehearsals in different ways, practicing breathing
techniques, blowing techniques, different approaches to
conducting. By the end of five years under Harry's
stewardship, Midtown Silver Band looked, felt and acted
like a professional unit. They had gone from a retiring,
small, un-ambitious town band to a group of people with
self-respect, proud and with a sense that they could achieve
more than they were. For the first time in Midtown Band's
history, and with some trepidation, Harry entered them into
their first adjudicated contest. The test piece was Life
Divine; the setting was Pontins Holiday Camp, Pwllheli.
They had won third prize, but judging by the noise in the

hall when the results were announced, you would have thought they had invented a machine that not only predicted horse-racing results, but which ran on water, and emitted beer!

It was in Midtown Bandroom that these events had been witnessed, and it was in Midtown Bandroom that the gathered throng now discussed how to fight its demise.

Delmie opened up the discussion to the floor and hands shot into the air.

"Yes, Steve?"

"Steve Pepper, Eb Bass", he began, announcing his name and instrument with what he thought to be an appropriate air of formality, "It's a disgrace. I've been in this band for ten years. Ten years I've given. This is my home, my front room, my office, my shed, my…my..."

"Driveway?" enquired James.
"Under stairs cupboard?" asked Toby Stephens, adding "Sorry, Toby Stephens, Baritone"
"…way out of the gloom and misery that makes up your every waking moment?" uttered Carl Davis, Bass Trombone. For which he received quizzical looks and an

embarrassed wife.

"...my life!" Steve expelled, and sat down, puffing.

Delmie chose the next hand in the air, "Dan, your go mate."

"Cheers Delmo", he paused and following Steve Pepper's lead he too introduced himself, "Daniel Parry, 2nd Cornet. Now I realise that compared to Steve I may be a bit of a Johnny-Come-Lately, but I've been here long enough to know I love coming to band, of course it sometimes gets in the way of other things, and we all miss the odd practice here-and-there to do something else..."

Harry looked appalled. Dan tried not to make eye contact. The crowd inwardly praised Daniel for his bravery.

"...but I love coming here and this Bandroom, when you walk in and straight away get that smell of instrument cases mixed with the slight musty aroma of an old room and you think, I'm going to play really well tonight. Well it's part of it for me, and I think we should fight to save it."

A ripple of applause went round the room, with the odd "Well said", "Good lad", "Dew, he was brave..." amidst the claps.

Delmie took over again, "OK, last one for now, then I want to ask our guest of honour, Alan Leather, who is a Planning Consultant that Lawrence knows, and who has agreed to help us out as long as we cover some sundry expenses..."

"And an hourly rate, it turns out", Harry muttered not quite under his breath.

"...and an, uh, and other expenses to be agreed by the committee, in preparing our approach to how we fight this factory. Yes, Ieuan?"

"Ieuan Efans, Percussion. Am I the only one who doesn't know what this factory is making?" He looked around, and noted that he clearly wasn't the only one. The Midtown rumour-mill had been rife with suggestions regarding this particular point, and everything from prosthetic limbs to nuclear missiles had been mooted.
"Ball-cocks,"
"I was only asking."
"…buoys and other plastic flotation devices, it says here," Delmie read aloud from the planning application in front of him.
"So this factory is literally a load of balls then?" asked Paul. A cheer went up from some of the younger element.

"...and other plastic flotation devices." Ron clarified. "Now, I'm sure our guest does not want to be kept waiting, he has important findings for us and I'm sure we will benefit from hearing what he has to say." Ron desperately wanted to impress Alan, the Planning Consultant.

"Right, good idea Ronald".

Ron winced. Delmie knew he would, and continued, "Over to you Al". Ron winced again.

Alan Nigel Leather stood up, a man in his mid-fifties but with a fine head of white hair, tanned skin from his golfing sojourns to Spain, and a pair of, what can only be described as Ronnie Barker glasses, the only thing Harry liked about him. He cleared his throat theatrically and began his address;

"Thank you Chair,"

"Does he always thank the furniture?" Eric enquired of Steve who sat next to him.

"thank you Committee and thank you all for coming tonight. When I was asked to look into this development on behalf of *Mill-town* Silver Band, I said yes immediately. Brass bands have always been close to my heart as my

Grandfather played French Horn in an orchestral ensemble..."

Harry gritted his teeth.

"...so I was delighted to accept the money for this project. Now, in all planning battles, we need to find out what the angle is. What do we use as our weapon? What shape is the sword we unsheathe and wave at the enemies'..."

"Balls?" interrupted Paul to much amusement. Ron was not impressed.

"...faces, as we cry, no! No to your abomination! So, as we have already heard, this development is a factory producing plastic flotation devices. There are some potential areas that will cause you problems with your objection, the main being that the factory will bring employment opportunities..."

Harry knew this would be a problem. There had been a trickle of redundancies recently in the town as small factories were closing, and larger concerns downsizing departments. Nothing dramatic yet but enough to make people nervous and want job security. At least two people in the band had recently been made redundant and Harry knew that others had been for 'assessments' with management, basically to determine what management could get away with in terms of redundancy conditions. Providing jobs in a small town is a big win.

"...and with that, the business of increased business for other businesses in the business community in the town. But, you will be pleased to hear that I have found the angle."

Alan paused to take a sip of water. He felt this made him look confident and in control, also it built the anticipation nicely.

"The environment!" he announced. Ron looked visibly impressed. He closed his eyes and shook his head in admiration, opened his eyes again, looked at Harry and mouthed the words "Brilliant".

Harry looked at Ron, gave him the thumbs up, turned to face the front and mouthed the word "Dickhead".

"What was that about a mint?" enquired Terry Horner, largely to himself.

Alan Leather continued; "The environment is a key battleground at the moment, a real hot potato. This is a plastics factory with its own incinerator. They would be producing emissions that are equivalent to having a four lane motorway running around Midtown, with nothing but double-decker tankers full of anthrax circling twenty seven hours a day."

Alan loved a good analogy. He had been trained by a mentor who had instilled in him the belief that people were inherently stupid, therefore much planning consultant time should be taken up imagining what might happen, then devising analogies which can be understood by 'the least intelligent of the masses'. He continued;

"The heat created and the CO_2 emissions would be equivalent to launching 8235 hot air balloons at one time above the town."

Those people in the crowd who were still grasping the point simply looked confused. Those who had now lost grasp of the point and let it to crash to the floor in splinters of misunderstanding were understandably perplexed.

"What? That sounds mental!" said an angry Owain Owain's mum, "I can understand the posters; I can go with the hate mail, but launching eight thousand-odd hot air balloons, at once?"

"That sounds very dangerous to me." chimed in Phillip Edwards, 1st Cornet.

"There's going to be an accident." Eric chipped in, who actually understood completely what was going on, but thought that this planning consultant was a complete buffoon and decided, for the purposes of his own amusement, to egg-on the resulting buffoonery instead. Voices, like ironic point-missing spears from the crowd, were now being hurled at the committee table;

"That's going too far. Nobody wants this but we don't want to risk lives in our protest, surely to God"

"I don't think he wants us to launch eight thousand hot air balloons."

"Well that's what he said!"

"They'll all be bumping into each other, won't they?"

"There's not enough room in the sky!"

"What if one crashed in the town because of this aerial *It's a Knockout!*?"

"Does it have to be eight thousand?"

"Think of the children!"

"Think of your Volvo" Eric joined in again.

Ron realised things were getting out of hand. This meeting had not been going to plan all night and Ron was visibly upset; "Sorry Alan, could I just interrupt you there sir. What's all the chatter down there? Can't you see that a man of high learning is trying to teach you something?"

Paul Harris answered, "Excuse me but I'll address my question to the Chair. What *is* he trying to teach us? All he's done is make up some spurious analogies to grab headlines. Can't he just say what the emissions will be and if they conflict with acceptable guidelines? And how we can use that information to form our opposition to this development?"

Harry spoke for the awed crowd; "Surprisingly eloquent Paul, and spot-on." he looked back at Alan.

Alan, realising he was losing his potential expenses decided he would go for scare tactics.

"Uh, well, by my calculations the amount of waste plastic coming out of this factory in twenty years will be the size of two Ben *Nevii'* in Norfolk!"

"Well as long as it's in Norfolk" James offered.

Ron spluttered, "Will you take this seriously!"

"Well sorry Chair, but it is difficult when all we are hearing is quite odd comparisons involving hot-air balloons and the twin-peaks of Ben Nevis, which don't mean a whole lot. Why can't he just say the figures and let us decide?" Paul reiterated his earlier point, again to the Chair, which again irked Ron further.

"John Coates, 1st Trombone. How much is Mr Leather being paid for this glittering insight?"

The atmosphere was tense and Lawrence felt he should step in and defend his friend, and himself to an extent, as it had been on his recommendation that they brought in Alan to build a case;

"Now John, we all know that consultants cost a lot of money if you want them to tell you what you want, and Alan is one of the best at that, I can personally vouch for his track record."

Harry shook his head.

"Um, thank you Lawrence." Alan said, not entirely convincingly.

"So, do you think maybe we could be presented with some facts and let us make our own minds up mate?" Eric asked.

Ron had had enough of people questioning a man who was clearly an expert in his field, "Well, there you go. You can win any argument with *facts* you know!"

The crowd went silent.

That silence was broken by Owain Owain's mum who had clearly been brooding for some time on her earlier misunderstanding. She made her feelings clear on this issue; "I pay my subs for the good of the band and for my Owain, and I would like to register a stringent objection to funding the 8000 hot air balloons mentioned earlier as part of this protest! That really is over egging an already extremely eggy pudding!   And another thing," she continued, wagging her finger aloft, "if, God forbid we lose this fight, are the council going to build us a new Bandroom somewhere?"

"Well," observed Alan with one final meaningless contribution, "that would appear to be the elephant in the room"

"Don't you talk about my mother like that", shouted Owain Owain, following-up with a wheeze of laughter.

The crowd laughed aloud at Owain, then went silent again, confused and even more bereft than before this meeting. Harry once again took control, and addressed everyone. "Right, well, I think we should end it there. We'll have a think about how we prepare our plans to object to this again, and come back to you. Alan, I don't think we'll require your services again, brilliant as they are."

James smiled.

"Always available if you need me Mr Jones.", Alan Leather responded, clearly missing the fact that he had made a right dog's dinner of the whole presentation. In fact, later that evening he would regale his Polish wife with how the crowd had been transfixed by his wonderful analogies, "You see Amannin, it's about reaching out, going beyond the confusing numbers, and speaking as if to a child with water on the brain."

As the night wore on, Harry and Mary sat at home too, as James, Emily and a few of the band enjoyed a speculative discussion in the Castell Coch pub.

"What do you think then?" Mary asked a quiet and thoughtful Harry.

"I think we've got a fight on our hands and that many people will see jobs first and Bandroom second."

And with this inevitable truth still fresh off Harry's lips, they both fell silent. Harry picked up the newspaper and Mary reached for the TV remote.

Chapter 3

Oceans (Goff Richards)

It's not usually Autumn or Spring that evoke the most powerful memories and emotions, this kind of nostalgia is reserved for either long hot summer days, or freezing, Christmassy wintertime. There was a kind of surefooted reassurance in the way the band coach wended its way through Snowdonia National Park on a crisp April morning, many of its occupants still half asleep, bleary-eyed, a combination of just-audible Radio 2 mixed with the low ever-present rumble of the coach's engine combining to fuel the atmosphere of pleasant nonchalance. The brown moor land stretched on into bare branched woods through a low-lying mist as Midtown Silver Band travelled to Rhyl for the annual entertainment contest.

As the final remnants of the lingering darkness lost their fight against the bright winter sun burning majestically over the eastern snow-capped peaks, James Jones idly drew pictures in the condensation on the window. As part of one of his little rituals, he cast his mind back to this very journey last year, and for at least 10 previous years. He would remember what was going on in his life at those times, the dramas in the playground, the onset of a new job, various girlfriends. And the memory of each year would have its own identity, whether it be music, relationships, clothing, hopes or dreams. This year, as James saw a pub whiz past the window, he experienced a mixture of feelings. Although everything in his life was as it should be, the lack of communication between his sister and father seemed to be developing into simmering resentment, and this made him ill-at-ease. He hoped things would settle down soon. He didn't want to be sitting on this bus in twelve months, looking at the mountains passing by and remembering this year as the time Dad and Emily went their separate ways.

His thoughts were suddenly shattered by an unearthly deafening boom in his right ear, which it took him half a second to realise was Phil Edwards bellowing "Sleeping Jim?" instantly accompanied by childish chuckling from the surrounding seats. James grinned after recovering from the shock, and replied "Yeah mate, it's your sparkling conversation".

Harry sat near the front of the bus, his thoughts much more focussed than those of his son. Not for Harry was the romantic reminiscing of this time last year. His mind was trained on one thing: today's performance. It had been an earlier start to the formal band year and rehearsals had been a bit rushed following Christmas and New Year. Harry was a purist, he was single-minded in his musical decisions, and for the most part he was usually right. This year he had made his mind up to close the Rhyl contest with "Akhnaton", a dramatic piece of music about an Ancient Egyptian Pharaoh. The climax of this particular piece consisted of the whole band reaching a thundering crescendo followed by an abrupt and sudden stop, during which a full-sized tam-tam would be struck, followed by the dramatic closing bars from the entire band at full volume.

"Whass' a tam-tam?" Lawrence ApDafydd on percussion had enquired of Harry when the piece was announced.

"It's like a gong only bigger, and with no definite note", Harry had knowledgably explained. Pleased with the definition he had himself previously obtained from Google after asking himself that very same question. "Just think of that half-dressed bloke at the beginning of the old films. He's hitting a tam-tam".

"Great!" Lawrence had exclaimed, "Maybe I can wear just my swimming trunks to play it. It is Rhyl after all". The band had guffawed loudly.

"Yes Lawrence..." Harry had replied, holding-court with his legendary sarcastic tones, "...but it's also entertainment. And what may seem entertaining to *you* may be anything *but* entertaining to everyone else". The band had guffawed again.

Harry had struggled in vain to obtain a tam-tam to use in the rehearsals for their closing piece, but had been promised that one would be on stage on the actual day of the contest, as he knew the trombone player of the band before them and had arranged "payment" in the bar following the performance. Lawrence ApDafydd had been practicing with a crash-cymbal during rehearsals and was looking forward to giving that gong, or tam-tam, or whatever Harry called it, a good wallop. As the journey continued, Harry made frantic last-minute notes, playing through the performance in his mind, oblivious to everything else as the coach rolled Rhyl-ward.

At the back of the coach, people had now woken up a bit more. The usual medley of games was going around to pass the time. Word Association had been exhausted, and Guess The TV Theme Tune had resulted in a heated difference of opinion based on soprano cornet player

Timothy Dann's insistent claim that the saxophone intro to Cagney & Lacey was played by one of the boys from Trehafren Band in the 4th Section. The players had now moved onto I Went To The Shop.

Phil Edwards on first cornet was trying to get the game going.

"Right," said Phil, "All clear then, I start by saying I went to the shop and bought something beginning with A, lets say Apple."

Everyone nodded. Phil pointed at Delmie.

"Then you carry on and say I went to the shop and bought an apple and something beginning with B, right?"

"Right" they all said. Phil sat back.

"Good. So, I went to the shop and bought an Apple"

Everyone looked at Delmie.

"OK, I went to shop and bought an apple and a….well…..a banana"

Delmic looked pleased with himself and turned to Lucy, the Flugel Horn player.

"I went to the shop and bought an apple, a banana and some cherries"

Everyone looked at Carl Davies who played bass trombone.

"What are you looking at me for, I'm not playing"

Everyone then looked at Eric Trefelyn. Now to be fair to Eric, he had been trying to follow the game and was willing to join in but he was a bit lost.

"Right, so, I say what you have all bought and then say what I want to buy"

Everyone said yes.

"OK then, I went to the shop bought an apple," he pointed at Phil.

"A banana," he pointed at Delmie.

"Some cherries?" he pointed at Lucy who nodded. Everyone looked expectantly at Eric.

"and ....uh...four candles".

Various people laughed and shook their heads in disbelief. Phil, who was a little confused at Eric's answer, spoke for them all "It has to begin with D; the point is we are going through the alphabet".

"Oh right, so apple, banana, cherries, right A, B, C." Eric said "Right got it now".

There was silence as everyone waited as Eric thought about his answer.

"Well?" said Phil.

Eric ventured a question; "Does it have to be fruit?"

The players groaned.

"Jesus Eric, just say something beginning with D!" Delmie shouted

"Aaw, I'm not playing then" Eric said in annoyance and folded is arms, "I can't think of anything beginning with D."

Delmie looked in disbelief at Eric, "You can't think of anything beginning with D? In the whole world?"

"How about dickhead?" Phil suggested.

The journey passed fairly uneventfully, and as their final destination loomed, the inevitable yell summing up utter excitement, someone trying to appear cool and composed but failing dismally, in five un-ambiguous words, was heard from somewhere near the front of the coach; "I can see the sea!"

As if Wales had won the World Cup, a roar of applause and an impromptu chorus of the 70's classic "Rock The Boat" erupted from the boys at the back, interrupted by a rudely awakened slightly bewildered-looking Ron Titley who yelled "Do you lot mind keeping it down, some of us are trying to get some kip!". The instantaneous unison response of 25 bandsmen, as if on cue, all replying "ooooooh"...in a rising then falling tone, and killing themselves laughing provided the only answer Ron was going to get.

The coach cruised into Rhyl and glided along the promenade, air-brakes like occasional softly-hit cymbals punctuating the deep drone of the engine and announcing its arrival. Resort towns at the end of winter are the bleakest places. The sea looked grey and menacing. The security grills on the shops and amusement arcades looked anything but amusing. In fact, the street looked angry, bored and tired like it never wanted to see visitors ever again. There were a few newsagents open and the pubs along the seafront already had groups of bandsmen loitering outside even at ten in the morning. That would be out of the question for Midtown Band though; Harry had a strict no drinking rule:

"You might think you're playing well after you've been drinking; you may even think you're playing better. But how many times have you thought you were taking home Audrey Hepburn only to wake up next to Audrey Roberts?" A wiser observation was not oft vocalised!

This rule was mainly adhered to, but it wasn't unknown in the history of the band for a few players to have gone on stage playing like Audrey Roberts!

Still, it was exciting. It was the seaside, however bleak, however cold, however unlike any actual summer holiday you'd actually want to find yourself on, it was Rhyl! An annual pilgrimage. The anticipation, the adrenalin, the fact there were seagulls flying around, all contributed to make it a good day, and as the coach drew to a halt in the car-park alongside 20 other coaches, each displaying the name of its respective band, Harry felt a wave of pride wash over him. "Here we are again", he thought. This was his world. This is what he knew. This is what he loved.

To the casual observer the coach looked at peace. Stood there impressively, gleaming in the end-of-winter sun, headlights looking seaward like the half-closed steely eyes of a mysterious stranger, its curtains now drawn as if displaying aloofness towards its fellow coaches. To anyone onboard the coach it was the complete antithesis of peace. Bags were being hauled out of overhead storage; a frantic melee of half-changed musicians ensued, replacing their "civvies" for their immaculately washed and pressed Midtown Band uniforms. An eye-watering mixture of deodorants and perfumes wafted through the gangway like a chemical cloud. Radio 2 was now replaced by the half-heard ends of sentences as the performers struggled to don their apparel in the minimum time, with the minimum room to manoeuvre. "Oi, that's my sock", "Ow! Mind your elbows", "Haw-haw-haw-haw...y-fronts!", and "Oh cock! I've come to the conclusion I've left my dickie-bow at home", culminating in everyone groaning and a couple of people coughing, as Eric un-ashamedly and with complete malice of forethought broke wind, like the sound of machine-gun fire cracking through a deserted valley. Finally the activity subsided, all conversation ceased, and 25 immaculate players prepared to disembark the coach, collect their instruments from the boot, and make their way inside the building.

As the band again lined up to take the stage the usual mix of jokes and arguments were going on. The contest was being held in the Rhyl Sun Centre and the corridor had a heavy stench of chlorine. Eric had a group of players standing around him, as he told story about a recent trip to Tesco. Apparently he had been shopping late one night and had noticed that there were a lot reduced items around and thought he could save some drinking money by filling up his trolley with them. He was explaining to those listening, that hc'd been halfway around the supermarket when he suddenly realised that they may all be reduced because they were past their sell-by date. The players knew all to well that Eric wasn't particularly good at remembering dates and times of things so he didn't really usually even have a clue what day it was.

"So anyway", Eric continued, "I decided to ask this bloke who was stacking shelves. There was hardly anyone in there anyway, there never is at that time of night."

Eric scratched his head, as if deciding whether to continue with the rest of the story. "Well, I asked this chap if he knew today's date, and he just ignored me! So I asked him again. Turns out he's Mutt and Jeff and can't hear a thing! So I ask him one more time…D A T E?"

The players were now more than slightly bemused by this. Apart from anything else they couldn't imagine Eric, normally very much a "big shop on a Saturday morning" man, choosing to do his shopping in the early hours. Eric continued;

"Anyway, I ask him again…DATE? And in the end I write it down on one of the boxes he's unloading. But when I do, he only starts backing away from me and shaking his head!"

"Why's that then?" Leighton Davis interrupts.

"Well", Eric replies, motioning with his hands to demonstrate further, "it turns out he thinks I'm trying to drop anchor in Pooh Bay."

"Uh?" Lucy Dann looked confused.

"Ah", concurred Leighton…"He thought…"

"Yes", Eric said, "I had to tell him…look I'm not asking you out you idiot, I don't want *a date*…I'm not trying to bum you man! I just want to know what the date is!"

Leighton wheezed with laughter, and the other players shook their heads and giggled.

"Anyway, then he grabs my hand and starts legging it through Tescos, pulling me along behind him!" Eric carried on. "So, we run from one end of Tescos to the other. I was knackered by the time he stopped!"

"So what was that all about then?" asked Lucy.

"Well, he'd dragged me all the way back to the fruit and veg, picked up a box of dates and gave them to me!"

The players all laughed out loud, suddenly going quiet as they noticed Harry glaring at them from across the foyer, as if reminding them where they were.

"So what did you do then?" Leighton asked.

"Well, I had to buy them didn't I", Eric said, "He was standing there watching. It was either that, or have him think I played League rather than Union! Worst thing of it all was, I don't even like dates, they give me the trots something chronic."

The players stifled laughter and shook their heads in disbelief. Steve Pepper and Harry stood together and were discussing the relative merits of sectional rehearsals versus full band rehearsals. James stood slightly apart from everyone else. Although the day was going great so far he was still uneasy, thinking about Emily and wondering why she had missed so many rehearsals that she had now all but completely dropped out of band. He could see why it may be awkward for her to discuss her reasons with their Dad, who was not known for his sensitive nature, particularly if there was a boyfriend involved. However, the fact that Harry was digging his heels in and seemingly taking her non-attendance personally was only widening a chasm that could now have been bridged. As well as being brother and sister James and Emily had always been good friends too, and despite, or perhaps because of, Harry's insistence that band played such a major part in their upbringing, the whole family as far as he was concerned were close and open with each other, and he was bothered that she hadn't even opened up to him about whatever was going on. Toby Stephens came over to James.

"Hiya, you alright? You look miles away?"

James couldn't be bothered to go into it with Toby now. It wasn't the time or place. So he just brushed it aside and started talking about the new wave-simulator in the Sun Centre pool. It was Toby that brought up Emily;

"By the way, how is Emily? Haven't seen her around for a while."

James mumbled that she was fine and that he thought she wasn't bothered about band anymore and that she was a girl, and what did he know what went on in a girl's head? Toby carried on though;

"Right, yeah who knows? But how is she, has she mentioned any of us at all?"

"What do you mean?" asked James.

"Well as she talked about us, or me at all?" Toby looked hopeful.

The conversation was interrupted as the doors at the end of the corridor opened and the band started filing through.

"I'll speak to you later Toby, good luck with that second movement part." James said as he left to join Roger so they could go on together. "That was weird," he thought as he walked away.

The audience applauded as Midtown Band sat down on the stage at the Rhyl Sun Centre. The principle players gave their respective colleagues discreet directions to move chairs closer and form the band into the positions Harry wanted. Lawrence ApDafydd stood behind the bass players who were sat in a row at the back of the band. Next to him was the tam-tam. It hung ominously on its stand and Lawrence regarded it. It was as tall as him and seemed like it almost had a personality of its own. Terry Horner on bass turned around and nodded approvingly at it, giving a little "thumbs up" to Lawrence, who then grinned, pointed to his trousers and mouthed the words "swimming trunks". The shrill sound of a short sharp whistle blast filled the hall, and everyone present, band and audience, knew the adjudicator was ready. A silence fell, as if the volume had been turned-down on anything human, and only the distant sound of the central-heating system in the background, and the occasional squeaking of a chair were to be heard. Everyone on stage was apprehensive. It was always the same. This was it, everything to play for, every chance to win still available. From the left of the stage came the increasing volume of footsteps. Harry walked on, took a bow, turned to face the band and raised his arms, baton held in his right hand. He let the moment linger as his eyes took a full sweep of all the players. Lucy was poised, her face betraying determination but also nerves. As Harry's eyes met her's, his right eyelid dropped slightly in a barely perceptible wink, and she forced herself to contain the involuntary smile she could feel on her lips in appreciation of his re-assurance. These were the moments when the already considerable respect the players had for Harry was elevated yet further. He knew that in order to win, his band needed to be not only totally focused but also relaxed rather than nervous, his eyes communicated his respect for them and instilled a belief in themselves that they could win this, they were capable, and if Harry thought they could win...hey, they could win.

Harry's right arm dropped like a whip cracking, and the band struck-up the first piece in this entertainment contest, "Hello Dolly". The band played well. Harry afforded individual rewarding grins throughout their fifteen minutes, not enough to induce complacency, but just the right combination of encouragement and respect. The 3rd cornets got a very discreet thumbs-up as they delivered a much-rehearsed passage which to the un-initiated was inconsequential, whereas to Harry, getting that passage right meant the difference between winning and losing. The 3rd Cornet players beamed proudly, spurred on by Harry's gesture, were determined to play the rest of the performance at the very peak of their ability. James couldn't help being in awe of Harry on these occasions. There may be some aspects of life that aren't Harry's forte, but training a band, communicating with the players, and generating a spirit of camaraderie and mutual respect certainly weren't one of them.

It was now time for the final piece. The audience had responded positively so far. Harry was pleased. He was optimistic. He knew the band had performed well, and not only well enough to win, but well enough by his own standards...which were another thing again! The opening was tight, the sound coming from the middle of the band was warm and full and Harry felt that this was a winning performance. He could almost imagine the Egyptians and slaves marching through the desert. This was the story of "Akhnaton". The volumes rose and fell, the differences in musical texture; mood and style unravelled depicting the whole range of descriptions necessary to tell the story. Regal Egyptians, slaves fighting for freedom, tender melodies suggesting a love story. The audience was silent, not wanting to miss a beat, as the piece entered its final section. A deep aggressive rumble from the basses signified the beginning of a slow dramatic crescendo swelling from within the belly of the band itself, now playing as if it were one entity rather than several individuals. The drama on stage was intensifying, the audience was enraptured. The increasing volume and accelerating rhythms only served to force the sound through any obstacle, moving ever closer to the inevitable finale. Lawrence stood next to the tam-tam, mallet in hand, waiting for his moment. As the climax drew ever closer, Harry's eyes flashed upwards, meeting Lawrence's and communicating everything they'd discussed during rehearsals in one almost telepathic moment. The band reached the pinnacle of the crescendo, a roar of hackle-rising, butterflies-in-stomach-generating bass-filled music filled the entire hall and Harry raised his baton aloft ready to signify the brief break during which the tam-tam alone would resound.

Harry's eyes fixed on Lawrence ApDafydd and the whole band were single-minded of purpose. The baton dropped and everyone stopped playing in a clean, almost machine-like cut-off. It took a split second for a range of band-practice advice to rush through Lawrence's brain..."you'll need to hit the gong harder than the cymbal"..."it's the most important part of the piece mate"...Chief amongst which was Harry's prime instruction just before going on stage "Give it all you've got Lozza!"

As the sheer volume and power of the band's last chord still fought its way into every corner of the hall, Lawrence, in a two-handed effort, brought the mallet into the centre of the tam-tam with a velocity that would not have been out of place if he was aiming to hit the winning six for South Glamorgan cricket team. And as contact was made, something very very unusual happened.

James, in the solo Euphonium chair, was sitting opposite the cornets, with Harry in the middle. It was the only occasion in James' life where he would honestly think time stood still. There was only one beat before the band would come back in, following the gong, to play the last two bars. But during that one beat, as James looked on, the four solo cornet players' heads, in complete synchronisation and in slow motion, turned towards Lawrence. Four jaws dropped, and four sets of eyes all projected one single expression; "What in the name of God, Jesus and Mary is that?"

At almost exactly the same time, a sound, no, a noise, not heard by human ears since Concorde made its final ever approach at Heathrow, not only filled the hall, it probably filled the whole of Rhyl. It was a noise that was pure acoustic energy, like a sonic wave consisting of a million different examples of sound ranging from the mating-call of the Blue Whale, to a thousand windows shattering simultaneously.

And as time remained frozen, the energy rippling across the surface of that gong translated into a boom of sound that just kept growing and growing and growing.

The back row of bass players was physically pushed forward and Phil burst out laughing as he saw the look on Terry's face. The audience had their fingers in the ears as the shattering sound filled the auditorium. In that split second James simply continued to look on, not believing what he was seeing or hearing.

Suddenly reality kicked in, Harry was now just waving his arms around to bring the band back in for the final bars. Almost on auto-pilot the band finished the piece, but they needn't have bothered. There are not all that many things in life that can drown out an entire brass band without amplification. But one stunned Welshman called Lawrence, one very large gong, and 200 cheering on-lookers, most of whom were wiping tears of laughter from their eyes, managed to give it a pretty good go on that chilly April day in Rhyl. As Harry and the rest of the band recovered from what can only be described as sensory overload, the true spectacle of the situation became apparent. Lawrence had belted the tam-tam with such intensity that the resulting shockwave had returned back through the mallet, all the way through Lawrence, and even into Ieaun, who had seen what had happened, ran across the stage from the Xylophone, and jumped on top of Lawrence who had just wrapped his arms and his legs around the gong in a vain attempt to shut it up. As the band stood up to take a bow, Lawrence and Ieuan, both still atop the still-vibrating gong, fired a pleading glance at Harry who gave them both a confirmatory nod. They let go and both fell to the floor. This generated a renewed wave of laughter and applause within the already delighted audience, and in an impromptu gesture, Harry beckoned Lawrence to the front of the stage to take a bow. Lawrence rather sheepishly accepted his moment of glory and stood next to Harry with the colour just starting to return to his face. It would only be later that the adjudicator's comments would be issued, immortalising in writing the climax of Akhnaton: "What an impact! What a gong! What did the rest of the band play for those last bars?"

It was less than thirty minutes later that the coach was once again maneuvering its way back through Snowdonia National Park, there was a lively atmosphere as people relived the 'gong moment', or the "tam-tam moment" as Lawrence would forever correct everyone, now that he knew what it was. Harry sat in his seat near the front, musing on the as yet unknown result. The band had left shortly after the performance, as there had been several requests to get home early enough to still enjoy Saturday night plans back in town. Everyone knew that due to the brass-band world having a grapevine to rival Moet & Chandon, the results would be with someone in Midtown almost immediately they were announced. Harry was replaying the pieces in his head, and hoping that despite them being accomplished, polished and memorable, the gong had not overshadowed what had been a good performance, and he didn't want it perceived as a comedy number. The band had been impressing Harry recently, and each performance seemed to be that little bit better than the last; it felt like they were building towards something. Perhaps, with this set of players, he could achieve "that sound", as he termed it; a sound he could not vocalise; a sound of near perfect harmony; the rarely achieved combination of instruments that all conductors dream of and aspire to.

Mary sat at home, in the kitchen having just filled the kettle and switched it on. She had decided not to go to Rhyl, intending to spend some time with Emily and try to get some sense out of her regarding her mystery man. Emily had left the house early though, and Mary's thoughts throughout the day were of the coming months. The Rhyl contest had meant another Saturday ticked off, and she knew there were many others coming up; carnivals, fundraising-concerts for the inevitable Bandroom campaign, yet more contests. She knew that Ron Titley was in the final stages of organising Midtown Band's first European trip, something that was intended to maintain interest both inside and outside the Bandroom, particularly as in these uncertain times, the band need as high a profile as possible in the community and beyond. She had to resign herself to the compromise; yes it would mean a holiday, but it was a band holiday. She doubted that Harry would want to while away the hours in a delightful French street cafe, sipping coffee and talking about the local architecture, with Eric and the gang in tow. He'd be in the street bars, sipping beer and talking about the news from home that Black Dyke had actually now risen to the status of 'Best band in the Universe ....Ever'.

Her thoughts drifted towards Tom, a not un-attractive man approaching middle-age who had recently started working in her department at the Town Hall. She considered that based on how smartly he was always turned-out and how cultured and well-mannered he appeared to be, he could probably even speak French and pull together a mouth-watering Crepe Suzette quicker than one could say "Charles De Gaulle"!

She looked at the kitchen clock, and caught a glimpse of the calendar next to it, making a mental note to remind Harry to phone his Mum, Gwladys, as it was approaching what would have been his late dad's birthday. The now boiling kettle clicked off, signalling time for Mary to enjoy a coffee and the peace of an empty house, before Harry and James returned to regale her with the events of the day, followed at some point by an increasingly reserved Emily.

Chapter 4

Hymns at Heaven's Gate (E Howarth)

Emily Jones sat inside the gleaming black limousine, subconsciously noting its exquisite leather and wood-trimmed interior, fleetingly appreciating the irony that on any other occasion a ride in a car of this quality would be a treat. But as she was wafted silently along Cefngoed High Street she couldn't escape feeling numb rather than excited. The High Street, so beloved by her and her brother during those sunny glorious childhood summer visits, was filled with people going about their early-afternoon business, yet Emily only saw the succession of boarded-up shops drifting by like forgotten souls on a long since abandoned schooner. The fading shop signs, mostly containing a family name, only served to add an uneasy poignancy; A funeral procession through a slowly dying town.

"You alright love?" Mary's voice interrupted Emily's reflections and she turned and smiled at her mother sitting next to her and holding her hand.

"Yeah, I'm alright" replied Emily, "it's just a funny day 'innit". Mary gripped her daughter's hand and they both looked ahead.

Harry and James were in the car in front of Mary and Emily, and the hearse carrying Gwladys Jones led the procession. James contemplated the strange tradition of the men and women having to travel separately from the funeral service to the cemetery as he too observed Cefngoed High Street through adult eyes. Maybe it had always been "going downhill", as his aunties and uncles had put it. But to James, and Emily, it had been where their Nan lived, they wouldn't have a word said against it, and as small children they'd both vowed to come and live here at the earliest opportunity!

"Be about 10 minutes now boys." This time it was James' turn to have his thoughts interrupted, however not by his dad, but by the driver.

"You've done well to stay in convoy through the High Street", Harry replied.

"Good Gawd, if we don't stay together Caradog'll have our guts for garters!" retorted the driver.

James grinned, amused at the notion, given his own experiences of the gentleman concerned. Caradog Pugh was born to no other role in life but undertaker. He stood just over 6ft, with a slim frame, an almost gaunt but paradoxically healthy looking face, and silver hair. To

James, who had been a pall-bearer that morning, Caradog had seemed to mysteriously appear and disappear like a helpful apparition, as though he instinctively knew the exact moment when those involved in the funeral would need help or advice. He had stood, resplendent in his black tail-suit, wringing his hands and beaming from under his thick eyebrows, not in a jovial manner, but in a way that contributed to his whole demeanour of "I know exactly what I'm doing, this day will pass without a hiccup". James, and for that matter everyone who had ever lived in Cefngoed, had known Caradog Pugh since he could remember. Caradog had always been the undertaker, and always would be.

The day had remained characteristically dry and bright for early May in Cefngoed, and the funeral service had gone well. Gwladys Jones was "old school" Cefngoed, known by absolutely everybody and much loved. There had been standing-room only by the time all the attendees had filed in, paying their respects to Harry. The hymns were of Gwladys's choosing, and the congregation had been in splendid voice.

The organist, replacing Gwladys as it happened, had been shocking. Apologetic glances were passed from the vicar to the immediate family. However, James and Emily had remembered their Nan's love of Les Dawson and his legendary piano playing, and had both commented to each other that she would have found this hilarious. Harry hadn't spoken much all day, except to exchange pleasantries with the family, and give the obligatory thanks to old friends who had made the effort to turn up. It all seemed such a long time ago when he himself lived in Cefngoed, and today even the presence of old school friends, Caradog Pugh included, did little to bridge the gap between his life then and his life now. To Harry they were separate worlds and although born a "Cefngoed boy" through and through, he'd always felt like a visitor when returning to visit his mother and father, after moving to Midtown when Emily was born. Today was no exception. As the procession, black as a bible and with unspoken dignity, left the outskirts of Cefngoed and began its steep ascent of the almost impossibly angled hillside roads, Harry couldn't help wondering how often, or even if ever, he would return to Cefngoed. James, Emily, and to a certain extent Mary, were all wondering the same thing as the pavement beside the road gave way to high stone walls, enduring an endless struggle to contain the foreboding bleak hills. The big cars, like modern day pit-ponies, hauled their cargo ever upwards until the road finally started to level once again. The stone wall to the left of the cars was briefly interrupted by the open cemetery gates. There was a steep drop on the right-hand side, and the now derelict "Owens' Garage" remained in its place almost opposite the entrance to the cemetery, unclaimed, undeveloped, just left to slowly decay, as if yearning to now be finally taken across the road. The cars drew into the cemetery and commenced an eerily final climb to the plot where Gwladys Jones would be laid to rest, at the very top of the mountain.

A damp mist rested in the floor of the valley as Harry looked down from the cemetery where he stood. The gravestones clung to the hillside, threatening to slide down the steep slope into the town below. Harry's thoughts were a confused mixture. At the moment he felt no loss, just the same numbness his daughter was also experiencing. He wondered if what had happened had not quite sunk in yet, and if there would be any spiritual faux pas if he devoted some thought to considering shifting the positions of the euphoniums and baritones to try and change the sound for the next contest. Everything seemed to be moving around him. Cars arrived, people made their way to the graveside.

The mist continued to stagnate around Cefngoed which now seemed to be miles below. He struggled to identify the feeling in his stomach. Was it loss? Was it guilt for not being with his mother at the end? Was it a misplaced nostalgia, enhanced by the unique not-quite-smoky, industrial aroma that he had grown up never noticing, but which at that moment seemed to signify Cefngoed? The vicar's words interrupted Harry's thoughts as the growing crowd of people were directed to a patch of ground just across the pathway. He could hear James greeting some cousins, and caught a glimpse of Emily and Mary getting out of their car. He looked back down at the coffin. He had got the call about his Mum while standing in the Midtown Social Club, leading the assembled throng in a very drunken chorus of "I am the Music Man". The band was celebrating their third place in the Rhyl Entertainment Contest and Harry had stumbled out of the club leaving the sound of singing behind him. His friends had just thought he had left because he couldn't think of what could follow "big bass, big bass, big bass drum" in the song.

It had taken Harry a good few hours before he sobered up enough to drive the 2- hour journey through Wales from Midtown to the Prince Of Wales Hospital just outside Cefngoed, where his mother was. The journey had scemed to take forever and not helped by the driving rain seemingly intent on thwarting him. Dawn had just broken when he reached the hospital, and he'd ditched the car in the first place he found. The fact it was an ambulance-bay had not even entered Harry's list of priorities at that precise moment! He'd run into the reception and was hurriedly escorted to his mother's ward. Ambient noise of trolleys chattering along, equipment bleeping, and the strange clinical smell all contributed to the apprehension as Harry had stood at one end of the room. The pleasant, bright ward had contained four beds. The fourth bed, the one nearest the window, had the curtains drawn all around it. Harry had looked at the slowly awakening ladies occupying the other three beds, hoping against hope that one of them was his mum. He'd felt a gentle hand on his shoulder and a shiver run down his spine. Somehow he'd known what was coming.

"Mr Jones? I'm very sorry. Your mother passed away peacefully 5 minutes ago".

Over the days between her passing and the funeral, Harry had tried to remember when he had last spoken to her. He had remembered a conversation on the phone;

"I've got to go into hospital on Thursday, nothing bad; they just said I needed a check over". Harry, half listening whilst rewriting the second cornet parts for "Slaidburn" so the new players from the junior band could play it, "I'm sure that should be a B-flat" he thought:

"Oh right", Harry had replied, "well nothing serious then."

"No, no but you know, just wanted to let you know", and those were the last words he'd heard his Mum say. The sound of slightly off-key tubular bells playing the first nine notes of We'll Keep A Welcome In The Hillside had interrupted the call, "Got to go Mum, someone at the door, speak to you later". Harry had put the phone down and started to get up to answer the door, but Eric had already come in;

"Hiya Harry, dew it's cold out tonight", Eric had rubbed his hands together. On hearing Eric's voice, the cat had looked up in alarm and on seeing Eric, had jumped from the seat where she had been sleeping and bolted out of the door and up the stairs.

"What's wrong with her?" Eric had asked.

Harry didn't know but the cat did. Ever since Eric had held her tail and jokingly threatened the cat with a lit cigarette up the bum, she had understandably been slightly nervous of him. That joke had been three years before, but the memory lived on.

And now, as he stood at the graveside, Harry was pretty sure that had been the last time he had spoken to his Mum.

Emily and James stood together, watching as the coffin, now resting in the ground with a peaceful air of finality, was being gently showered with handfuls of dirt as those present took their own moment to say goodbye to Gwladys. James looked past the crowd down into the valley below and remembered how he, his sister and their Nan would have walked up to this spot during many a visit over the years, enjoying a birds-eye view of the road snaking it's way in and out of Cefngoed, and playing a few rounds of the "car colour" game. As James now, years later, watched the cars ascending and descending, his mind wandered. Who was driving that silver convertible in the distance? Where were they going? Where had they been? What was their life all about? Why can't it be 10 years ago again, with Nan sitting here watching with me?

Emily nudged James as she stood next to him. "Remember the car colour game?" she asked, grinning over her face, but her eyes full of tears. James nodded, eyes firmly forward. He knew if he either looked at her, or opened his mouth to talk it would be the end of the composure he was doing his best to maintain. He remembered his Nan's strict orders over the years; "I don't want people crying and wailing at *my* funeral!" she'd often insisted, "I want everybody to have a nice day, and remember me when I was alive, not go on about me dying!" James and Emily had always giggled, dismissing with childlike naivety the fact that their Nan would one day leave them.

Mary too was experiencing mixed emotions. As a mother-in-law, Gwladys had played a major part in her life, and obviously the lives of her children. They had never been particularly close, but she felt a gnawing emptiness as she stood coffin-side. Maybe it was because a chapter in her own life had closed? Maybe it was a maternal instinct to share in the sense of loss her children were obviously experiencing, Emily in particular who had been inconsolable upon hearing the news of her Nan's death. James had accepted it quietly, and had shown no particular emotion. Mary knew how he was feeling however. In that respect he was very much like his dad, channelling emotion into passion and energy, usually in band practice. Emily was generally the same, however on this occasion she had almost fallen to pieces. The sound of Emily's voice struggling through sobs on the morning of Gwladys's death still haunted Mary; "Why couldn't she have stayed with us a bit longer?" Mary couldn't answer her daughter's question.

The funeral crowd was breaking up now and heading back to the Salvation Army hall for some drinks and sandwiches. Harry stood looking down at the coffin as the first drops of light rain, which had held off all day, started to speckle the coffin lid as if the elements were sending a message, being gently tapped-out in Morse code, that it was now time to leave. Mary came and stood next to Harry and put her arm through his, "Keith and Arthur are off now, they asked if you were going to listen to their rehearsal tomorrow night but I said I didn't know whether we would be staying down", Mary spoke to Harry but kept her eyes on the coffin.

Harry heard her and grunted a response but his mind was elsewhere. He was still almost light-headed from the carnival of thoughts and emotions taking place inside him, surprised and a little shocked by long-forgotten feelings returning like a bizarre archive of his lifetime; his mum wiping his nose with her apron and burning the Sunday roast, hiding from her under the table in the pub as she sold the "War Cry" and collected money for the Salvation Army and her knowing full well he was there and not saying anything apart from asking his friends, with an amused look on her face, "Harry not with you tonight boys?".

Of course, all his friends replied in unison, "No Mrs. Jones", and Harry had watched as her legs moved away from the table.

He also had the feeling of guilt at not saying goodbye and not telling her what a good Mum she had been. Whether he would have actually done it, given the chance, is debatable, but the guilt was there.

Mary looked up at Harry. She was confused by Harry's expression and couldn't read his thoughts, "Shall we get going then love? People will be expecting you at the hall." She tugged slightly at his arm but Harry just swayed a little towards her without really moving. It was not his mum that was keeping him there now, but a boy standing at the cemetery gates down at the bottom of the headstone-speckled slope, a boy who Harry could have sworn he'd seen somewhere before. Through the mist of rain that was now covering the graveyard, Harry and the boy stood looking at each other. It was a good four or five hundred yards to the gate and the rain hindered his vision, but Harry could see the boy wearing grey shorts, a shirt, tie and blazer which looked exactly like the Cefngoed Grammar School uniform he used to wear. The boy pulled something out of his pocket. From where Harry stood it looked like some cards, possibly cigarette cards, which Harry found slightly odd as he didn't think cigarette companies still made cards like the ones he used to have of his football heroes. He remembered cherishing those types of cards as a lad, and promising himself that one day, he would score the winning goal for Wales in the world cup.

Mary pulled at his arm again. This time Harry started to walk with her and finally, silently said goodbye to his Mum. He looked towards the gate but the boy was gone. The Jones family stood together, alone in the ever-thickening rainy mist, the view of the valley now barely visible, each contemplating a different aspect of the day, but ultimately sharing one sobering thought; "There goes yesterday".

"Who's that?" Mary suddenly asked, her voice breaking the silence like a brick through a window. A figure was slowly becoming apparent through the rain, still around a hundred yards away but walking towards them, becoming clearer and clearer as it advanced. James's first thoughts ran to Caradog Pugh, and he could almost hear the gothic cadences of full all-stops-out church-organ chords which always mentally accompanied Caradog's arrival. But it wasn't Caradog. As the figure continued to materialise, its right hand suddenly shot up in the air, five fingers extended. "You lot alright for a lift back?", a familiar voice bellowed, as Eric Trefelyn hoved into view in front of them.

The Jones family grinned, as if catapulted back from the edge of a cliff top descending into melancholy, and reminded quite inadvertently by the red-faced, white-haired, portly Welshman that life goes on.

"One of the cars is waiting to take us back mate", replied Harry. And as if the day had been reduced to nothing but a series of events through which Eric had been deliriously swept, towards the enticing beacon of a good 'nosh-up, Eric yelled back, "Right-oh, see you the other end for a sausage roll then!"

His words still echoing around the desolated windy mountain top, the Jones family laughed out loud for the first time in days, eternally grateful to Eric for decimating the complentative tension with one throwaway comment, delivered with unwitting comic genius.

As the family walked down the hill, towards the gates where the car was waiting, red tail-lights visible through the rain, and wisps of white steam spewing from the exhaust, Harry couldn't help noticing that there was not another soul anywhere, not even a parked car. And he briefly wondered who the little boy peering through the gates had been with, as they all climbed into the black limousine and headed down the steep hill leading back into Cefngoed town.

At the Salvation Army hall the funeral guests were loading up paper plates with sandwiches and sausage rolls. The usual comments could be heard rising above the low hum of voices;

"Good spread this…"

"Is that pie any good Herbert?"

"Bit crumbly"

"She always knew how to put on a good spread, always looked after you"

James and Emily shook hands with countless well-wishers and had to hide their smiles as each one notched up another square on Funeral Bingo. They had decided on the drive over to play a game, based on bingo, but using the phrases they knew would come up at the wake;

"She'll be missed Jim"

"It was a good service"

"Vicar did a good sermon, respectful"

"She's gone to a better place"

When someone said to Emily, "She had a good innings", she actually did laugh but quickly brought her hand to her mouth to cover it and just nodded. James saw this and had to turn away and cover his smile. He thought to himself, "Nan would have liked this", not the morbid remembrance but the humour within her grandchildren at her funeral. It seemed that death had always been a part of Nan's life and always treated with a degree of humour. When James and Emily had gone to stay during summer holidays and Christmas', there had always seemed to be someone who had just died or who was, "not looking too good…"

During most phone calls Nan had either been to, or was planning to attend, a funeral. And seemingly, part of the attraction of going to these funerals was firstly, that every single funeral in Cefngoed had, as part of the catering, one of Nan's corned beef pies, and secondly, she always seemed to pick something up for herself. James had met her once at the train station and commented on the coat she was wearing only to be told that it had belonged to Mrs. Ackerman who died last week and whose husband had given Nan the coat. During another phone call to Emily, it had transpired that her new deep fat fryer was also gleaned from a recent funeral and that's just how it was. Perhaps it was her age, or the fact that Cefngoed did seem to have more than its fair share of the elderly, or maybe she just had a particularly philosophical outlook, but death was part of life for their Nan and her friends and just because people were gone that didn't mean you didn't carry on and make best use of the things that were left, including time.

The only time James and Emily had seen her really upset at a funeral was at their Bampi's. There had been no smiles that day and no jokes. It was the day that their Nan's heart broke and, even though Emily and James never saw it, it was from that time on that their Nan had often sat crying in the evening looking at Bampi's chair in the corner and hearing his voice in her head.

James sat down at the side of the hall and silently said goodbye to his Nan with a tear in his eye and a slight smile on his face.

Harry and Mary mingled and the hum of voices lessened as people shook hands with Harry and kissed Mary on the cheek. As Harry made his way through the throng, all he was thinking about was a comment Emily had said as they were all getting ready that morning, not meant as such but possibly the most profound comment of the day, "I wonder who'll make the corned beef pie for this one?", she had said, and now Harry was wondering about that and also promising himself that he would start to build some bridges with Emily, he may even be able to persuade her to come back to band, if for no other reason than they could do with her on Repiano Cornet!

Emily had also sat down at the side of the hall, away from the crowd. Her black dress still fitted her well and to all surrounding her she had a good, young woman's figure. It was only if someone were to look very closely could they see the slight tug of the dress around her middle as Emily started to show.

Emily, who for the previous week had been making a concerted effort not to draw attention to herself, absentmindedly put her hand on her stomach and gently stroked as she privately said goodbye to her Nan and, for the first time, silently said hello to her child, her numbness now overtaken by an irony involving one life ending and another beginning.

Mary looked across the hall to make sure her children were bearing up alright, spotted James laughing and chatting with two uncles who had turned up in long black coats reminiscent of some kind of South Wales mafia, and smiled. Then she noticed Emily, sat alone, reading a list of esteemed Salvation Army soldiers in a frame on the wall, as the chattering crowd, and indeed the world revolved around her. She saw Emily's hand on her stomach, remembered the weeks of wondering what was wrong with her, and suddenly her distraught comments of the morning of Gwladys' passing fell into place. As Mary's hand tightened around her plastic cup she wiped a tear from her eye. She would wait for Emily to come to her.

Emily sat, looking at the list of Soldiers, noting her Nan's name amongst them. Through fear, Emily had kept her pregnancy to herself but knew that her body would give her secret away soon. The reason she had initially missed band rehearsals was due to wanting to spend as much time as possible with whom she felt to be her first "real love", however the reason had changed when she had discovered her "condition", a revelation that had been combined with the gentleman in question performing a disappearing act David Copperfield would have been proud of. The excitement of illicit rendezvous had been replaced by fear, confusion, and a feeling that somehow everyone could tell she was pregnant simply by looking at her. Harry had mistaken these feelings for stubbornness, or idleness and this had started the unease between them, particularly as

Emily could not bring herself to tell her dad the truth. He thought she didn't care about Midtown Band anymore and in a way he was right; he had seen his daughter throwing everything he had taught her back in his face. She had seen that Midtown Band wasn't the biggest thing in her life, or in anyone's life and this feeling growing inside her was one of combined panic and love bigger than anything she had felt before. It was possibly the loneliest time in Emily's life as she sat there surrounded by every remaining member of the family, compounded by the fact that the one person in the world whose reaction to her news was guaranteed to have been one of delight, was no longer with her.

As Harry took his place in the queue for the buffet and sidled along in front of the long paper-covered table, he grinned as he saw Eric smiling at him, already piling his second plate high. Eric was pointing approvingly at the sausage rolls and stifling a laugh, predicting his friend's amusement and glad to be lifting his spirits. Harry's eyes fell upon a splendid corned-beef pie taking pride of place, centre-table, in a blue and white patterned pottery dish with a lid adorned by a cow's head. Emily's question was answered; Mrs. Ross from across the street had made it in memory of Nan. He would have to let Emily know.

Chapter 5

Deep Harmony (Handel Parker)

Midtown Bandroom and its car-park was a flurry of activity, enhanced by nervous tension preceding the contest later, and the high-spirits that go hand-in-hand with a sun-dappled June morning. Even at 8am, the lack of clouds, the absence of a breeze, and the horizon emphasised as if by some divine spotlight, all contributed to the promise of another glorious day.

The crunch of instrument cases and percussion kit being wheeled across the gravel, the excited chatter of players and their families, and the starting of car-engines were all set against a backdrop of Radio Midtown emanating from the ageing stereo in Steve Pepper's Volvo. Four bass-players and their basses were swallowed up by the capacious estate, and it stood there ticking-over, Terry Horner in the passenger seat, one elbow out of window, the other helping to shovel a bacon roll into his mouth, Leighton Davis and Eric Trefelyn in the back, and Steve himself in the driver's seat, door still open, Ron Titley leaning in, earnestly discussing directions as if part of some elaborate "pre-flight" checks.

"Now, you've been briefed", Ron explained, "you have the directions as provided and photocopied by myself, our ETA in Rhymney is 10-hundred hours, I now make it approximately 8.02. What do you make it?"

Ron wagged his finger accusingly at Steve's watch.

"Well, I make it about five-past-eight Ron", replied Steve, "but Myfanwy reckons we'll be there by half-past-nine."

"Who's Myfanwy?" came Ron's response.

"She's the woman who tells me where to go!" explained Steve.

"Don't *all* women tell you that?" Eric's dulcet tones drily enquired from the back seat, resulting in guffaws from Terry and Leighton.

"She's my Sat Nav, Ron", Steve continued, "I've typed in our destination, and now she'll tell me exactly the quickest way there".

"Will she, will she?" muttered Ron, unimpressed that his lovingly-prepared directions were somewhat redundant, "Good, good...anyway, see you there, I've just got to see Jim and Roger before they go", he concluded, pointing at the red van waiting directly in front of Steve's Volvo, loaded with percussion, sheet-music, stands, mutes, and driven by James Jones. With his new objective now in mind, Ron gave the Volvo's roof a rapid double-tap with the palm of his hand as if granting permission or clearance to leave the car-park at will, and stepped away as Steve closed the door. The Volvo's occupants rolled their eyes as the officious Ron strode over to the driver's window of the van in front, gave it a purposeful triple-knock with the knuckle of his index finger and struck up a conversation with James; "Now, you've been briefed, you have the directions as provided and photocopied by myself..." An on-looking Terry Horner guffawed once again from the Volvo's passenger seat, imagining James' expression.

As the unlikely flotilla of vehicles drew out of the car-park, each faithfully hauling its own payload of people and instruments, Harry and Mary were already more than half way to Rhymney in Harry's car. If ever there was an atmosphere that could supposedly be cut with a knife, then a particularly sharp knife would have been required within the environs of the Jones' Mondeo that morning. The speakers delivering Harry's in-car Black Dyke band compilation had not been interrupted by a single syllable as the two occupants were each lost in an uneasy contemplation, borne from the recent news of Emily's pregnancy. It had been a week now since she had broken the news to her parents, and Harry had reacted badly. Mary had been preparing for it since she'd guessed what was going on at Gwaldys's funeral but she was still angry with Harry over the way he had spoken to Emily, and that anger along with Harry's shock had meant three days and one car journey of frosty silence. Emily had managed to hide the growing bump via a tenuous strategy involving loose clothes and staying out of everyone's way, but from a distance Mary had been keeping an eye on her progress.

Harry stared intently at the road in front, taking in every semiquaver Black Dyke had to offer, vainly seeking some respite from reality. Mary, her eyes fixed on the dashboard, wished she could think of a suitable opening sentence and at least impart to Harry that she wanted to somehow make him feel better about it all, while at the same time trying to bury feelings of simmering resentment that Harry himself was not saying something to make *her* feel better, and couldn't help wondering how Tom from work would handle this situation. She was sure he would know exactly what to say. "He would understand" she thought. Her relationship with Tom had been growing and she felt like he was a good friend now who often confided in her. From what he'd said, it appeared that sometimes his wife could be difficult and he had told Mary that his wife didn't always "do the things he wanted her to." Mary had imagined his tea not being ready, or his shirts remaining un-ironed, and she remembered thinking it was a shame as he did work hard. The beaming sun, and roads full of optimistic summer Saturday drivers only seemed to emphasise the gloom as Harry and Mary motored onwards.

James meanwhile, was having a great time. He was usually asked to take-on any van-driving duties given his current part-time profession as a delivery driver, and he always enjoyed driving the band van. Pop music was blaring out of the radio, Roger was regaling him with accounts of his latest drunken nights out around Midtown, other band-members' cars were overtaking, their passengers waving and generally kicking-back. Both James and Roger bellowed with laughter as Delmie Evans' Astra roared past, crammed with people, the bare buttocks of an as yet un-identified player pressed against the rear passenger window.

"Still going the right way are we?" James asked, basically knowing the answer.

"Oh yes", replied Roger Lloyd-Evans, "you can say what you like about Mao Tse Ron, but he does knock out a cracking direction".

James chuckled.

"Yeah 'maaan", continued Roger in, for no particular reason, an appalling attempt at a Jamaican accent, "we'll be 'der in about half an hour".

A red Saab convertible hissed luxuriously past them, a bespectacled Carl Davis, serious as ever, at the wheel. No waving, no display of buttocks, just Carl, stoically poised, probably reveling, thought James, in the fact that no-one had been drawn to share his car on Ron's passenger rota for the contest. James remembered his dad's character-analysis of Carl and grinned to himself; "Yes, he may be a miserable git, but he owns his own King Trombone and he hasn't missed a practice in 5 years". James' grin suddenly gave way to a frown as he wished some of Harry's dry humour could be sprinkled in Emily's direction, now more than ever. The scenery was spectacular as Mid Wales gave way to South Wales, and the sides of the valleys surrounded the ribbon of road that would take the band convoy towards Rhymney, this year's venue for The National Eisteddfod.

The Eisteddfod is an annual landmark event in Wales established across decades of tradition; a festival to celebrate the traditions of music, song, storytelling, creativity and craft, a celebration of Welsh and Celtic heritage, an aspirational platform for generations of Welsh musicians, artists, poets, and craftsmen, not to mention cooks and bakers. For the course of the festival, the showground transforms into a sea of tents and marquees housing exhibitions of children's drawings alongside established artists, craft stands ranging from one-man operations to small industries and food stalls selling everything from burgers to traditional barabrith. Central to the festival are the competitions and of utmost importance to Midtown Band is the band contest.

The band had elected to drive to this particular contest, the hiring of a coach having been discussed and dismissed due partly to some people being on holiday and in fact the whole concept of Midtown Band actually competing in this contest being thrown into question during an argument in band practice where Carl had suggested that it might be a "bit of a wasted journey" if they didn't come in the first three again. James noted, as the playful convoy slowly took its place, the short length of dual-carriageway now reducing to single once again, and the cars slowly out-running the van and disappearing from view one by one.

A lorry now dominated James' rear-view door mirror, and as the bends in the road gave way to a nice straight, James afforded a little more weight to the accelerator and the van slowly gained speed. Another glance in the mirror indicated that the distance between the van and the lorry was increasing. James couldn't stand these drivers that were almost on your rear bumper. Cars flew past in the opposite direction and as James' eyes left the mirror and concentrated on the road ahead, he couldn't help thinking he'd noticed something odd. He glanced at the mirror again. Sure enough there was something poking out of the lorry's right-hand side, something obscured by the heat-haze rising from the tarmac, but seemingly growing in size. James kept one eye on the mirror, the other on the road, as this mysterious object became more and more apparent. There were no cars coming the opposite way at the moment, and the road remained straight, all the way to the horizon. Suddenly James realised what this object was. It was a car, slowly edging out from behind the lorry in an attempt to overtake.

"Don't overtake here, for the love of God", James mumbled, appraising the length of the straight and the likelihood of cars suddenly coming the other way, in one succinct never-to-be-heard snippet of advice. The sun on the mirror, and the haze distorting an already reflected image meant that it wasn't until the car actually fully committed to the manoeuvre that the vehicle's identity then dawned on James, who could only look on in disbelief as, like some kind of bizarre yellow giant land-crab, Steve Pepper's Volvo gradually introduced itself.

"Oh my god...." James verbalised, "that dickhead's going to take-out the entire bass section. Look at this!"

Roger leaned over from the passenger side for a better look at James' driver's-mirror. The Volvo was now in full view as it attempted to come alongside the lorry, like a surreal collection of bass-playing pirates planning to board it. James and Roger's jaws dropped as the big car very very slowly made progress, clouds of white smoke billowing out of its rear and the ample frames of Steve and Terry becoming visible behind the windscreen in the distance. James could only wonder what was going through not only Steve's head, but also his passengers'. Roger suddenly gasped. A bus was hurtling towards them in the opposite direction, on a direct collision course with the Volvo. Had Steve seen it? There seemed to be little urgency. No sudden application of brakes, no reduction in the Volvo's momentum. The gap between the bus and the Volvo was closing rapidly. James started sweating, he honestly thought there was about to be an extremely serious accident at any moment. As he looked on, the Volvo, as though with no particular instinct for life-preservation, started to slowly sidle inwards towards the lorry it was trying to overtake. James was sure he could see Steve Pepper's round expressionless face indicating nothing more than mild irritation as the heat-haze, almost as though a reverse-play version of the last 20 seconds, once again claimed the Volvo as inch-by-inch it disappeared back behind the lorry. The bus arrived and shot past the lorry, missing Steve's car by inches, accompanied by flashing of headlights and obscene hand-gestures from the bus driver. James and Roger sighed with relief. Steve's passengers sat eyes wide, knuckles white as they involuntarily gripped their seats, and Terry's foot eventually stopped stamping on imaginary brake pedals. Steve's only comment was brief, as he calmly uttered;"What was that pillock flashing for?" And as the Volvo cruised past a sign that read "WC 200yds", Myfanwy summed up Terry, Eric and Leighton's thoughts in one instruction "Please take the next exit".

Gorffennaf Park, on the outskirts of Rhymney, was like a bustling town in its own right during Eisteddfod weekend. The expanse of grass was all but covered, leaving a network of green avenues via which one could navigate all the festival had to offer. A collection of musical styles, from classical to rock, but all in Welsh, colluded in a melee of background noise, under-pinned by a throbbing bass. People scampered in, out and between every tent, soaking up the experience. Harry and Mary had been at the Park for a while before the rest of the band started arriving. They had sat in the car, occupying one of the few remaining spaces in the field-come-carpark, marshalled in by volunteers wearing high-visibility vests with the word "Croeso" emblazoned across the front. Both Harry and Mary heard little of the car-radio still playing, as they both silently thought of Emily. It was Mary who decided to break the deadlock, "We just need to be there for her Harry, she has obviously been scared of telling us."

Harry opened the car door; "I'm getting changed." he said, and got out, closing the door behind him.

Mary just sighed. "Tom wouldn't be like this."

Harry was rummaging around in the boot for his band shoes as the first of the Midtown Band cars started arriving. It was fairly obvious who they were due to the horn being beeped in time to 'We Will Rock You' on the stereo and a pair of trousers flapping out of the sunroof. As the car stopped, Toby Stephens got out of the back. He was just in his pants, and looking annoyed.

"Nobheads!" he shouted as he retrieved his trousers from the sunroof and pulled them on. One of the marshals suddenly strode over, waving his arms.

"Great," thought Toby, "he's about to do me for indecency at an Eisteddfod".

However the marshal ignored Toby, walked around the car and started talking to Timothy Dann, who was driving.

"Sorry butty", he said, in a broad Welsh farmer's accent, "there's no more spaces here; you'll have to use the overflow car park up there". He pointed to an area about fifty yards away which had been fenced off.

"But there's cows at one end of it", Timothy correctly observed.

"That's right", grinned the marshal.

"Won't they charge us?" enquired Timothy with slight trepidation.

"Nah, they normally let you in for nothing!" bellowed the marshal before laughing loudly and waving them on. Timothy shrugged, followed the marshal's direction and drove into the overflow car park, shortly to be joined by Delmie's Astra, Carl's Saab and the rest of the band, James and the red van bringing up the rear.

Harry shook his head at the somewhat undignified arrival of his troops, but was relieved. "At least the band boys are here now", he thought. He would have a respite from the topic of Emily, at least for a while.

There was however, one car noticeable by its absence. "Where's Steve?" asked Harry.

"He was behind us until about 40 minutes ago", said James, trying not to think about the fact that it was possible Steve may have again attempted overtaking at the most ill-advised time, this time with disastrous consequences.

"Come on then Ron", Harry continued, "let's go and see what time we're playing. Everyone else, back here in half an hour so we all know what's happening".

And with that, the band, in their own little groups, went their separate ways to have a look around.

"Blimey, it's a lot bigger this year", Rachel said to Lucy as they ambled along the wide grass-way between the tents.

"Yeah, everything is still written just in Welsh though for some reason", moaned Lucy as they wandered into the next tent en-route. A few of the band boys were already inside looking at the various items on display, and a very po-faced woman standing behind a table at one end. The table had a number of products on it made from animal skin, ivory and bone, the most notable of which were some small statues about four inches high next to a small sign which said: *"These ornaments were made from the tusks of a bull elephant. This magnificent animal was slaughtered to make these statues which retail at £5 each in the West"*

As the band all stood around expressing their disgust, cornet-player Phil Edwards arrived talking to James. Now to be fair, they had been deep in conversation and had just followed the band boys into the tent. As they stopped talking and reached the little table, they both just started looking at the display.

Phil couldn't believe what he was seeing. There was a handbag on the table made of crocodile skin, with an actual baby crocodile's head fixed on as the clasp. Phil reached out and picked up the bag.

"Look at this!" he exclaimed, "How cool is that?"

For a second there was silence and then everyone in the tent burst into laughter.

"What's the matter? That's really cool, look the clasp is a little crocodile head", Phil looked at the po-faced woman who was most definitely not laughing. In fact she was now looking less po-faced and more furious. Just to pile on even more insult, Phil addressed her as though speaking to a Spanish waiter in a loud, exaggerated voice thinking that she was probably full-on Welsh and didn't understand English;

"How much is this?" he shouted pointing at the bag.

The band came running out of the tent in fits of laughter followed by Phil looking bright red, walking backwards and trying to explain that he didn't know what she was talking about, and could she stop shouting now please. Even though Phil didn't speak a word of Welsh, the reason for her furious ranting and the collective hilarity of the bandsmen became all too clear as she pointed at the sign above the tent's entrance, which simply said "World Wildlife Fund".

Back at the car-park, Harry was getting concerned. Midtown had been allocated an early time to compete and there was still no sign of Steve Pepper and the basses.

"Where is he?" Harry vocalised his thoughts to Mary, Ron and the slowly increasing number of players making their way back. Phil, James, Lucy and Rachel were last to arrive back at the car-park, and a worried Harry was holding an impromptu meeting.

"We're due on stage in 25 minutes," he explained, "and unless they show up here like-but-fast we're not going to have any basses." The band fell silent. Yes, they all wanted a nice day out, but they were there to compete. They'd all sacrificed other activities to attend rehearsals, learn and practice parts, and they were not ready to see all that go up in smoke.

"Can some of us double-up and play the bass parts?" suggested an ever-logical Lucy.

"Good suggestion", replied Harry, "but I've racked my brains and can't see how we can make it work". Lucy knew that Harry would have not only racked his brains, but exhausted every possible avenue to find a solution.

"In that case", said James, "we're going to have to borrow". There was a sharp intake of breath from the players. Under the rules, bands were allowed to borrow up to two players from another competing band. Harry had already arrived at this conclusion but just didn't want to admit it. "Who's on just before us dad?"

Harry swallowed hard, and as if it pained him to do so, he looked over to the left where a fully-uniformed band were disembarking their coach and preparing to head to the main stage tent. James' heart sank. Glancrumlin Adult Products Band; unfortunate for two main reasons; firstly their all too descriptive sponsorship, secondly their conductor; Edwin Goodwin, who Harry hated with a vengeance.

"Do I really have to ask that…" Harry almost choked on his own words, "…man, if I can borrow two of his basses?" He already knew the answer.

James felt for him. This was the man who had unfairly, in many people's opinion, pipped Midtown to first place on one too many occasions. The man about whom Harry had oft commented, "You can't trust a man who conducts with his arms above his head", and "He looks like a reject from Swan Lake".

"Well, it's either that, or we can't play", said Ron. He was correct.

Harry gritted his teeth, forced his lips into the most convincing smile he could, and strode over to the nearby coach. Edwin Goodwin saw Harry coming, grinned broadly and held out his hand. "Edwin!" gushed Harry, "How the devil are you?" Midtown band looked on, unable to hear the conversation but noting a selection of strange movements from Harry, who had his back to them. First he pointed at the ground, and then his arms shot out as though imitating an aeroplane. He looked as though he was laughing. At one point he briefly turned to face Midtown, his smile turning to a furious snarl as he mouthed the word "cretin", smile instantly returning as he turned once again to face Edwin. The conversation concluded and Harry strode back to where his own band stood.

"We're good", he said. "Two Glancrumlin basses will wait on stage. Johnny Quango and Johnny Ryder. The two Johnnies. Lovely".

Midtown Band was relieved. Even though a rival band's players would be playing alongside them on stage, it was an unwritten law within banding that those players would perform to the best of their ability, as though with their own band. It was a rule that no bandsman would ever break.

Forty five minutes later, an anti-climax dogged the mood of the band as they vacated the stage.

"Ok, so it didn't go so well", a sympathetic Mary said as Harry met up with her post-performance. She knew better than to patronise him with fluffy critiques about how "nice" it was, and how it "sounded as if they should win".

"It was alright," said Harry, "but we could have done better. It just wasn't our day. Those two basses did well though; I owe them both a drink".

Mary offered to drive the car home if Harry wanted a pint. An offer Harry readily accepted.

Back at the car-park, the band was busy changing out of uniforms, putting instruments back into cars and generally wallowing in an air of despondence. They knew they had technically played well, but it had lacked sparkle. It had fallen short of what Harry felt to be a winning performance. Harry arrived and made his customary little speech; "Alright everyone, I think we all know how that went. It's just one of those things; let's concentrate on the next one now. Meanwhile, I know we all came here in cars, so can I just remind everyone that if you have driven and you intend having a few beers..."

Lawrence Ap Dafydd interrupted, chiming in "We're organising a race to Pontlottyn later!" The band burst out laughing, and it served to somehow lift the despondency.

"Yes, yes" continued Harry, "be that as it may, I was going to say, get someone else to drive your car home". The band once again dispersed, all feeling bad for Harry. They knew that he liked to win, but they also knew that it was more about the performance as far as Harry was concerned. Mary decided to join some of the band girls as they wandered around the showground. Not many of the wives, husbands or families of the players had come along on this occasion, and she knew Harry would be catching up with old band cohorts.

Harry made his way to the bar, the band boys stuck around the car park deciding who wanted to go straight home, who wanted to stick around, and how to organise transport for everyone accordingly.

"Where are they all though?" Toby Stephens asked, referring to Steve and the basses, "it's a shame we can't phone them" he reminded them all of Harry's feelings about mobile phones at band events.

"I thought Terry Horner had one of those things that go in your ear", said Ron, "I've seen him walking around Midtown talking on it".

"You mean a blue-tooth headset", volunteered Carl Davies in his usual dour tones.

"They're good they are", said Lawrence, "I'm thinking of getting one".

"Why?" said James, bemused. If anyone was interested in modern technology and gadgetry, it wasn't usually Lawrence.

"Dunno mate", said Lawrence, "thought I'd treat myself to a phone that goes in your ear. I just feel I should have one".

Ron frowned, Lawrence's dry humour totally lost on him and Carl. Lawrence continued, discreetly nudging James in the side with his elbow as he spoke. "Or, I might even get one of the ones that go in your eye."

James stifled a giggle as Ron and Carl looked confused. "What are you talking about?" said Carl, "You can't get one that goes in your eye!"

"Yes, they were on about them last night on tele, they're called eye-phones apparently." explained Lawrence. James burst out laughing.

"Idiot", contributed Ron. James decided to give Lawrence his advice. "You don't need an i-Phone mate, they're more for…" he paused to locate an example.

"Businessmen?" offered Ron. "Social networkers?" added Carl.

"…cocks." confirmed James, eliciting another round of chuckles. Ron and Carl were glad they hadn't admitted ownership of the said devices.

Carl finished packing his uniform away and closed the boot of his Saab.

"How come you bought a convertible then Carl?" asked James, genuinely curious. "I mean, you don't quite seem a convertible kind of person".

"Well I'll tell you for why", replied Carl in his usual dreary manner. "it's so, on the hottest day of the year, when I pull up at the traffic lights in town, roof down, I can glance over at the guy cooped up and sweltering in the car next to me, and just for that brief moment, his life is just that little bit more crap than mine."

"And on that note…" James left his conclusion hanging as they walked towards the festivities of the Eisteddfod.

Harry was sat in the bar, nursing a pint of bitter. He'd just been chatting to an old friend from South Wales and was about to walk over and join a group of people he recognised. As he walked from the bar, Eric Trefelyn suddenly appeared at the entrance of the beer-tent and walked in waving at Harry.

"What happened to you lot?" Harry began, as they both sat at a table.

"I'll tell you in a minute, right now what are you having, the usual?" replied Eric, placing his folded jacket on the table and getting up to go to the bar. Harry nodded. It was still relatively early on in the day and the beer tent was only half full. The bright sunlight permeated through the canvas roof making the tent warm inside. The air wafted with cigarette smoke and Welsh voices debating everything from the choice of Dylan Thomas as the opening reading of the festival, to the price of beer. With a couple of pints of Felinfoel in his hands, Eric returned to the table and resumed his seat.

Straightaway, Eric adopted a serious tone, "What is it mate?"

"What's what?" Harry answered coldly.

"What has made you act like a bear with a boil on his arse for the last week?"

Harry took a sip of his pint, put it on the table, and looked Eric in the eye. His oldest friend would be the first person to hear the words come from his mouth. He swallowed hard, realising he was nervous as hell and then just said it, "Emily's pregnant."

The low hum of chatter just continued on in the beer tent. The sun still shone outside and Eric just picked up his pint and took a sip. Harry had been waiting for the world to crash around him when he uttered those words, but everything just seemed to carry on. Eric watched Harry for a second and then spoke quietly and confidently,

"Don't blame her Harry."

Eric was known to everyone as bit of a joker and a bit of a drinker and not known for any great insights on life, but the way he was came from that insight. He had been in the pit when a roof collapsed trapping five men who died in the coal dust. He had seen his community ripped apart during the miner's conflict, seen the inside of too many hospitals and lost friends and family along the way. And throughout his life, Eric had found that laughter and a sense of the ridiculous provided escape and a way to cope without going under. Of course beer and cigarettes helped as well, but everything that Eric had seen in his life had given him a deceptive wisdom that most people never saw.

In four words Harry realised how close he and his friend were. Eric had looked into Harry's eyes and seen the past week written there. Harry still got angry though, "What do you mean don't blame her? Who should I blame then? She won't tell us who the father is so I can't go and give him a hiding, who's left to blame Eric?"

Eric picked up a beer mat and showed Harry.

"See this Harry? This is how big that baby is inside Emily now. Pretty soon that baby is going to be here and it'll be you're grandchild. That baby growing inside her may only be this big, but it's still part of you Harry. Remember when James was born, you and Mary thought it was the scariest thing ever? That's what Emily's feeling now, and from what you just said she's hasn't even got the father to help her."

He put the beer mat down and took another sip of his pint. Harry looked down at the table, "I've not done very well with this Eric."

"You've acted like anyone else would have. You can only be yourself mate. You're not a saint, and most importantly it's not too late. You've just got to be there for her now because she'll remember, and once you blame her for this….." his words trailed off into the growing background noise and both men just sat quietly together.

Harry's thoughts were broken as a sheepish Steve "it wasn't my fault" Pepper suddenly arrived, out of breath, at their table.

"Been looking for you everywhere Harry", he gasped.

At that particular point in time Harry just didn't have the energy to be angry, but was nonetheless quite curious to find out what Steve's excuse was for making himself, and the entire bass-section, two hours late, particularly after spending the last three weeks boasting about his new Sat Nav.

"Come on then," said Harry wearily, "let's hear it."

"Well", began Steve, "who would have thought there were *two* Rhymneys…?"

Chapter 6

A Tale As Yet Untold (Philip Sparke)

The July morning seemed uninspiring. Glorious sunshine during the last few weeks had given way to misty drizzle. However, the eighty people congregating on the Midtown Silver Bandroom car-park at 7am could not have been in higher spirits.

Thanks to the stalwart efforts of Ron Titley, Midtown Band was going to take their first foreign tour. Through his various twinning committees and Rotary Club contacts, Ron had arranged with the town of Lorient in Brittany a series of concerts and joint entertainment evenings within the town, and the surrounding villages, over the course of two weeks. The concerts would form part of Lorient's annual Cultural Festival event. Since the plans were finalised, the band had been gearing-up for the trip by arranging fundraising concerts, raffles and press coverage to attract sponsorship. They had not turned down any engagement which would swell the coffers, and although the trip itself would involve many concerts, for the players it signified a reward for months of hard work and a break from the ever-present and ominous discussions about the Bandroom's future. The Mayor of Midtown and most of the town councillors were also going along, as were spouses and families. Ron Titley beamed. He was in his element standing on the car-park, surveying the culmination of his efforts, along with the town dignitaries. He had just finished handing out the itineraries he had prepared and personalised with the coach number and even the seat number allocated to each traveller, and all that remained now was for the two coaches to arrive.

The Jones family stood amongst the others, suitcases and uniform-covers on the gravel. James was excited. He loved travelling but did not have the means to do any at the moment. After dropping out of Cardiff University due to a decision 18 months into the course that Hospitality and Tourism just wasn't for him, he had returned to Midtown and announced that he was going to travel the world, decide which country he'd like to live in, and basically move there. Mary and Harry had been sceptical; an attitude which had annoyed James, but which had been proven over the last three years. Far from doing any travelling, or devising a strategy which would allow him to fund his dream, James had taken whatever part-time, temporary job had come his way, turning-down solid opportunities for on-going employment with prospects, for fear of being "tied down", and had ended up frittering away his weekly pay-packet in The Cock or the Starlight Lounge. Mary had not been amused, and still wasn't. She knew what James was capable of, and was worried that his non-committal attitude would continue as the years flew by. She also knew how unfulfilled Harry felt, despite the pride in his work he displayed, at the factory. For years she had encouraged him to have enough belief in himself to find a way to be professionally involved in music. Harry however, had always looked upon music as a passion, almost a religion, something that was separate from the necessity that was "work". At the moment, James wasn't that passionate about anything. Even banding was little more than a "hobby", albeit an enjoyable one. He lacked Harry's drive. Harry felt it would be hypocritical to be too judgmental about James, who was only displaying the same lack of career-ambition as Harry himself, and as long as James was turning up for band and playing euphonium, well it couldn't be all bad.

Mary sometimes felt like knocking some sense into both of them. Harry needed to have a frank discussion with James about his future, and James needed to take some kind of responsibility. Maybe the trip to France would broaden James' horizons a little, show him that the world outside Wales was nearer than he thought, and give him the incentive to finally reach out and grab it, something that Harry had also planned to do years ago when he and Mary were first married, but had never come to fruition.

Emily stood next to Mary. Her morning sickness had eased off recently and she was very much looking forward to the tour. For her it was a change of scene, a representation of leaving behind the mess she felt her life had become, if only for two weeks. And maybe, in the less rigid, holiday-like atmosphere, her and her dad would find a way to build a few bridges. Today, the Jones family was extended. Part of the Cefngoed contingent, namely Mary's sister Megan and her husband Iestin, one of Harry's childhood best mates, had booked a place on the France trip. Megan and Iestin were always good value, and Emily was delighted they were there. They had driven from Cefngoed last night, stayed at the Jones' house and were now both stood, waiting with the rest of the party, obscured by white billowing smoke from their third cigarette that hour. Megan and Iestin were the type of people that seemed to engage "holiday-mode" as if they'd flicked a switch. The switch had been well and truly moved to the "on" position upon their arrival in Midtown last night. Both of them had wallets full of cash that it was their sole intention to blow indiscriminately during the following two weeks, both of them were laden with cigarettes, and each concealed a hip-flask brimming with vodka which they intended to drink and replace with "duty free" at the earliest opportunity. James and Emily often joked about Megan and Iestin's status as "die hard" holidaymakers. Some people just knew how to be on holiday, and this couple was not short of practice. They would find a way to save up and get involved with any trip going, whether Cefngoed British Legion, city-breaks with friends, 3-day mini-cruises, collecting vouchers from the newspapers, they would be there, and there would always be stories to tell afterwards.

"Here they are!" shrieked Owain Owain's mum from her self-appointed position at the car-park entrance. She began waving her arms above her head as if guiding an aeroplane down. Even though the coach firm supplied the regular transport of Midtown Silver Band, she felt it her duty to alert them of the Bandroom's location as they made an appearance, travelling down the main road. A general murmur, increasing in volume, broke into a cheer involving clapping and whistling as the first coach suddenly rumbled and hissed its way onto the car-park, gravel crunching under-wheel, and huge wipers sweeping droplets off the windscreen. Coach No.1 was driven by the company's owner, Wyn D. Day, who grinned at the cheering crowd and gave a quick double-blast of the horn as he drew the massive gleaming blue and silver coach to a halt. Coach No.2 immediately followed, and at the wheel sat regular band-driver Lloyd Wenby, also grinning, as Gwladys Jones would have put it, like a bag of chips, and delivering a sharp salute to the applauding group.

"OK everyone", Ron shouted as he walked sergeant-major-like in front of the crowd, arms outstretched, flat palms pushing against an invisible wall, willing everybody to be quiet and listen to him. "If we could just have a bit of order, yes, yes…shut-up now, everyone…"

"Who's this dick?" Iestin leaned in towards Harry and spoke without moving his lips.

Harry laughed, instantly taken-back to a classroom 30-years ago when Iestin had asked the same question as the new English teacher walked in, only managing to evade detention when being overheard, by telling the new member of staff that Harry's name was Dick, and he was simply trying to find out who it was that had just walked in.

This piece of quick-thinking had resulted in the new English teacher referring to Harry as Dick for the first 6 months of the school-year, and even after enquiring why he was listed as "Harold" on the register had simply been informed by Iestin that in Cefngoed the shortened version of Harold was in fact Dick.

"It's Ron Titley, the band Secretary", Harry whispered back, "bit of a pillock if the truth be told, but he's harmless enough, and to be fair he has pulled it out of the bag organising this trip."

"Could everyone allocated to Coach No.1, that's Coach No.1, please move all your luggage here", continued Ron, clipboard now in one hand, the other pointing at the gravel he was standing on, "then make your way onto the coach, making sure I tick your name off the list as you do so."

Forty of the assembled crowd started shuffling forward, bags in hand, uniform covers over shoulders. Coach No.1 was apparently going to be where most of the actual players would be travelling, along with partners. This would leave Coach No.2 for the supporters, the dignitaries, and other associated family members. A pile of suitcases and uniform covers were slowly loaded into the large hold-space, along with instruments, music stands and a box full of music. Uniforms were stacked neatly in the small area next to the boot, labelled "Crew compartment", and one by one people made their way onto the bus via the front-door, each announcing their name to Ron who stood by the door, peering over the top of his spectacles at his clip-board and theatrically ticking each name in turn. Steve couldn't resist the opportunity, and when it was his turn to board, he informed Ron;

"Stephen & Gillian Pepper, E-flat Bass player and dinner-lady", giggles followed.

The Peppers boarded, and this then set the trend;

"Daniel & Rachel Parry, cornet player and cornet player", suppressed titters were audible amongst the queuing passengers. Ron just rolled his eyes, anything to get everyone on the coach. Carl Davis and his wife were next to go aboard. The humour of the faux-formal announcements was lost on Carl who would never have knowingly joined in with such juvenile matters, so thinking this was simply protocol, he also announced;

"Carl & Alexandra Davis, Bass Trombone player and…"

"Cracking bit of stuff!" someone bellowed from the waiting queue. Everyone cheered and whistled. Carl turned round, shaking his head as if disappointed by the fact he was associated with such an uncouth collection of individuals. Alex, who looked like she'd been poured into her tight short black dress, large designer-sunglasses perched on top of her long blonde hair adding to an image which suggested she'd be more at home on the arm of a premier-league footballer, also turned her head towards the queue but was giggling at the comment as another tirade of wolf-whistles greeted her.

"…and massage-therapist!" corrected Carl, as Ron hurriedly ushered them onto the coach.

Gradually the coach filled up, the luggage-hold doors were slammed shut, and the engines of Coach No.1 fired into life. It rolled slowly forward and a roar of applause followed inside, but suddenly it stopped again. The rest of the travellers, preparing to board Coach No.2 looked on as Coach No.1's door suddenly hissed open, Terry Horner jumped out and began hurriedly jamming half a pie into his mouth, explaining as best he could, through the medium of hand-gestures and spat-out pastry crumbs that "Windy" says there's no hot food allowed on his buses.

"What was that?" Terry yelled up at Wyn D. Day who had shouted something from the driver's seat.

"Oh, on his *coaches* I mean", continued Terry at a nonplussed Ron.

Half an hour later both coaches were traversing Mid Wales, heading for the English border and the onward journey to Southampton. Coach No.1 lazily weaved its way along the roads, as if conserving its energy for the nearing motorway, whilst in reality giving Coach No.2 a chance to catch up so the remainder of the journey could be completed in convoy. Activity onboard was already varied, and noisy. A very early poker-school was in its infancy, based around one of the few opposite-facing seats with a table between. A few of the lads were enjoying the "I went to the shop" game, and others were singing along to the radio. The remainder were either chatting, or managing to catch up on some sleep, aided by the gentle motion of the coach, and the low, soporific hum of the engine. Players' husbands and wives knew better than to expect anything less than the gambling, the singing, the playing of stupid games, and in fact most of the spouses were joining-in. Those who thought that any time on the coach would even remotely resemble a romantic interlude were only kidding themselves. The drizzle was easing off, and the condensation on the windows was slowly clearing. It was now threatening to be another bright sunny day. A whistle, becoming apparent over the engine noise, was solidly and deliberately rising in pitch, signalling the extra power being pushed through to the mighty wheels. The hedgerows and roadside verges started to speed up and were, in no time, replaced by the extra lanes of the approaching motorway. The journey was now well and truly underway.

It was still relatively early in the day, and motorway-traffic was not a problem. The morning sun now made its presence felt in no uncertain terms, and the coach, like a galloping horse was frivolously swallowing up the miles. James sat by the window, next to Roger, chatting about everything and nothing. They had just concluded a debate with some of the others, about which James Bond film was the best. And in an unlikely display of animation and in-depth knowledge, Carl Davis had managed to put across some quite convincing arguments, peppered with quotes and even a not unaccomplished impression of Sean Connery. "Perhaps this is the side of him Alex sees", James had whispered to Roger, "God knows he must have something more to him than we ever see if he can pull a bird like her."

"Yeah" Roger had agreed, before dryly adding, "either that or he's got an enormous crotch-rocket."

James had laughed out loud, constantly amazed by Roger's ability to always come up with a new and surprising but somehow perfect definition to match the circumstance. In this respect he was ahead of his time, and wasted in Midtown.

"Here's the others!" Delmie suddenly shouted from the back of the bus, and as everyone's head turned to face the right-hand windows, Coach No.2 drew alongside.

Everyone on Coach No.1 waved and shouted, as if their cohorts on the other coach could somehow hear them, and as the two coaches navigated a short stretch of motorway in parallel, the occupants were granted a brief glimpse into each other's world. Those on Coach No.2 were treated to a real-life silent movie, the narrative of which was an observation of modern-day society as forty carefree holidaymakers gesticulated their enthusiasm, their shouts reduced, by two thick windows separated by a metre of motorway, to mimes. Every member of society was represented, and to the un-initiated would look like the most cliché collection possible, ranging from the unemployed roofer to the successful businessman, and encompassing the student, the parent, the yob, and possibly even the tart. Alternatively, those on Coach No.1 were presented with a snapshot, a notably static image, of a group that courted respectability; smartly dressed, newspaper-reading, boiled-sweet-sucking adults whose thoughts were only interrupted during the exchange of intelligent comment. As James waved, he spotted Mary and Harry near the front, who both grinned and waved back. Sitting behind them was Emily, eyes transfixed on the window, face locked in an expression which James recognised instantly, and which imparted "For the love of God can I be on your coach instead!" James grinned back as sympathetically as he could at poor old Em. And the rows of seats continued; councillors, people's nans, the Mayor...

In the midst of this group, as if someone had let a chimpanzee loose in a library, Iestin had his hands pressed up against the window, and was licking the glass, performing his extremely politically-incorrect depiction of a confused mental-patient. Those on Coach No.1 roared with laughter, partly at the impersonation but mainly at the unlikely forum within which the artist worked, and as his act progressed into the realms of feigning a frantic hammering on the glass in a vane attempt at escape, his audience looked on, delighted, and roaring with laughter. Iestin's manic actions suddenly ceased and he turned to face Ron Titley who sat in the seat behind, next to

Councillor Ellis, lips moving. Everyone on Coach No.1 saw a frown appear on Iestin's face, and Ron's arms suddenly folding, accompanied by a shaking of his head, and more lip-moving. Iestin suddenly faced the window again, this time with his tongue jammed forward into his chin creating an under-bite as he rocked back and forth, his finger, below head-rest level, pointing at Ron. And as Coach No.2 slowly accelerated and passed by, Iestin was afforded a final cheer as his audience watched him secretly giving a repeated 2-finger gesture, again below seat-back level, to an oblivious Mr Titley.

The following hours, as the twin coaches passed through the Midlands, then eventually into the South West, continued in the same vein. And as Coach No.1 arrived in Southampton, a sleeping Norman Lightfoot sported a face full of make-up, and Toby Stephens retrieved his trousers, resembling a strange double wind-sock, from the sunroof where they had been since just south of Milton Keynes. Although he did attempt to get into the spirit of things with his indignant cry of "Les nob-heads!" as he eventually got them back on. Those on Coach No.2 folded up their newspapers, put away their books, and generally reflected on a pleasant journey which had served to raise their awareness of current affairs and contemporary fiction. The coaches were now finally parked next to each other once again; engines now silent apart from the occasional ticking as they cooled off, as if settling down to snatch forty-winks on the dockside before it was time to drive onto the ferry. The passengers on their respective coaches were now united by shared excitement about the ferry crossing, and all were eager to get to France.

The front-door of Coach No.2 hissed open, and Harry walked down onto the coach-park, made his way around the front of Coach No.1, and into the now open door. As he boarded, the ambient noise of chatter, people pulling bags out of overhead storage, beer cans being deposited in black bin-bags, all ceased. Only Steve Pepper could be heard as he customarily announced,

"Our father, who art in Heaven",

The rest of the band, plus partners, instinctively joined in, and shouted "Harold be thy name!" followed by cheers and whistles.

Harry grinned, and made his way half way along the aisle.

"Right. Listen up everyone. We are going to be here for a while now waiting to get on board the boat. If you want to go outside to stretch your legs then fine, but stay near the coach. Norman, that really isn't your colour 'butt".

Laughter rippled round the coach and Norman, still ignorant of the fact he was sporting mascara, blusher and lip-gloss just laughed along, not sure why, but equally not wanting to appear foolish.

"So, whatever you do, make sure you're back here in two-hours. That's when we'll know what's happening." Harry continued, he then turned to have a word with Eric, and the players commenced standing up and stretching. The coach park was a huge expanse of grey, disappearing under containers, lorries and cars, and eventually ending with a drop into the sea, and as Harry, Eric, Steve and Terry stepped off the coach, the late-afternoon wind whistling in from the estuary hit them.

"Blimey, it's a bit windy" Terry noted. They all nodded.

"Right, where can we get a drink?" said Steve rubbing his hands.

"Well, all the cans have gone, we'll have to go and find somewhere." Eric said and started walking away from the coach. "You coming 'butt?"

"I might catch up with you", replied Harry, "I'd better see what Mary and the others are up to". And with that, he went back onto Coach No.2, although unable to deny how welcome a quick pint and a laugh with the boys seemed, especially given the uninspiring atmosphere of the journey there.

"Eh, Harry said not to go too far from the coach" shouted Steve, as the small group headed towards the coach-park's exit.

"Look, we're going to be ages waiting to get on. We'll find a pub, have a drink and come back. No-one will even notice we're gone." Eric kept walking followed by Terry and a worried Steve.

Emily had taken the opportunity to grab some time on Coach No.1, and was sat next to James, looking out of the window. Her stomach was now plump and round and the news had been broken to the players that she was expecting a baby.

"Where are they going?" James asked, watching the trio getting smaller and smaller as they sauntered over the tarmac.

"Where do you think?" Emily answered absentmindedly.

James turned around.

"Delmie, fancy sneaking off for a drink? Rog' what about you?"

Delmie was up in an instant, as was Roger.

"Lucy? Rachel? You coming?"

Rachel got up and climbed over Lucy but Lucy said she wasn't bothered and was going to stay on the coach.

"Can I come?" asked Emily still looking out of the window.

James looked surprised; "Course you can, I just didn't think you would want to?"

James was imagining a pregnant Emily in a smoky, busy pub being constantly bumped by half-drunks. Emily thought James was trying to protect her from comments and looks from people, and decided she'd had enough of that recently and changed her mind.

"Don't worry. I'll stay here." she said and dreamily watched the lorries arriving and queuing up on the dock.

As Delmie, Roger, Rachel and James left the coach Lucy came and sat next to Emily. They chatted for a minute and then fell silent. Emily had never really been close friends with Lucy but she appreciated her coming over and even more appreciated the fact that there had been no questions about the baby. All everyone wanted to know, of course, was the identity of the father. But Emily had not said, and didn't think she ever would.

Toby Stephens watched Emily through the headrests. They had been starting to get close before Emily's pregnancy and Toby had hoped for a relationship, but since she had stopped coming to band, things had cooled off. He planned to use this trip to rekindle something, and in fact he had convinced himself that should things develop between them, he was ready for the responsibility of looking after both Emily and the baby!

Steve, Eric and Terry had walked for about ten minutes before finding a decent pub that stocked real ale. They were soon joined by Delmie, Roger, Rachel and James.

"Bloody hell Jim, you better make sure your Dad didn't see you" Steve said nervously, still not quite sure whether they'd strayed "too far from the coach".

Eric stood by James at the bar.

"How's Emily, Jim?" he asked quietly.

"Alright. I think she's alright"

"How's your mum and dad?"

James let out a sigh.

"Well you know dad Eric, he doesn't want to talk about anything if it isn't to do with band and Mum just looks worried all the time."

"Give your dad time Jim. That's his little girl, and suddenly he's seen her become a woman."

James picked up three pints and turned around, "I know Eric, but she is still his little girl and he his still her dad and she needs him now, not when he decides that sectional rehearsals can take a back seat to his own family". He walked off feeling bad. Eric had only been trying to help.

The next hour involved a lot of drinking. A few more players entered the pub, followed by, of all people, Ron Titley. He was accompanied by a group of councillors, and at first there was unease as if the headmaster had just discovered a party in the Common Room, but Ron looked relaxed and was soon joining in with some of the banter.

"So Ron, is the good lady wife not coming along to France then?" Eric inquired.

"She'll be rendezvous-ing with us next weekend", said Ron, pleased with his inclusion of a French word, and nudging Eric to emphasise the little joke.

"Ophelia will be flying over and meeting us for the second week", Ron continued. "She won't entertain the idea of travelling on water since she watched The Poseidon Adventure on video." He shook his head solemnly, "Even Wild Willy's Water Ride in Rhyl is something she can now only ever dream of experiencing, and as for the Log Flume in Porthcawl, forget it. She even shuddered last Sunday when I put a gravy-boat on the table at dinner time."

"Steve" whispered Terry, "Let's get Ron a drink"

"What for?" Steve answered in surprise, he had never brought Ron a drink in his life "he's got all his councillor mates with him, they can buy him one."

"No mate", urged Terry as surreptitiously as he could, "you don't understand. Let's get Ron…a *drink*"

"Ah…you mean a *drink*", said Steve, the penny now dropping with regards to what Terry was getting at.

"Well, surely it's our duty to ensure he has a good time" said Terry with a wink as they squeezed through the players at the bar and asked for half a pint of lager and lime, which was what Ron drank. They also ordered three vodkas. Steve instantly gulped a third of the lager and lime which he immediately replaced by pouring the vodkas in.

Terry walked over to where Ron sat, "There you go mate" he said.

Ron was delighted and somewhat touched by the gesture and for the first time felt part of the gang. He thanked Terry and puffed his chest out with pride.

Terry looked over to Steve and slowly nodded his head. Steve gave a private "thumbs-up" in reply.

Mary and Harry sat together on Coach No2.

"I bet they've all gone to a pub" thought Harry. Mary put her hand on Harry's.

"Why don't you go and ask Emily if she's OK. She's sitting next to Lucy over there" she said hopefully, pointing at the neighbouring coach.

"I won't interrupt them." said Harry and continued staring out of the window at the same patch of tarmac that had transfixed Emily. It is quite amazing how a grey landscape of nothing can hold so much attention, but at least half the coach passengers and indeed half the other passengers in other coaches stared at the ferry dock. Some absent minded, some intense, some putting faith in the grey concrete to reveal answers to problems they had been carrying around with them.

Harry just thought of Emily and how they had all been before the pregnancy. He wished he could go over and say something to her. But what? He didn't know how he was supposed to feel, or act, but he did know that it just made him feel angry thinking about it all. It was easier, for the moment, to carry on as they were. There was a lot to think about; the trip, the potential demise of the Bandroom, the Albert Hall. What was he expected to do? He looked behind, wondering if Megan and Iestin were interested in some fresh air, secretly hoping to bump into the others and enjoy a swift pint. But his sister-in-law and her husband were fast asleep, leaning on each other, each clutching an empty hip-flask.

At the pub, James looked at his watch and stood up quickly, "Jesus Christ look at the time. We'd better get back." Most of the players heard, finished their drinks and started to vacate the pub, negotiating their way through the ever-increasing crowd as evening loomed. Getting Ron out would be a different matter.

"Bloody hell Terry, what have we done" said Steve as suddenly the pub was once again treated to a rendition of Delilah from Ron who was sitting on a bar stool, shirt unbuttoned to the waist, with his arm around one of the local lushes, belting out a third rate impression of Tom Jones.

His comb-over was now hanging down the side of his head and his glasses balanced precariously on the end of his nose. The councillors had made their excuses half-an-hour ago, using the pretext of "visiting the Gents".

Terry went over to him. "Come on 'Tom, we'd better get back to the bus".

Ron looked at Terry with drunken eyes, "I won't have that!" he scolded, wagging an accusing index-finger, "It's not a bus...it's a..." he paused, "what is it now?"

"Coach?" said Terry helpfully, trying to conclude the conversation and get Ron back in time.

"No, I wasn't wearing one", replied Ron, somewhat incoherently, "And anyway, this is Delilah!" He planted a kiss on the woman's cheek leaving a heavy dusting of foundation and blusher on his mouth, then commenced another chorus.

Terry grabbed his arm. "Come on Ron, remember your position"

Ron looked angry, "My position", he shouted, then, as if surprised by the volume, repeated it in a whisper, using his other hand to tilt Terry's head closer, "my position…is sitting here, with Delilah and I'm never leaving!" He started singing again and put both his arms around the woman's waist. She lolled back and forth as he gently swung her around dropping cigarette ash on his shoulder from the fag hanging out of her mouth.

Terry and Steve looked at each other, back at Ron and then just walked out, leaving Ron, who paused between verses only to shout "Titley's better!" at the bar-man in what could be construed as a statement of self-congratulation, but which was actually an inebriated attempt to order Tetley's Bitter.

"He'll be alright." they both agreed, remembering overhearing the Councillors saying they were going to the toilet, and sure they would help Ron back. Plus, they figured that Ron, who had, after all, organised the whole trip, would soon realise where he was and would get back to the ferry. However, they overestimated Ron's ability to handle his drink; he had no ability in that department whatsoever.

But Ron *didn't* realise where he was or what time it was, and was even somewhat confused about *who* he was. He didn't stop drinking or singing for another four hours. Neither did he realise that Delilah was in fact Derek. He also failed to realise that due, ironically to the absence of his own clipboard, everyone on Coach No.1 had thought he was embarking the ferry on Coach No.2, and vice versa.

Harry stood, as yet unaware of Ron's situation, with many of the other band members, leaning against the railings of the ferry as it began its voyage on a breezy Saturday evening. Passers-by and friends of other passengers waved the ferry on its way, and as Harry waved back he noticed a boy standing amongst them, studying what appeared to be a map. As the well-wishers slowly got smaller and smaller as the ferry sailed forward, Harry struggled to remember where he'd seen the boy before, and was certain is was the same boy he'd seen at the cemetery on the day he'd buried his mum. "Maybe he knows someone in the band?" Harry now started surmising to himself, "and that's where I know him from…" But somehow he knew that wasn't the case. The boy had an almost ethereal property about him, as if connected with Harry, who even now was reminded of his own childhood ambitions to see the world, ambitions which may have been fulfilled starting with Harry's idea to emigrate during the early 1980's but which had been forgotten, and overshadowed by his acceptance into the National Youth Band of Wales. And as the dockside crowd disappeared into the horizon, replaced by opportunist seagulls chasing the ferry hopeful of being thrown scraps of food, Harry and the others walked inside. For them, the trip had just begun.

Ron Titley however, the stalwart protector of Midtown Band's decency and decorum, had quite literally missed the boat. A boat which he had booked as part of the trip he had so diligently and painstakingly organised down to every last uniform button, now sailing "sans" Ron, who was drunk beyond redemption and getting-off with a not very convincing transvestite in an alley behind a dockside pub in Southampton.

Chapter 7

Call Of The Sea (Eric Ball)

Midtown Silver Band and its guests, after concluding the seemingly obligatory ceremony of standing on deck in the freezing night, watching land disappear as the ferry slowly made its way out to sea, were now spread out around the ship. Due to a combination of availability and price, given the unenviable task of arranging travel for eighty people, the sea-crossing was to take approximately seven hours, arriving in Dieppe around 5am. The band had agreed that cabins would have been an unaffordable luxury, and there would be enough opportunity to catch up on sleep while back on the coach. Most of the band had agreed, and were enjoying the excitement of the night crossing. Some were walking laps of the ship, others were reconnoitering the various bars, cafes and amusements aboard, and a group of the more seasoned travellers were claiming the most suitable chairs and settees randomly dotted around the decks, attempting to get comfortable enough for a few hours sleep, with the aid of blankets and various inflatable pillow-type devices they'd cunningly brought with them from the coach.

James was still leaning on the rail, watching as the coast faded into the dark night and the twinkling lights of Southampton were swallowed up. He concentrated on the white trails of frothed water following the ferry. Like a tractor making its way across muddy ground, the ferry seemed to be in just a few feet of water, leaving tracks in its wake, as the engines made their presence known with an authoritative, rhythmic growl. James concentrated hard on these tracks. He wanted to focus on something relatively stable so as not to follow Delmie's example, standing a few feet away. Lucy rubbed Delmie's back as he vomited continuously over the side of the ferry.

"Oh, you poor thing" said Lucy with genuine concern, as Delmie emitted another spine-tingling roar, followed by a particularly abrupt request that she leave him alone, at which point she left him to throw up in peace.

Harry was sat with the basses around one of the tables in "The Atlantis Bar"; a large function-room where circular tables dominated most of the space, the first row of which formed a crescent around a dance-floor in front of the stage. The room was packed full of holiday-makers, every table was occupied, as was most of the floor-space. Coloured lights flashed in time to "Dancing Queen" by

Abba, the song currently being pumped into the room at a volume making it necessary to slightly shout in order to be heard. The lights demarcated the dance-floor, which along with their counterparts on the stage, and a massive slowly rotating mirrored-ball hanging from the ceiling, provided a lively bustling party venue for, as the sign next to the entrance indicated, strictly over-18s. Norman Lightfoot and Owain Owain stood outside in the corridor, longingly savouring the illicit sounds of laughter, music, glasses clinking, and incessant chatter each time the door briefly opened to allow someone in or out.

Harry was only on his second pint but the rest of the boys were still reeling from their earlier drinks, and the effects were evident.

"I'm not saying that at all...no, not at all", Eric was pointing a wavering finger at Terry, his eyes half closed, his other hand clasping a pint of bitter. "I'm not saying...", he was interrupted by an unexpected and particularly audible belch, adding an almost demonic timbre to his next three words before returning to normal, "...*he was better* than Jenkins, I'm just saying on a good day he can kick with the best of them." He nodded earnestly, pleased with the point he'd made.

Steve got up, swayed a bit and then sat down again.

"Haven't got your sea legs yet Steve?" Harry smiled as he spoke.

Steve just nodded, gripped the table and hauled himself up again.

"Same again lads" he announced rather than asked, and stumbled off into the crowd towards the bar.

"How many have you lot had?" Harry asked, making himself heard above the melee, and starting to smile as he was already enjoying the holiday-atmosphere of the lively bar.

Terry and Eric looked at each other "Not as much as Ron." Terry said and burst out laughing. Eric grinned and looked at Harry with half closed eyes.

"Ron? What, Ron was drinking with you lot?" Harry was incredulous "Where is he now?"

Again Terry and Eric looked at each other. They just shrugged their shoulders and looked back at Harry, any explanation being fortuitously delayed by some activity on stage. The lights throughout the Atlantis Bar had now dimmed, highlighting the dance-floor and stage, where a large wooden easel on the right-hand side displayed a poster advertising the cabaret act that would entertain the bar that night; a two-piece husband and wife combo from

Stockport. The wife, much taller than her husband, appeared on the poster wearing a glittering short dress, too much make up and Anita Dobson hair. The husband had a waistcoat made of the same glittery fabric, short blonde hair and stood, looking moody, with his puny hands resting on his keyboard. Above them, in a red and yellow fire-effect typeface, was the name of their group; "Flame!", whilst at the bottom of the poster was their strap line; "A Band On Ship!" Their act was to consist of songs from the shows, re-workings of popular hits and some classics for the older crowd.

An amplified voice boomed through the room, replacing "Dancing Queen" and announcing; "Ladies and Gentleman, Sailors and Sea-Dogs, please put your hands together...for Flame!"

Everyone in the room started to applaud, only to be instantly interrupted as the voice continued, totally shattering the atmosphere as the room-full of drunk passengers was now in silence, apart from a few lingering claps, the odd cough, and the distant voice of Steve Pepper somewhere at the bar explaining "No, *top*...I said lager *top*!" The announcement then needlessly started to point out that Flame would usually comprise Jerry London and his wife Tara, but tonight Tara had been struck down with a mystery illness and couldn't perform. As the audience started to look more and more confused, and began resuming their conversations, the voice continued explaining how he had gone to see her shortly before going on stage, to find her sweating and shivering and not looking very well at all, and the ship's doctor had been delayed and couldn't diagnose her or give any medication.

"So please welcome to the stage..." the voice boomed, accompanied by a sudden whistle of feedback causing everyone to instantly cover their ears and groan.

"Jerry London, one half of Flame!"

A few claps from the more polite members of the audience greeted Jerry as he appeared from behind the curtain, strutting to the synthesizer and microphone at the centre of the stage to the beat of "Disco Inferno".

"Thank you, thank you" he shouted, before pressing a few buttons on the synthesizer which resulted in the introduction to "Wake Me Up Before You Go Go" filling the room, and Jerry bellowing

"Everybody...Jitterbug!...Jitterbug!"

For every other reason than musical value, the audience clapped, cheered, and a group of women from one of the front tables grabbed their handbags and ran onto the dance-floor.

So Jerry continued, on stage on his own, behind his keyboard, doing his best to pull off a show. It was usually Tara that was the lead singer, with Jerry throwing-in a bit of backing vocals, and he was actually relishing the opportunity to get in front of the microphone, enjoying the spectacle of a full dance-floor with the majority of the audience singing and clapping along. The fact that everyone was on the first night of their holiday, were all pretty much hammered, and would probably have danced and sang-along to Saddam Hussein singing "Macarthur Park" didn't occur to him. Between "Love Me Do" and what he felt was going to be an utterly rip-roaring version of "Thunderball" Jerry decided to read out some announcements he had been given from the audience. He addressed the crowd in his somewhat soft effeminate voice, with a broad Yorkshire accent;

"OK everyone; hope you're all having a good time. Just got some announcements to read out for yourselves. Right what's this one here..." he leafed through the bits of paper in his hand, while the audience clapped and whistled.

"Right, this one's for Debbie and everyone from Tan-o-matic in Totton." A cheer went up somewhere in the crowd from a party of women, "Have a good time on your holiday girls, oh that's nice."

Jerry leaned in close to the microphone "By the way, I have noticed that a few of you have asked how Tara is. That's lovely, that really is lovely. You're all such nice people. She's fine, she's fine..." he continued in total sincerity, "...she's probably finally seeing-off the attack of the 'squitts she had mid-week. It's been a trying couple of days, I've had about 4 hours sleep since Wednesday, and no amount of Cillit Bang is going to sort out the toilet in our cabin, but I do thank you for your concern, I really do."

A ripple of laugher went round the crowd. He put on his cabaret persona again.

"Right who's next, oh yes, what does this say now?"

At this point Steve Pepper, who had left his round of drinks at the bar whilst visiting the Gent's and had subsequently embarked on a drunken, directionless expedition, struggling through the crowd via both ends of the room, was eventually arriving back at the bar and was just in front of the stage as Jerry read out the next message;

"I can't quite make this out, but I think it says, from Sheila, she is on her wedding anniversary with her husband...*Cyclops* it looks like, and she would just like to say that her husband is a..." Jerry paused to read the message, allowing two seconds, which was all Steve required, to shout out "Twat!" at the top of his Welsh voice.

There was a brief silence and then uproar as the Atlantis Bar collapsed into fits of laughter. Jerry tried to restore order but was drowned out by the laughing and cheering from the crowd. Harry, and the rest of the basses, still sat at their table, howled with laughter. There were tears in Eric's eyes, and even Harry, who was still sober enough to see what was coming, couldn't help laughing at, if nothing else, Steve's perfect comic timing; if only such timing could be applied when he played the semi-quavers in *Tam O'Shanter's Ride.*

There were a couple of people that were not so happy though; namely Sheila and her husband who, it turned out, was a site-foreman from Birmingham, who'd lost one eye years ago in a fight over a kebab, and was known to the whole of the West Midlands as "a bit of a loony". He pushed his way through the crowd and planted a right hook on Steve which sent him flailing into a group of drinkers at the bar, a group that included Lloyd Wenby, driver of Coach No.2. Lloyd, who was not renowned for his patient demeanour, or his diplomatic prowess, turned round, threw what was left of his pint over Sheila's husband and without a second thought began purposefully beating him up.

Lloyd would never look for trouble, but equally would never pass-up the chance to get involved in some if it came his way. From somewhere near the back of the Atlantis Bar, nicely-sozzled percussionists Lawrence Ap Dafydd and Ieuan Efans strode across the dance-floor and began trying to drag Lloyd off his adversary.

Jerry, deciding his piece-de-resistance would now probably fall on unappreciative ears, shelved "Thunderball" and launched into his own version of "Saturday Night's Alright For Fighting", as more fists started flying and glasses started smashing.

"Yeah, that's right", shouted Sheila's husband as Lawrence grabbed Lloyd to pull him away, "Get this nutter off me, then take your boyfriend and get lost!"

"Now, now, there's no need for that", replied Lawrence, and mainly for the benefit of the surrounding onlookers, felt the need to add "...and he's not my boyfriend."

Ieuan agreed, also stepping in to grab Lloyd's other arm, who was still attempting to get a few final punches in.

"I'll smash your Brummie face in if you carry on", yelled Lloyd, restrained by Lawrence and Ieuan, but intently staring at Sheila's husband like a perplexed Rottweiler on a short chain.

"You're just a bunch of losers", continued the husband in his thick West Midlands accent, attempting to tuck his shirt in and straighten his collar, "you shouldn't be allowed in here, in fact you should all be banned!"

However, over the racquet of Jerry London just a few feet away, and the dancing, cheering crowd, Lawrence misheard, released Lloyd, stepped towards the surly Brummie and asked "What was that you said about the band?" before his right hand shot forward, connecting with Sheila's husband's chin, once again sending him to the ground.

Ieuan also rushed forward, "What was that Loz? He was slagging-off the band was he?" and waded in to join Lawrence.

"OK boys, OK", Lloyd Wenby suddenly piped up in an inexplicable about-turn; "there's no need for all this is there? Fighting's not going to solve anything." as he began separating the three men.

Sheila was now stood, hands on hips, glaring at her husband, and Steve Pepper, who in his drunken haze had managed to extricate himself from the situation in blissful ignorance was stood at the bar, explaining "No, *two* cheese and onion, and *one* smoky bacon".

Harry stood up and surveyed the carnage happening in front of him.

"Anyway, I'm off for a walk, better see where the others are", he announced above the music. Not particularly impressed that some of the band had been involved in a fight before even passing the Isle Of Wight, but suitably relaxed enough not to care, as long as their valve-fingers or drumstick-holding-hands were still operational.

"Right you are mate", Leighton shouted back.

"Hang on", Eric called over, "I'll come with you".

And with that, Harry and Eric wandered out of the bar leaving everyone to sort themselves out, and wondering how many more "classics" Jerry London could muster up in the absence of his wife. A wife, as Harry overheard later from one of the crew, was not suffering with a stomach upset at all. In fact, and unbeknown to her husband, the ship's doctor had pretty swiftly diagnosed her with a particularly virulent strain of Chlamydia, a consequence of her being not just the cabaret act, but the ship's 'welcome wagon' for any new male members of staff. She had secretly bedded all the crew at least once and looked forward to those long days stuck in dock when the French dock-hands would handle her with very little care and attention indeed and actually had the famous Tara London on their list of favourite British attractions.

"Alright boys", Harry shouted down the corridor as he spied James, Roger, and a considerably happier-looking Delmie walking towards him. "What's happening?"

"We've just had a bit of grub", said James, "Mam and everyone are in the Nautilus Room, there's some bloke playing piano, Lawrence's missus was singing 'As Long As He Needs Me' when we walked past".

Harry laughed, "Most of the boys are in the Atlantis Bar just down there", he pointed, "there's a bloke playing keyboard, and they've got Guinness on at £2.00. Is Iestin and Megan up the other place as well?"

"Yeah", laughed Delmie, "he's a boy, that Iestin!"

"Where's it by?" asked Eric, "up on the next deck is it?"

"Just up the stairs, turn left and it's right there, opposite the Purser's office", Delmie said.

"Oi, what are you boys up to?" Harry suddenly shouted, feigning anger, as Owain Owain and Norman Lightfoot suddenly tore round the corner.

"I'm James Bond", began Owain, "and Norman's a foreign spy."

"Fair enough", Harry replied, "have you had something to eat?"

"Meeting my mum in half an hour at the Frying Dutchman Cafe", said Owain.

"Right-o then", said Harry, "see you later." And with that the two boys ran off down the corridor.

"We're heading to the Nautilus Room then," said Harry walking away, "upstairs you say?"

"Yeah", shouted back James as they walked off, "see you later!"

As Harry and Eric walked up the stairs at the end of the corridor, they noticed someone standing out on deck looking into the darkness. As they reached the next floor they could see that it was Emily, standing outside, hair blowing in the wind.

"I'll see you in there, butt. I'm just popping round the corner for a fag", Eric said, "then I'm off to see if there's a bog around here somewhere, unless I have to find the poop-deck", he grinned at his friend. Harry knew exactly what Eric's game was, and as he was left alone, every instinct within him was telling him to open the door and go out, talk to Emily and put his arm around her, but he couldn't. He was angry with her, he was angry that she had wasted her life for some brief moment of pleasure or stupidity or whatever it was, and he couldn't explain to her, without getting angry, that she had destroyed their bond as father and daughter. He couldn't explain to her that his role had been to protect her from the bad things in life and he had failed. He couldn't explain to her that he loved her so much that it would kill him to acknowledge that someone had robbed his daughter of the chance to live a young life free of this burden.

Eric's words came back to him from the Eisteddfod "Don't blame her Harry".

His hand rested on the door handle, but as he began to turn it there was a clatter of feet running up the staircase. James, who had lost the fight with his stomach just as he was about to enter the Atlantis Bar, came charging past Harry, burst out of the door and emptied his stomach over the side of the ship.

"James!" Emily shouted at him as he stood right next to her.

"Sorry" James managed to splutter back before going again. "I don't know if it was the burger and chips, or that bloke in the bar singing My Heart Will Go On, but I didn't half come over queer just then".

Harry decided he'd leave them to it, and go to the Upper Deck to get some fresh air for a few minutes before he went to find the others.

Suitably refreshed and head slightly clearer, Harry headed to the Nautilus room. Upon opening the door, he was greeted with a sight that made him bend over, hands on knees, wheezing with laughter. The room, judging by its decor, was the ship's more upmarket, serene, wine-bar type venue. Clad in light tasteful wood, smart bar adorned with a piano-keyboard design, thick carpet on the floor, and lots of low settees, armchairs and coffee tables. One entire wall was floor-to-ceiling windows providing a panoramic view of the sea, whilst the other focal point in the room was a raised platform upon which stood a white baby-grand piano. A man who looked to be in his early 50s was sat on one of the high stools at the bar, dressed in a white dinner-jacket, treble-clef motif on breast pocket, obviously the player of the white piano, a piano which at present had Mary's sister Megan sat at it, hammering away while Iestin, cocktail in hand, stood in front of it leading the crowd in a chorus of "We'll Keep A Welcome In the Hillside". There were around fifty people in the room, all sitting down with glasses of wine and cocktails, all clapping their hands in time to the music. Two tables in particular caught Harry's eye; Mary, The Parrys, Toby Stephens, Denise Lewis, and an assorted collection of very merry bandsmen's wives and partners were all singing away, arms around each other as they sat encircling one low table, while right next to the piano a group of Japanese businessmen, all smartly dressed, were sitting around their respective table, being "conducted" by Iestin as they attempted to learn and join in with the song, congratulating themselves with pats on the back and handshakes each time they got a line right, and encouraged by none other than Eric, sat right in the middle of them.

"Hiya love!" Mary shouted as she spotted Harry at the door, "come on" she patted a spare area of settee. Harry gave her the thumbs-up and motioned that he'd head to the bar first. He tried to see the state of people's glasses on the "band table" and as far as he could see they all appeared pretty well-stocked and straddled by actual bottles of wine.

"You do beer, butt?" asked Harry as he arrived at the bar.

"Non monsieur", replied the barman, "for the beer, you will need to be in the Atlantis Bar, he is downstairs".

"OK", said Harry, sighing, "what about them bottles?"

"Ah oui, we 'ave the, how you say, bottled lager?".

"Lovely", said Harry, "I'll have one of them, the Stella if you've got one".

The barman handed over a bottle and a glass, and Harry replied;

"Mercy, mercy," as if begging to be treated with some kind of clemency.

He walked over and took his seat with the others, just in time for the final line as Megan concluded the song with a flourish, and Iestin led everyone, including the Japanese businessmen in the last few words, "...when we come home again to Wales!" A round of applause followed, and the Japanese group were on their feet clapping and shaking each other's hands, and bowing towards their esteemed mentor, Eric. Iestin and Megan made their way back to the table, both clearly the worse for wear but handling themselves remarkably well.

"I was looking for you in the Atlantis Bar downstairs", Harry greeted his friend.

"I know, we were all on our way there when we spotted this place, it was Happy Hour when we arrived", said Iestin, "House White 1 Euro a glass, so we told old Jacques we'd have ten bottles", he motioned towards the barman.

Harry laughed and began explaining where everyone was, following questions from Mary and the others.

"The only people I haven't seen around are Ron and Carl", concluded Harry, "in fact I haven't seen Ron since Southampton, but some of the boys said they'd been having a drink with him at some point."

"What about James and Em?" Mary asked.

"Yeah, they were both outside just now", Harry said, "looked like they were getting some air." He decided that discretion was the better part of valour and left out the details about James' Technicolor yawn over the side of the ship.

Iestin and Megan had obviously been brought up to speed regarding Emily's situation, and Harry wondered to what extent he'd been portrayed as "the bad guy" in his handling of it all. But everyone seemed their usual amiable selves, so Harry sat back as the pianist, who had concluded his break, took his seat at the piano and launched into a very twinkly instrumental of "Moon River", embellished with scales and runs at every juncture. The group struck up various conversations, all mainly centering round their forthcoming arrival in France, Harry and Iestin caught-up and reminisced, Mary and Megan seemed to be having a very intense, private discussion, and most of the others were dipping in an out of the various chats taking place. Iestin nudged Harry as they spoke, and motioned towards the Japanese contingent sat at their table by the piano. They all appeared to be very much struggling with something. Heads were being shaken angrily, snippets of Japanese could just be heard above the piano at which they occasionally pointed, and one man was sitting, head in hands, feet rapidly stamping the floor as if foxed by some ancient oriental conundrum. Eric, still amidst them, just seemed to be shrugging a lot, as he sat with his arms folded.

"What's the matter with them?" said Harry.

"Gawd knows mate, they're a good laugh though, I was talking to one at the bar, they all work for a hotel chain, and have some business or other in Dieppe tomorrow", explained Iestin.

"Mmmm," replied Harry thoughtfully, "maybe everything's not quite going to plan with them all, the way they're acting at the moment."

Suddenly, one of the Japanese men jumped to his feet, punched the air with both fists and triumphantly shouted "Breakfast At Tiffany's!"

"Ahhh", the rest of the table shouted, clapping wildly, then all shaking hands once again.

With that, Eric stood up and made his way to the bar, and Harry also took the opportunity for a refill.

"They got there in the end then", said Harry as they waited for Jacques to serve them.

"Yeah, Breakfast At Tiffany's", grinned Eric "of course I knew what film it was from all along, but I thought I'd let them struggle with it."

"Right, course you did mate, course you did" Harry chuckled.

"Did you talk to her then?" Eric then asked.

Harry knew exactly what Eric was talking about and replied sharply "Leave it out mate; I'll have enough of this off Mary later, and probably throughout the trip!"

"Fair enough, butty", Eric put his arm on Harry's shoulder, "just keep in mind that you've still got the chance to sort all this out with Em, and in the spirit of where we are, you don't want that particular ship to sail. Now, where are these drinks?"

As the night wore on, one by one everyone at the table made their excuses and decided to walk up to the next deck, which was where most of the opportunities to grab a sofa, or arrange some chairs suitable for sleeping on, were to be found. Mary and Megan went to find Emily, Harry, Eric and Iestin decided to have "one for the road", and before long the Nautilus Room was more reminiscent of the Marie Celeste.

Harry opened his bleary eyes in the early morning light. It looked grey outside as he peered across the row of seats to the window. He shifted his body and winced at the pain and stiffness in his bones. Stretching forward, he looked around at the other passengers to see if he could see any familiar faces.

Mary was a few rows behind looking uncomfortable with her face pressed against the chair fabric, and a blanket half pulled around her. Next to her lay Emily, then Megan and Iestin, both snoring and occasionally grunting as their bodies subconsciously counted-down the minutes remaining until their next duty-free cigarette. Mary had spent half the previous night telling Megan about Tom from work. It was a conversation that had been a tug-of-war between the Spirit Of Ecstasy and the Devil's Advocate, summed up by Megan's sage advice "We all think the other man's grass is greener sometimes, but watch out for him that's all I'm saying Mare" Megan had warned "Apart from anything else he sounds too good to be true, to me".

Harry took stock of the band members he could see, idly wondering once again where Ron was, then went back to a restless doze. Presently, everyone was awakened by the public-address system, crackling throughout the ship, announcing their arrival in Dieppe.

As everyone boarded the coaches, the ship's incessant engines and the oily mechanical smell of all the vehicles doing nothing for the delicate heads and stomachs of many, the mood on Coach No.2 was subdued. They had been made to wait for 20mins because their driver Lloyd was late. Eventually Wyn D. Day, the driver of Coach No.1, had to open up the coach while they waited for Lloyd to appear. Most people either attempted to get back to sleep when they found their seat, or were nursing hangovers with bottled water and packets of Resolve. Only Carl Davis, usually the most dour and unsociable band-member, seemed refreshed and full of energy as he skipped up the steps and into the coach, greeting everyone with a cheery "Bonjour!", followed by his wife.

"Where did you get to then?" inquired Toby, "we didn't see you all night"

"Well" continued Carl annoyingly cheerily, "we didn't fancy crashing on chairs and that, so we got ourselves a cabin."

For a moment or two, Carl was the most hated man on Coach No.1 as the aching, un-showered, tired bandsmen watched him jauntily promenade along the aisle, before taking his seat with a satisfied sigh. The women on the coach were jealous of the hot shower, comfortable night's sleep, and change of clothes the couple had obviously enjoyed. The men on the coach were all thinking one thing; "You jammy git!", partly for the same reasons as the women, but mainly because all of them would have given their hind teeth to spend a few hours in a cabin with the lovely Alex as she also shimmied along the coach in what looked like sprayed-on black leggings and a very tight white t-shirt.

The coach deck was crammed with coaches and it was obviously going to take a while to disembark, so everyone just sat in silence waiting to get off.

Steve Pepper was grimacing as he prodded his swollen lip and eye with his finger. He could only partially remember what had happened, but felt sure he must have been the victim in it all. James held his stomach, sighed a lot and tried not to look as ill as he felt, Roger sat next to him fast asleep. Meanwhile, on Coach No.2 the atmosphere was much the same.

"I don't understand it." said Harry to Mary after walking the entire length of the coach twice, and talking to Wyn, "Both Ron and Lloyd the driver are missing."

Mary looked around at the rows of seats "What are we going to do? Are we sure they're not over on the other coach?"

Eric Trefelyn, who had been doing a final sweep of Coach No.1 walked up Coach No.2's steps and quietly said to Harry and Wyn,

"We've got to get off the boat Harry, now."

Eric, whilst trying to enquire amongst the ship's crew about the location of the missing Lloyd and Ron, had just been involved in some French-Welsh relations which had not gone particularly well, and he was decidedly edgy. The crew had heard about the trouble in the bar last night, were convinced that the Midtown Coaches were full of trouble-makers, and were determined not to have any trouble this morning. Their conclusion had been largely exaggerated by a tip-off from a one-eyed West-Midlander who had informed them "they only picked on me last night because they thought I was French". At present, the crew were angrily circling Coach No.1 armed with spanners and wrenches in a show of strength, like a pride of lions preparing to take-out a doomed hyena.

"What do you mean we have to go now? Who's going to drive the coach?" Harry asked.

"I will" Iestin stood up.

Harry, Mary and Megan all looked at Iestin "You will?" they said in unison.

"Yeah, I'll give it a go. I've driven most things. How hard can it be?" Iestin said, bubbling with confidence and making his way down the aisle. Wyn looked doubtful, but was starting to think he had little option. He could see what was going down, and he knew from experience that Customs would only need one small excuse and both coaches would be held at the dock for hours.

Wyn and Iestin made their way off the coach and over to where the other one stood, Wyn gave Iestin a crash course in the controls whilst Harry sat down nervously watching through the window. He still didn't know where Ron and Lloyd were, and after a brief confab it was decided that if they were both still aboard the ferry, they would at least find each other, and Lloyd had the address and phone number of the eventual destination. Lloyd also had a mobile phone, which at present seemed like it was switched-off when Wyn tried to raise him. Eric, and the basses were starting to experience a feeling of dread, deep in the pit of their stomach, none of them said as much but they each had an awful feeling about what must have happened to Ron at least. Especially, as it had become apparent during last night's various conversations that he wasn't on either of the coaches when they boarded the ferry. Wyn was now slightly more relieved about Iestin taking captaincy of one of his coaches. It seemed very much like they were both speaking the same language and as Iestin turned the key, the coach's engine roared into life. Harry decided to swap coaches in order to sit near Iestin and help guide him out of the ferry. Wyn took his place in the driver's seat of Coach No.2 and finally they were both ready to move out.

Coach No.1 lurched forward as Iestin applied pressure to the accelerator and continued lurching down the coach deck, down the ramp and on to dry land. As the coach made it into the day light everyone breathed a sigh of relief. "See, just like driving a big car really" Iestin said proudly. The two coaches, nestled amongst the others rolling off the ship, nervously crept along the tarmac. Iestin, as instructed by Wyn, handed a document through the window to the waiting Customs Official manning the booth at which Coach No.1 had now arrived. The French official looked at the document, and then looked at Iestin. Harry gulped, wondering what kind of offence it was to impersonate a coach driver, whilst having no licence, probably resulting in no insurance, and on the wrong coach. Iestin looked relaxed, as always. Harry remembered from school that Iestin was a born blagger. He had got away with everything from putting cling-film over the toilet in the teachers' staff-room, to stealing a bush-baby from Bristol Zoo during a school-trip and managing to get it back to Cefngoed. This hiatus of a few seconds, as the coach stood there, ticking over, awaiting instructions, seemed like hours to Harry. Finally, the man in the booth, imposingly dressed in uniform, peaked cap, and topped off with large intimidating Foster Grant sunglasses, opened his mouth to speak. Harry held his breath. The Official handed the documentation back to Iestin through the window of the coach, accompanied by one single word which slowly left his lips.

"Merci."

The barrier in front of the coach lifted, and Iestin, as gingerly as he could, once again applied pressure to the accelerator and slowly inched the coach forward. As they cleared the dock and turned left, onto the road leading towards Dieppe, Harry looked up at the ceiling, pursed his lips and gave a long focussed sigh of relief. Iestin grinned, looked in the mirror and saw Coach No.2 now also leaving the Dock. He saw a brief flash of Coach No.2's headlights, and a thumbs-up from Wyn. The passengers remained in somewhat blissful ignorance and remained lost in their own tired little worlds as the coach picked up speed. Iestin opened his window, extended his arm and gave Wyn a reciprocal thumbs-up, as they drove past a huge sign on the right-hand side of the road. "Bienvenue vers la Francais". Iestin, turned his head slightly, grinned at Harry, still standing slightly behind him, holding onto one of the front seats, and said. "Welcome to France, butt!"

Chapter 8

The Frogs Of Aristophanes (Granville Bantock)

As Iestin steered the blue and silver behemoth away from the docks, the morning sun was still low in the sky. Sheets of blinding light were saturating the windows on the left-hand side, and the tired, irritated occupants were doing their best to improvise solutions. Hats over faces, hands in front of eyes, magazines stuck to the glass with heads jammed against them, all provided temporary and insufficient relief from the merciless glare. Only a few had mustered up the energy to unbutton the curtains and slide them across, the others still maintaining futile attempts to avoid the inevitable admission that they were in fact awake now.

Harry, now perched on the edge of the front passenger seat, next to a dozing Toby Stephens and Norman Lightfoot, glanced in the large rear-view mirror perched outside on the left of the windscreen. There were now a few trucks between them and Coach No.2, and Harry indicated to

Iestin that perhaps they should let the others overtake at the next opportunity.

"Definitely mate", agreed Iestin, "I haven't really got a clue where we're going. As soon as we clear this bit we'll find a place to pull in".

The road ahead, as far as the eye could see was a fast-moving carriageway that looked to be going around Dieppe. Traffic was building up, mainly as more coaches, trucks and cars were now rapidly disembarking the early ferries and heading inland.

They motored on, the reassuring hum of the engines somewhat heightened by the lack of noise within the coach itself. Eric Trefelyn, seated near the back, slowly heaved himself up, stretched and yawned like an ageing German Shepherd with hip problems, and started to plod his way down the aisle, steadying himself using the seats as he went.

"Alright?" he greeted Harry and Iestin as he reached the front, and stood, hand on the back of Harry's seat.

"Yeah mate", Iestin replied, "according to Wyn there's some Services about an hour north of Dieppe. We'll all pull in there and sort ourselves out."

"Soon as we can, we'll let the other coach past so we can follow them", Harry added.

"Lovely", said Eric, "still behind us somewhere are they?"

As the three of them glanced once again in the rear-view mirror, it started to dawn on them that Coach No.2 was no longer in view. More and more vehicles had managed to join the carriageway behind them, and even though there was a fairly unencumbered stretch of road disappearing into the distance behind, there was now no sign of Coach No.2.

"They're probably back there somewhere", said an optimistic Iestin.

"Unless they got off at one of them exits we passed", said Eric.

"Well, if they have, I've got the directions here", said Iestin. "We'll meet them as planned. Can't be that hard to find can it?"

Harry suddenly had a sinking feeling, and wondered whether to tell the occupants what was going on just yet, or let them relax a little bit longer.

"Mobile phones!" Eric suddenly blurted out. "Someone on the bus must have a mobile. We'll ring someone on the other coach and find out where they are!"

Harry shook his head, "All our phones are in the suitcases. It was one of the things listed on Mao Tse Ron's briefing notes, in case other passengers kept getting disturbed."

"Well, we'll just pull over and get one out then!" said Iestin, "that's no problemo, as they say in France!"

"Yeah Butt", replied Harry, "only one problemo with that, guess which coach all the suitcases are on, and guess which coach is carrying all the instruments and that?"

"Ah", replied Iestin. "Anyway, I'm sure we'll be alright if we follow the directions."

They rolled onwards, Iestin at the wheel, Harry and Eric pouring over the A4 sheet of directions Wyn had put together, originally for Lloyd's benefit. The problem was that these directions were written in English, whereas all the French road signs were, unsurprisingly, written in French! As Iestin looked forward, over the roofs of the cars in front, he could see the main carriageway about to terminate a few hundred yards ahead, at what appeared to be a T-junction.

"Right boys", he announced, "we'll have two choices in about a minute's time. Left or right?"

Harry and Eric, scratching their heads, were still not ready to commit to this kind of complex decision, not at this point in the proceedings, and as the junction was finally upon them Iestin brought the coach to a halt, reminding everyone of his unfamiliarity with the vehicle by jamming the brakes on in what was to become his trademark manner, as if he'd thrown an anchor out of the window. Passengers lurched forward, cups flew off arm-rests, a delicate James and Delmie simultaneously reached for the first receptacle to hand, and both suffered their first vomit-fest on foreign soil, at least on this trip.

"What the Dickens is going on?" a belligerent Carl Davis yelled from his seat. "My missus nearly went down on the floor then!"

"Bet that's not all she's been down on recently!" someone shouted and a chortle resounded through the coach.

"Sorry everyone", shouted Iestin, "we're just deciding which way to go".

Harry looked at the directions then back at the sign. Car horns started beeping behind them.

"Which way man, you've got the map haven't you?" Iestin was now getting a little itchy.

Harry just stared out of the window. The sign going left read "Toutes Directions", the sign going right read "Autres Directions", and Harry didn't have a clue what either of them meant.

"Umm, left" he said "No hang on, right"

The horns were beeping constantly now and some French drivers had got out of their cars and were walking to the front of the bus.

"Someone tell me which way? Or we'll end up dead in Dieppe before the trip has even started!" Iestin shouted, by now convinced that all French people were just waiting to beat someone up. Harry suddenly had an idea, and grabbing the microphone mounted on the dashboard he asked,

"Right, is there anyone here that knows any French?" before hastily adding, "and no comments about Carl's missus please!"

Leighton Davis suddenly stuck his hand up.

"I know how to order two beers, and I can ask where a good place to go fishing is."

"Thanks mate, thanks for that", replied Harry rolling his eyes.

"What about eggs?" Lawrence's wife suddenly shouted, genuinely attempting to be helpful, "the French never have two for breakfast because they say one egg is un oeuf!"

Harry could see he would be getting no help from the passengers, so concluded that the decision rested solely with him. French motorists were now banging on the side of the coach, and the situation was not helped by an extremely hung-over and irritable Steve Pepper half-way along the coach sticking two-fingers up at them through the window, and mouthing obscenities while his wife glared at him and tried to grab his arms.

Harry, now simply wanting to extricate the band from this situation as quickly as possible, took a gamble and announced "Left, toots direction, left!"

Iestin heaved the steering wheel and popped the clutch. The coach leapt forward and Delmie offered up another paper-bagful of stomach-contents. The coach headed up a long hill as it left Dieppe, the docks and the beautiful church on the hill behind it.

Within minutes, the town had given way to countryside with rolling meadows and gentle hills, only accompanied by wide expanses of farmland all around. Now pretty much all awake, the passengers were starting to enjoy the trip once again. Conversations were beginning, Rachel Parry optimistically and topically opened a session of "I went to the *supermarché*, and I bought...", and Terry Horner mumbled, "Good God I'm hungry!"

"Didn't you eat last night?" asked James who was in the seat directly in front of Terry.

"No", replied Terry mournfully, "we stayed in the bar till 1, and then the Frying Dutchman was shut, and didn't open again till 5 when we had to meet at the bus! All I had all night was a bag of pork-scratchings and a pickled egg."

"I might have some sarnies in my carrier-bag", Denise Lewis interjected, "I can't vouch for them though, they've been there since we left Midtown."

"Oh, 'ave a look will you?", an optimistic Terry asked. Denise reached up to the overhead storage, and produced a very squashed carrier-bag containing what looked like a lump of foil.

"Yeah, I've got some here", Denise said, "I don't think you'll want them though."

"I will, I will", replied Terry, "I think I'm dying of hunger here."

"But the butter has gone all congealed with the ham", Denise added, screwing her face up in disgust.

"That's my favourite kind!" Terry pleaded.

"And they're all squashed and out of shape", a doubtful Denise concluded.

"That's just how I like them", Terry grabbed the package out of Denise's hand, and began enthusiastically transferring the contents into his mouth, with hums of contentment and appreciation.

On the other side of Dieppe, Coach No.2 thundered through the French countryside, in the opposite direction from its brother. Wyn was convinced that they would catch up with the other coach at any moment, and was still wondering what had become of Lloyd Wenby. There had been no phone-call on Wyn's personal mobile as yet, and he'd left his business phone with his wife at home in case any bookings came in for her to deal with. As Mary watched the fields going by, she day-dreamed for a little while about living there. Emily was also watching the world go by and had felt happier since being in France, as if all her problems had been left behind in Britain. She had spent a lot of the previous evening with Toby Stephens, chatting about anything and everything, sharing jokes and making up nicknames for some of the band members. She wished that Toby had been on Coach No.2, as she'd really enjoyed his company on the ferry, and thought he was a really good friend.

"I wonder where the others are." Mary turned around to speak to Emily who was now sitting next to Megan.

"Dunno Mare," Megan replied, "but gawd help them if Iestin's still driving. He's alright with the controls, but he's got less direction than an ASBO case!"

The three women gulped, imagining Harry, Iestin and James on a magical mystery tour, being driven by an unlicensed, very hung-over brickie, the sum of whose life ambitions culminated in a desire to one day learn how to juggle live hamsters.

Emily laughed to herself, even though the situation with the other coach was mildly worrying, at least no-one was talking about the baby, or the father, and she could at least for the moment enjoy some freedom from it all. Suddenly something jerked her back to reality; a kick inside her, stronger than ever. Further down the coach, the councillors were all wondering where Ron was, and the rumours were starting.

"I reckon he got on the wrong boat", Councillor Ellis suggested.

"Nah, I should think he had some urgent business regarding the situation with the Bandroom", said the Mayor, "I mean, you know how precious his time is, and how thinly-spread he is". Ron had obviously presented these people with a seriously exaggerated description of his role as band-secretary! The other passengers enjoyed the spectacle of the passing villages and hamlets, and basked in the generally sedate and calming environment of their coach. Owain Owain sat next to his mum scowling. He had never been so bored in his life, and was not impressed that his mum had not allowed him to travel on Coach No.1.

Iestin meanwhile, at the helm of the other coach, cruised along the wide open road confidently, whistling and humming "We are the Self Preservation Society" from the Italian Job. Harry and Eric, still perched immediately behind him, looked on with furrowed brows, all too aware where the coach finished-up at the end of that particular film. Harry continued studying the map and looking at road signs as they whizzed by. It had been an hour and a half since they had left Dieppe and there was no sign of the place they were supposed to meet the other coach at. Harry leaned forward and spoke to Iestin. "Next place we see, we'd better pull over Yessy".

Iestin saluted Harry in acknowledgment, and sure enough as they cleared the next bend, a small snack-bar was visible about half a mile down the road. Iestin pulled the coach into the almost empty car park, taxied over the gravel and pulled up as squarely as he could with the far wall, before turning the engine off and letting the coach slowly wind-down to silence.

Harry stood up and addressed the coach "Right, comfort break everyone, back here in half an hour." He turned to Iestin "Well done Butty."

Harry, Iestin and Eric were the first to set foot onto the car-park. Iestin lit two cigarettes, passed one to Eric and stepped away from the coach's shadow into the morning heat of Northern France in the summer. "Not bad this international coach-driving lark. Should have done it ages ago" he thought to himself as he exhaled a plume of blue smoke.

In the snack bar there were ten plastic tables with four chairs each. Within about five minutes of arriving, the place was full of hungry Midtown Band players all addressing the one and only waitress there with a mixture of French, German, English and Welsh, as orders were taken. The waitress was only doing this as a summer job to get some money, and also in order to avoid having to help her family on the farm. She was from rural France, knew very little English and most of her usual clientele were French truck-drivers. She reached the table were Harry, Eric and Iestin sat.

"Bonjour. Prise de la natte I votre ordre?

The three just stared back blankly, and then Harry ventured an answer;

"Bonjour...we would like...three..." he held up three fingers "...cups of tea?" he said hopefully.

"Tea? Oui, et pour manger?

Harry held up the menu as he and Eric both tried remembering as much French as they could.

"Deux ouefs and sausicon, bacon? And, uh, well, just tomatoes?" Harry made the shape of a big round ball when he said tomatoes and added "Red? Rouge?"

The waitress wrote down what she thought was the order and smiled sweetly at them, they had tried at least. She ventured to the next table where Steve and Gilly Pepper were sitting. Gilly, who had been surveying the menu and half listening to what was going on, confidently put her menu down. "Do you want me to order for us both?" she asked her husband.

Steve put his cigarette out in the ashtray, looked surprised and just nodded.

Gilly turned to the waitress who was poised with her pencil at the ready, and with every syllable perfectly enunciated, said, in a loud Welsh accent;

"Two egg and chips please love".

Terry Horner, still ravenous, sat with Leighton Davis.

"Tell you what mate, I don't half fancy some turkey and chips for some reason", Terry said "I wonder if they've got any."

"Turkey?" asked Leighton, "why turkey?"

"Dunno mate, just fancy it. I'll ask Claudette now", he replied, inventing a name for the waitress, and beckoning her over.

"Avez vous..." began Terry, "...any turkey?"

The waitress looked blank. "Tur-key?" she repeated, not having a clue what he was talking about.

"Yeah, you know, turkey", said Terry, thinking that this would somehow increase her understanding. He then began flapping his elbows while attempting to sound like a turkey, much to the amusement of the others. The waitress, now becoming slightly impatient, and noting the number of people still waiting to be served, glared at Terry, folded her arms and raised one eyebrow.

Terry looked at Leighton hoping for some support, and suddenly through his own tenuous logic whispered, "Oi mate, what's *chicken* in French?"

"I think its *le coq* or summat", replied Leighton, thinking back to textbooks many years ago.

"Good.", Terry turned back to the waitress, holding his arms apart trying to depict something large. "Turkey. It's like a big chicken? Like a...a...grande coq?" he explained. The waitress shrugged, and the onlookers laughed even more at the hapless Terry who was just becoming redder and redder.

"Look love", Terry suddenly lost patience, "I just want a big cock. That's all I'm asking for." The others couldn't help but to burst out laughing, and even the waitress who didn't have a clue what was going on, could see the funny side.

Leighton beckoned her over, pointed at the all-day-breakfast on the menu, and calmly said "Two of these please darling", deciding that it was just better if he did the ordering.

As everyone finished their food and started making their way out of the snack bar the waitress breathed a sigh of relief. Most orders had gone well she thought, there had been some misunderstanding over an order for four Cokes, which she had heard as 'croques' and brought out four rounds of cheese on toast to the bewildered table, but luckily the one they called "Terry" had managed to find a home for them.   Apart from that she thought that these people from Payes De Galle were OK. Out in the sunny car park Iestin and Harry had a map laid out on someone's car bonnet and were studying it carefully, and one by one the whole entourage crowded around offering suggestions on where they were and how to get to the place they should be.

Harry had come to the conclusion that they should have followed the sign 'Autres Direction' after all. No-one particularly wanted to turn back and there was general confidence that they could find their way to the rendezvous point without doing that. The men all agreed that turning back was something they would not be doing.

"Why don't we just ask someone?" Alex Davis inquired.

Harry just looked annoyed at the very suggestion, and carried on looking at the map.

"You go and ask someone if you want" he said gruffly.

A lorry had pulled in to the car park and a large man was clambering out of the cab. He turned round, pulled his trousers up around his waist and lit the cigarette that was dangling out of his mouth.

"Tell you what", Eric volunteered, "I'll go and ask this chap."

With that, he turned around, fag in mouth, and trudged over the gravel towards the man. The band all followed, as if wishing to lend Eric moral-support in his task of having to ask directions from someone in foreign climes, leaving Harry, Iestin and the map behind.

"Bonjour" hailed Eric cheerily "Bonjour".

The man just nodded and looked around at the sea of hopeful faces approaching him.

"Ca va?" Eric said thinking he was doing well. The rest of the crowd murmured impressively at Eric's prowess.

"We are from Wales?" Eric said loudly, drawing a map of Wales in the air in front of the bemused man and then pointing out of the car park to where he thought Wales might be. The man looked over his shoulder then back at Eric.

"Where are *vous* from?" Eric slowly said, pointing at him hopefully.

"Leeds" the man answered in a thick Yorkshire accent.

The band all collapsed laughing and James headed off to get Harry and the map.

About five minutes after talking to Martin the lorry driver from Leeds, Midtown Band in Coach No.1 was headed to Dieppe. There was apparently no option but to turn back.

Over on Coach No.2 Wyn was now getting concerned. They were just pulling into Hercule Buckmaster Services, which had been the agreed meeting point, but there was no sign of the other coach. The passengers chatted, looking forward to an opportunity to stretch their legs; Megan was gasping for a cigarette, and looking for a chance to refill her hip-flask. Terry Horner's wife was wondering if Terry had managed to get something to eat, and their son little Jack was looking forward to seeing his dad. As Wyn drove through the coach-park section of the services, he purposely avoided many of the available parking spaces, opting to take the coach to the very bottom end first, and then drive back up and park, hoping against hope that he'd catch a glimpse of his other coach, with a collection of Welsh bandsmen outside it. But it was not to be, and as he expertly swung the huge vehicle straight into a space, he had to consider what he would say to the passengers. The air-breaks hissed co-operatively, and the engine, like some kind of huge beast preparing for slumber, slowly decreased in volume and pitch till all that remained was a final subtle shudder to be followed by silence.

"OK everyone", Wyn announced, "If we could all be back here in one hour please. They've got quite a lot here, somewhere to eat, toilets, phones, cash-machine, they've got it all".

"So where are the others?" Mary inquired, vocalising the thoughts of the majority of Coach No.2's passengers. "I can't see them anywhere".

"I should think they'll be here any minute", Wyn replied, "and if not, we'll wait till they are. They've got pretty good directions."

Mary and Megan looked at each other doubtfully, but realised they had little choice but to see how it all looked in an hour. Emily decided to go and have something to eat with Owain Owain and his mother via the ladies loo, Mary and Megan intended visiting the shop at the earliest opportunity to compare British and French motorway services, others in their own little groups slowly disembarked the coach and strolled across the coach-park beneath the warm late-morning sun. As Emily chatted to Mrs Owain, she noticed a couple of women pushing buggies containing babies, and couldn't help reflecting that this time next year that would be her.

The occupants of Coach No.1 were deflated. The fact they had to backtrack for over an hour, just to be where they started, had not gone down well. No-one was interested in who bought what from the *supermarché,* no-one described themselves as "The music-man who comes from down your way", and everyone's trousers remained steadfastly away from the sunroof. James, who actually felt better after being sick earlier, looked through the window at the scenery now travelling in the other direction, and wondered, like his mother, if he would ever live somewhere like this. He was angry with himself for letting his travelling ambitions slide. He had taken the easy option; a part-time job here, some cash-in-hand work there, a few pints and a curry every week, and all his friends conveniently available in band practice. Not a bad life some might say, but James knew he was capable of more, especially while he was still young. He knew his mum was worried about his future, he also knew his dad was worried that he may lose his euphonium player, but most of all he knew he needed to take control of his own future, make some decisions and stick to them. His thoughts of leaving had been emphasised by changes that were happening around him. He wanted to be a good uncle to Emily's baby, not just someone who was there, in the house, waiting for the pub to open or for band practice to start. He wondered if the seemingly inevitable demise of the Bandroom would herald a new era for the band, in which players would slowly drift away in the absence of their community's "heart". A twice-weekly visit to a borrowed room in the art gallery or the high-school would not have the same appeal as the Bandroom did, over the years. There would be less chance of passers-by, visitors, and prospective new players popping in and contributing to the band's future in whatever way. Maybe it was time for him to leave after all, and what was that banging noise?

"Can anyone else hear that?" James said in an irritated tone, to Roger.

"Yeah, now you mention it, it sounds like something banging underneath the bus", said Roger.

"Yeah, I can hear something too" said Delmie.

"And me" agreed Toby, suddenly appearing like a meerkat above the head-rest of his seat.

"Great, on top of everything else, the bus is falling apart now" James folded his arms in contempt and looked out of the window. As everyone started trying to pinpoint the knocking, something caught James's eye. Outside the window, just below where he was sitting, it looked like one of the massive luggage-doors had started to open as they hurtled along.

James sat open mouthed and started to point out of the window.

"What's wrong mate?" asked Roger nervously.

"The…the bloody boot is opening!" he exclaimed and all the players rushed to the window to see.

"Stop the bus!" shouted Delmie "Stop the bus!"

Rachel Parry went running down the coach to tell Harry.

Down in the bowels of the coach's boot, the shock James had just experienced was incomparable to what was being experienced by the person who, upon waking up in the dark after spending over seven unconscious hours on top of a load of instrument cases, mistaking the rumble and the motion for the engines of the ferry, had just managed to crack open the luggage-door lock from the inside using the stone-removing implement on his pocket knife. Only when he managed to roll his bruised, aching body against the door which suddenly gave way and began to open, did he realise what was happening. Managing to grab hold of something before actually rolling out, ears suddenly filled with the sound of wind shrieking around the luggage area with a noise that wouldn't have seemed out of place emanating from the voice of a maternally outraged banshee, there was suddenly tarmac rocketing past, less than two feet below his nose, specks of gravel being thrown up at his face, and blinding light suddenly forcing its way into his eyes. And only then, in that split second when the door began to open did he realise that the rumbling was not the ferry at all, but the sound of a coach, speeding up a French motorway, being driven by an over confident Welshman. As he struggled to grab hold of the bottom of the door and pull it back closed, while at the time hanging on for dear life lest he roll out of the 70mph coach as it fairly rattled along the autoroute bypassing Dieppe, he caught a brief glimpse from an all too unnatural angle of the side of the coach, and the glistening windows up above. At the same moment, Carl Davis spotted him from his vantage point half way along, and with an expression only *he* would come up with shouted to everyone onboard, "Steady the buffs…it's Lloyd!"

There was a collective sharp intake of breath as everyone now observed the terrified driver clinging to the door, flapping about below.

"Oh my gawd!", shouted Iestin who had been looking for the most convenient place to stop. And, forsaking convenience for pure urgency, he hastily located the hazard-lights switch, and as smoothly as he could, began to bring the mighty coach to a halt.

The smell of exhaust fumes, and the heat of the engines hung in the air as Harry, Iestin and Eric jumped out of the now stationary coach, ran along its side to where the open luggage-door was, and half-carried a very shaken Lloyd Wenby onboard.

Harry turfed Norman and Toby off the front seat, and Lloyd gratefully sat down, catching his breath. Given the fact he'd almost been killed a few minutes ago he seemed in remarkably good spirits, which were only improved when Iestin offered him his hip-flask which was still a quarter full. Even better, Lloyd was able to provide not only directions, but an effective cross-country short cut to the rendezvous point, and in just over 45mins, Iestin was finally bringing the Midtown coach to rest next to its twin at Hercule Buckmaster services.

The occupants of Coach No.2 sighed with relief, as 2 hours late, their compadres' coach pulled up. Iestin spotted his wife, grinned and gave her a wave. Megan couldn't help giggling. If anyone always lands on his feet it's Iestin. The inevitable questions followed, and it turned out that the one-eyed nutcase from Birmingham, not content with how the previous night's altercation had concluded, had followed a slightly drunk Lloyd down to the coach-deck on the ferry around midnight, and while Lloyd climbed into the boot to retrieve his "emergency drinking fund" from his case, had slammed the luggage-door shut, intending to lock

Lloyd in, but unwittingly knocking him out as it hit his head.

"Oh yeah," confirmed Lloyd "I saw the Brummy git at the last minute, and if I ever see him again…"

"Ok mate", said Wyn, "you pop in to the services and grab a quick shower, I'm sure Iestin won't mind driving up to Lorient if you can navigate?"

"No worries", Iestin replied, and for the remainder of the journey stuck to the tail of Coach No.2 like glue. Harry resumed his seat next to Mary, and Toby Stephens took the opportunity to go and sit next to Emily, fully intending to pursue what he felt to be their blossoming relationship.

It was early evening when the two coaches drove into Lorient, slightly late but still in time to check into the hotel that Ron had booked, all enjoying a quick wash before making their way along to the welcome ceremony and buffet that was to be laid-on by the town officials. The civil townsfolk of Lorient were very pleased to be hosting the band's visit, and it would possibly prelude a twinning project that had been mooted by Midtown's mayor, who, Harry noted, seemed to be taking a back-seat when it was time for some actual official duties in the main function-room of the hotel. Following a speech by the Mayor of

Lorient welcoming the band, as ambassadors of Wales, to their town, all eyes inevitably looked towards Harry when it was time for a Midtown representative to reciprocate. Harry sighed, and Mary sympathised. She knew how much he hated this kind of thing, which was ironic as he could be quite a natural diplomat. It was a skill honed over many years of adopting compere's role as well as conductor at hundreds of band concerts, but it was a skill Harry didn't like using in what he felt were contrived situations. He didn't like politics at the best of times, and believed they had no place whatsoever in music. Yes, he was happy to be in Lorient, and was truly grateful for such a warm welcome, but he felt that far from solely being about the music, he could see the Midtown Mayor and the councillors ingratiating themselves with their French counterparts, and couldn't help feeling that if they could devote as much effort into trying to save the Bandroom, or providing funding for new instruments, then things might be a bit better all round. Basically, he suspected they only supported the band when it suited them. Nonetheless, he adjusted his tie, approached the small stage that had been erected, walked up the three steps and shook hands with the Mayor of Lorient. Along with the two Midtown coach parties, the reception was attended by Lorient's councillors, various cultural representatives of the town, and members of the public who were interested enough to turn up. All told, a crowd of approximately 150 people stood before Harry as he cleared his throat to speak.

"I would just like to say," He began, "merci".

The crowd clapped and laughed affectionately.

"We in Midtown are very much looking forward to sharing our music with our good friends here in Lorient," another cheer interrupted him, "and we hope we can entertain you as magnificently as you have welcomed us tonight. Once again, merci".

Mary smiled as a huge round of applause, filled the room. The words had been a perfectly simple, dignified and sincere combination. And she knew Harry would have hated every second of it. Harry stepped down from the stage, discreetly rolled his eyes at Mary, and accepted a glass of wine from one of the waiters wandering around with trays. And finally, Harry, along with everyone else could relax. Drinks flowed, acquaintances were forged. Emily stood with Toby, enjoying herself and briefly forgetting her problems. James, opting not to drink tonight, stood with Roger and Delmie, enjoying the event and looking forward to exploring Lorient over the forthcoming week. Mary was relaxed, both her children were smiling,

Harry had completed his official obligations, at least for tonight, yet she couldn't help wondering what Tom was doing right now back in Midtown; a dinner party? A night at the opera, or maybe some other sophisticated pastime?

Eric, Terry, Leighton and Steve knocked back their first wines of the evening and were, for their own sheepish reasons having coincidentally similar thoughts to Harry, who after reluctantly delivering his speech, which should have been the duty of the band-secretary who would have relished it, wondered "Where the Dickens has that Ron berk got to?"

Chapter 9

Dreams And Aspirations (Tony Cliff)

Every day of the following week would take-on its own identity. Far from the expected regime of breakfast, travel, lunch, afternoon concert, travel back, dinner, as per Rulebook Ron's itinerary, the nature of the outdoor concert venues actually gave everyone a chance to gain a brief glimpse into the way of life in French towns, villages and hamlets. By Wednesday morning of the first week, an informal routine had established itself. To give Ron his dues, he had managed to arrange the daily concerts in the most beautiful and interesting locations, taking on-board the suggestions of Lorient's Council. Monday had involved breakfast at the hotel, a 25min drive to a small wine-producing village where a lunchtime concert had been held in the square. Farmers and wine-makers had flocked from the outlying area, and had given the band the most enthusiastic welcome and support before a sumptuous buffet was revealed, complimented by copious amounts of locally produced red wine. The buffet had lasted almost all afternoon, during which the band members, none of them able to speak much French, had managed to befriend and converse with the villagers, none of whom spoke any

English, all managing to successfully communicate via the universal languages of music and alcohol. The afternoon had concluded with the coach ride back to the hotel in Lorient, an hour's relaxation sitting by the outside pool, and then dinner in the restaurant followed by a disco lasting till midnight. If there had been any doubts about the success of the trip, they'd been eradicated on the first night as the band, their friends and families, danced the night away pausing only to order more drinks from Pierre, the regular barman at the hotel. Those that weren't dancing had chatted, sat out by the pool in the moonlight, some had opted to explore Lorient, and following a similar day on Tuesday the template had been established.

Wednesday morning saw a bleary-eyed James and Roger wander into the restaurant for breakfast at around 0830.
"Good god, I'm tatered!" Roger announced as he took a seat next to Eric, Steve and Gilly Pepper. The kitchen door opened to reveal the clattering of plates, and seemingly urgent orders being barked in French, as Pierre, who never actually seemed to leave, appeared carrying two more coffee-pots in each hand and placing them at strategic positions on the tables dotted around, all occupied by Midtown folk.

"Ah, bonjour Pierre!" James cheerily announced.

"Hello Jeem", responded Pierre grinning, "you would like tea, or cafe, I mean 'cawfee?'", he asked, most of his English pronunciation being learned from American cop shows.

"Coffee for me, mon ami", James replied before asking the rest of the table in general, "So what's happening today then?"

Harry, Mary, Emily, and Toby Stephens were sitting a few seats along.

"We're off to this farm", Harry announced between mouthfuls of egg on toast, "It's about half an hour on the coach".

"Usual arrangement is it then?" James asked his dad, "meet at the coach at 1030?"

"Yeah, that's right", Harry continued, "those non-players who don't fancy it can stop in Lorient if they want".

"You coming Em?" Toby asked hopefully.

"Yup, I'll be there", said Emily, who had not felt more relaxed and at ease with herself for weeks.

"I'll save you a seat then", replied Toby, who by this time obviously had a major crush on Emily, which had not gone un-noticed by many of the band who took every chance to make exaggerated kissing sounds, which for some reason always led to amusing armpit noises, each time Toby walked into a room.

James was relieved to see that Harry and Emily were at least tolerating each other now, even if not directly communicating. They were sharing dining tables, exploring the local area in the same groups, and James hoped this was at last the beginning of some long overdue bridge-building. The buzz of conversation filled the restaurant as the large party, most of who were tired and, to differing degrees, hung-over, enjoyed breakfast and one-by-one gradually finished, got up, and left.

It was around 11am when the two coaches bumped their way down the single track that led into Ferme d'Église, a smallholding which offered a traditional French cafe/restaurant, woodland walks, and a children's zoo comprising, chickens, rabbits, geese, goats and sheep. There were also pony-rides and, at certain times of day, wine-tasting. The sun, as it had been all week, was very bright, and very hot. Band jackets had not been worn at all yet on this trip, and Midtown players were very visible as they alighted the coach, and investigated the small collection of shops forming the centre of the farm. A sea of bright white shirts and black trousers indicated their presence, as in their own groups they decided to have a look around.

Mary and Megan made a beeline for the craft shop, an obvious souvenir opportunity, and were soon rubbing shoulders with many of the other Midtown supporters who'd had the same idea. A significant amount of French tourists were also wandering around the place, and it was to these that the band would play at around 1pm.

Harry and Iestin decided to go and have a look at some of animals, while Eric Trefelyn and the basses at present had not moved from the coach. This wasn't really their kind of place, and they were contemplating a plan of action to kill some time before lunch at midday. A consensus was reached, and they all made their way down the steps and out into the sunlight, heralding an expedition to find a place to sit and light up a cigarette each.

James and Roger had decided to try and spot some local "talent", and were slowly completing their first circuit of the busy central courtyard, deciding to pop into the craft shop, and the farm museum en route, to see what they could see.

"French", whispered James, nudging Roger and motioning towards a slim brunette studying a 100-year old plough mounted on a plinth.

"Nah mate", retorted Roger, "I'd say Italian if anything."

"What about Cowboy Boots over there?" James said, discreetly pointing at another attractive brunette wearing tight blue jeans and tan leather ankle boots.

"Yeah, she's definitely got the look of Francais about her", giggled Roger childishly, "Hang on though, what about her?", he pointed at the back of a very tall blonde with shining hair in a pony-tail, dressed in black jeans and a jacket, examining the leaflets on a stand near the door. "She may even be Swedish. Wherever she's from she looks alright to me."

Just as James was about to answer, the blonde turned around and walked towards the bookshelf, revealing an almost chest-length beard, side-burns Father Christmas would be proud of, and eyebrows so bushy they looked like they may be providing a home to a family of starlings.

James wheezed with laughter, "Yeah beautiful mate, I didn't realise you were that way inclined".

Roger frowned. "Yeah, yeah, well it's a mistake anyone can make innit", he said, hoping that this wouldn't be shared with Eric and co, who wouldn't let him forget it, probably ever!

Harry and Iestin were standing next to the rabbit enclosure. Hoards of young children were waiting for their turn to cuddle and stroke one of the large floppy-eared bunnies who, as Iestin amusingly termed it, "worked there". Iestin, who had always been fascinated by wildlife, sat on a bale of hay, chatting to Harry while holding a particularly large and contented looking black and white rabbit.

"That takes me back", said Harry, "Remember you had that bush-baby away from Bristol Zoo when we went with the school?"

Iestin laughed out loud, "Yeah, flippin 'eck, that's like 35 years ago now. And it's a wonder I didn't catch pneumonia that day as well!"

Harry couldn't help laughing remembering that during the afternoon of the day in question, he'd spotted Iestin actually swimming across to the penguin-island, fully clothed, in order to "have a look at a penguin".

"What happened to that bush-baby in the end anyway?" Harry asked curiously.

"Quite a sad story as it goes", began Iestin in his Cefngoed drawl, "I kept him in the garden till Mam found out, and then I took him up Cefngoed Mountain and let him go. He was doing great for a good few years until that nut-job old farmer's widow up there shot him thinking it was that black-panther people reckon they saw. Idiots."

Harry put his face in his hands and shook his head; only Iestin.

"Are you allowed to go back to Bristol Zoo yet?" asked Harry, remembering the zoo-keeper's final instruction as he'd ushered a soaking Iestin onto the school-bus in the afternoon, unaware of the furry rodent hidden in Iestin's bag, and yelling "and I don't want to ever see you here again!"

"I wouldn't want to go anyway", said Iestin, solemnly remembering the bush-baby and its fate, "too many memories mate, too many memories."

It was nearing midday, and a suitably nicotine-satiated bass section made their way into the cafe, where a lunch had been pre-arranged for the players. The four stalwarts, each briefly eclipsing the sunlight as they walked through the open door, took their seats on one of the two long tables awaiting them. Other players drifted in.

"Do you think them ponies speak English or French? Carl Davis suddenly announced as he sat down.

"Dunno Carl", Denise Lewis answered as though it had been nothing other than a perfectly reasonable question, "French I should think, why?"

"I just been for a ride on one, and the bloke leading him along wasn't saying all the normal words, he was talking in French. But the pony still understood him."

"Fascinating that is Carl", Lawrence Ap Dafydd interjected with a sarcastic glint in his eye, "What language do you suppose the goats speak?"

At which point, a usually quite shy and retiring Norman Lightfoot, who had been listening to this byplay, said, "I suppose it depends on what they teach their *Kids* at school?"

"Weyhey!" Eric and the basses shouted in unison. This was the band's stock response for any corny, yet aptly delivered line. The table roared with laughter, and Norman beamed, basking in the response to his comment.

Plates full of crusty bread rolls arrived as an introduction to the ploughman's lunch that was about to be served. The remaining bandsmen had now drifted in, and were enjoying the jugs of iced-water that had also been provided. There was giggling from the end of the table nearest the door as a particularly large and confident-looking goose waddled in, observed the two tables full of bandsmen, and continued waddling down the gap between them, despite the yells of "shoo!" and clapping of hands of the cafe's staff.

"Awww, he wants some food", Lucy Edwards said.

"Don't encourage it", said Carl, as everyone else giggled at the goose's audacity.

"Hey, I'll give him a bit of this bread now", announced Eric, "watch this; I used to do this with my cat."

And as everyone watched, Eric slid his chair out from the table, and squatted on the floor, hands on knees, with a crust of bread sticking out of his mouth for the approaching goose to come and take. Everyone giggled. The goose marched straight up to Eric, having now spotted the prize dangling out beneath his large red nose. Eric grinned as the goose's head, tilted quizzically to one side, came closer and closer, and as the band looked on, Eric suddenly squealed with pain.

The goose, had not only swallowed the bread, but, thinking there may be more from the same source, had grabbed Eric's top lip with his beak and was refusing to let go.

"Ow!" shrieked Eric, now kneeling, rather than squatting, and yelling unintelligible words which could only have been pleas to remove the large bird from his lip.

The band was, for a moment, shocked. No-one quite knew what to do.

Harry suddenly bellowed frantically "Get it off him, for goodness sake someone get it off him. Think of the consequences, this is serious!"

The nearest band members leapt to their feet, and began clapping at the goose, while others tried to grab it and pull it off Eric's face. The staff in the cafe went to find a steel bucket they could bang with a spoon, which apparently the goose hated.

"I can't believe this!" Harry continued at the top of his voice, "For the love of god get it off him!"

"Ok dad, ok, take it easy", shouted James down the table, impressed by his dad's concern for his friend, but realising that a panicking Harry was not helping the situation, "it's not going to kill him is it, he'll be alright, I mean it's not a killer-goose is it!"

"I know that!" bellowed Harry back at him, "I'm just wondering how he's going be able to play those staccato quavers in The Keel Row if that thing knackers his lip!"

James rolled his eyes, and the others stifled a chuckle. It had been said before and it would be said again, Harry would never change.

Within seconds, the banging of spoon against bucket was enough to send the goose running and flapping out of the cafe, leaving a slightly bruised Eric sucking the top of one of the iced-water jugs, and muttering to himself about how he was in no doubt as to what he'd be eating this

Christmas, and as the band enjoyed their ploughman's, James's jaw suddenly dropped as he saw a figure standing in the doorway. An extremely pretty girl, who appeared to be in her early 20s, stood there in an outfit supposedly depicting a traditional farmers' wife. James admired her large brown eyes, and jet black hair, and fired a quick glance over at Roger who was mouthing the word "French" silently back at him, while nodding slowly and earnestly.

But to their surprise, as soon as she opened her mouth to speak, none other than an East London accent filled the room, "Right then, I'm looking for some big strong men to come and help me."

The ensuing stampede, as the band boys fought to clamber over chairs, hurriedly ram bits of cheese into their mouths, and generally aim to make the journey from the table to where this girl was standing as quick as possible, left Lucy, Rachel, and Denise alone at the table, rolling their eyes.

It had turned out, that one of the exhibits on the farm, a high-sided traditional hay cart, had fallen over and lay in one of the adjoining fields looking very sorry for itself indeed.

"What's your name then? You're not from round here are you!" James asked the girl, struggling to keep up with her as she strode over to the cart in her floral dress.

"Charlotte", she shouted back, "Nah, I'm from Walthamstow, here on a gap year."

James was impressed, and made a decision that there was no way he'd be leaving here today without finding out a little bit more about this fantastic girl.

The twenty bandsmen stood next to the large, fully laden cart lying on its side.

"Now", Charlotte confidently instructed, as she flicked a lock of black hair off her face, "If you could all stand on one side of it, grab the edge, and slowly lift it, as it gets high enough it'll eventually right itself using its own weight."

"Right you are love", Eric replied, forgetting about his sore lip.

The boys all lined up, and slid their fingers under the edge of the side lying on the grass.

"Right", instructed Harry, "after three..."

"Alright Haz", Eric shouted back, "it's not *Morning Has Broken* mate!"

The band laughed out loud, preparing to lift and tip the massive cart, and its load of hay, back onto its wheels.

"One, two, three...lift!" Harry's voice boomed as each of them slowly pulled the wood away from the ground, and began walking underneath it as it slowly tilted up into the bright sunny air. Stood between Lawrence and Ieuan, Eric heaved and pushed, as the cart slowly started to tip.

"Right", Charlotte shouted, "One big push should do it now!"

The boys all shouted at the top of their voices, gave one final lift and push forward, and the mighty trailer suddenly shot up in the air away from them as, with one long loud creak, it's balance went past the point of no return and it crashed back onto its four wheels, leaving the twenty bandsmen stood at the bottom of its 10-foot side. A round of applause from the bandsmen, and quite a large group of assembled onlookers, heralded a successful job, but as Lawrence turned left, and Ieuan turned right, both intending to congratulate Eric, all they saw was each other. For a moment they were confused. Barely a second ago had Eric been standing between them pushing for all he was worth. It only took another second for the row of bandsmen to realise that the group of spectators were frantically pointing and shouting towards the top of the cart. In unison twenty heads all looked up, to be greeted by the sight of Eric's feet sticking out of the hay atop the cart, flailing about, trying to ascertain their bearings. It wasn't until ten minutes later, when a cursing Eric was finally recovered and helped down that it became apparent what had happened. As gravity had forced the cart out of the bandsmen's hands and back onto its wheels, Eric's belt had somehow become caught on one of the metal brackets along the top edge of the cart's side, and as the cart had righted-itself, Eric had been hauled off his feet, catapulted over the top of the cart, ending up head-first in the hay, 10-feet up.

The band, all now helpless with laughter, struggled to maintain any sort of composure and dignity, not so much due to what had happened, but at Roger's reaction as he actually lay on the floor, shaking and inconsolably sobbing in a fit of hilarity, as if this had triggered memories of every single thing he'd ever found funny.

At 1pm, the band was ready to perform. An appreciative audience sat on deck-chairs around the square stage which had been assembled in front of the courtyard. The sound of brass filled the hot summer sky and provided a backdrop to the hustle and bustle of the holiday makers exploring Ferme d'Église. Each piece of music concluded with clapping and cheering from the audience, and the deck-chairs, the al-fresco stage and the sound of the farmyard animals interspersed with children's laughter only added to the informality, and the relaxed atmosphere of today's concert. James, as he stood at the front of the stage playing his solo "Blaydon Races", managed to catch Charlotte's eye as she marched past with a group of delighted young children on their way to see some lambs. He was elated when she smiled back and gave him a little wave. He would not be leaving today without speaking to her. Harry was enjoying the concert. The band had played well at every engagement so far this trip. He was proud of their professionalism amidst the holiday atmosphere. Working hard and playing hard is something that's not easy to achieve, but *playing* hard and playing hard is even more difficult. His thoughts were only interrupted a few minutes later when a flaccid-lipped Eric did in fact manage to totally fluff the quavers in the Keel Row as predicted, and as he threw Harry an apologetic glance, Eric was sure that over Harry's shoulder behind the last row of deck-chairs he could see that goose walking along looking across at him from a distance.

Two hours later, the coaches were once again rumbling along the single track, but this time heading back towards the main road that would return them to Lorient.

"So", said Roger as he sat back in his seat trying to position himself at the optimum angle beneath the air-conditioning vent, "you managed to have a chat with her did you Jim?"

"Certainly did mate, certainly did", replied James, also sitting back, hands behind head. "In fact I'm meeting her on Monday!"

"Yeah?" said an impressed Roger, "Splendid work my friend, splendid work. Where you meeting her to?"

"Here", said James, "we haven't got any concert on Monday, so she's told me which bus I catch to get almost here. I have to walk the final half mile, but it'll be alright."

"Cracking", said Roger, "so is she up for it?"

James laughed, "Dunno mate, we were just talking about gap years and stuff, and in fact Gille who runs the museum was talking about an opening for me if I want it. He's looking for someone to start in the New Year when one of the other guys goes back to Britain".

"Whoss' it pay?" asked Roger.

"Not all that much, but there's free board and lodging, so that's alright innit. And apparently there's even a band in the next village that always needs players."

Actually, it did sound alright to Roger, particularly as the delightful Charlotte would presumably still be around.

"So, you gonna go for it then?" he asked James what would appear to be the 64,000-dollar question.

"I dunno yet", James replied, his head already considering pros and cons, mainly of his own invention as he played Devil's advocate with himself.

"Good god man, what's not to know?" said Roger, "I'd be there like a shot!"

"Well, it wouldn't be the same would it" James pondered out loud.

"What, music all in French you mean?" Roger said, and James eyed him with suspicion

"No" continued James as if struggling to convince even himself of his reasons, "they'd all be…"

"French?" interrupted Roger.

"No, well yes but not that, I wouldn't be…"

"French?"

"No!" James elaborated, "it wouldn't be the same band life, in Midtown Band we're all..."

"Not French?" Roger enquired, inwardly killing himself laughing.

"Flippin heck man, it's not about being French or Welsh or anything. It's about all the good times over the years. We all remember Terry's hand getting stuck when he dropped that pasty down his bass. What about Steve sleeping in his

Volvo and getting stuck on that sandbank when the tide came in that year in Abertowyn? We know all the jokes, all the stories, there'd be none of that."

Roger suddenly knew what James meant. Midtown band was so engrained in their lives, past, present and probably future, that no-one ever really considered what life would be like in a different band.

"Knowing that Carl's wife will always be available for a sly snog at the end of the night if all else fails!" Roger added.

"Exactly, that's exactly it!" James enthusiastically remarked, "That is, exactly it!"

A silence fell between the two friends as their respective words were contemplated, only to be briefly interrupted as they both felt it necessary to peer over the tops of the seats in front of them for a brief glimpse of Alex Davis, sitting by Carl and reading a magazine in her sexy little summer dress.

As they arrived back at the hotel, everyone prepared for another night in the bar; a couple of hours to sit by the pool and relax, another splendid dinner, then 5 solid hours of drinking, dancing and singing. Pierre would resume his position as barman, he was now even getting quite familiar with everyone's "usual". The disco did not have the most contemporary selection of music, but by the time it was 10pm and 80 people were all joining in the chorus to "Let It Be" in front of the flashing red and green lights, no-one really cared. Iestin and Megan were in their element, Harry could think of no place he would rather be, surrounded by his band, no work the next day, and tomorrow's concert being his biggest worry. Mary was also relaxed, she was happy to see Harry and Emily having such a good time, even though they seemed to have reached an impasse in their own diplomatic relations, but she couldn't help wondering if feeling comfortable and content were poor substitutes for feeling excited and exhilarated; feelings she was sure Tom's wife regularly enjoyed, despite Megan's contradictory words of wisdom. At midnight, when the disco wound-up for the evening, everyone agreed it had been another great day, and as they once again all trooped to bed, they hoped that the rest of the week would continue as it had begun. No-one was disappointed.

Saturday began with a lie-in, because the format of the day was to be a little different. The concert was to be in the early evening in the gardens of the Mayoral residence; a very large detached property on the outskirts of town, followed by a reception at the hotel, once again attended by the local dignitaries. Those that felt inclined strolled down to breakfast at around 9.30, followed by an announcement from Wyn the bus driver that he would be taking one coach to Finistere and Lloyd would be taking the other coach to Queven, and basically everyone had the choice of where they wanted to spend the day. Many of the boys decided to stay in Lorient, enjoy the pool, have a wander around town, and use the day to recover before the evening's events. Most of those that took up either of Wyn and Lloyd's offers were the couples, including Toby and Emily who now appeared to be spending every possible moment together. James grinned as he noticed Iestin and Megan boarding one of the coaches and pausing to check the status of their hip-flasks. Harry and Mary also boarded, with Mary intent on visiting some shops to see what was on offer. Those remaining in Lorient more or less had a quiet day. Whether lazing poolside, or strolling around the town, the hours seemed to disappear, and it seemed that in no time at all the voices of those that had gone on the coach trips were to be heard once again in the hotel reception, signalling their return and the onset of late afternoon and early evening. The band would forego dinner in the restaurant tonight, in favour of the post-concert bash, to which the Mayor's wife was to employ the new catering firm she herself was developing. It was to be their first major event, and both she and the Mayor were keen for it to go well.

The concert in the Mayor's garden was a sedate affair. Harry felt once again that it was an event designed to "tick a box" rather than to enjoy some good music, nonetheless he encouraged everyone to play to their usual high standard, and he was pleased when they acquitted themselves with due aplomb. He was annoyed that none of the dignitaries wandering around the grounds were particularly listening, and didn't even seem to notice the end of one piece and the beginning of another. However, it was an opportunity for everyone to enjoy the spectacle of the beautifully kept gardens, and was an apt prelude to the reception that was to follow. When the band concluded their final piece, Harry made no secret of the fact that he didn't intend to "ponse around here" for ages, and encouraged everyone to get back on the coaches as soon as possible, an attitude which the majority of the band and supporters shared. Midtown Mayor and the councillors were the last to board, relishing any opportunity to further strengthen relations, the attraction of regular trips here at the expense of local rate-payers being a strong one. However, they too knew that the majority of those they'd been schmoozing at the concert would also be at the reception, and so had no problem with getting back to the hotel in readiness.

As the boys walked into the function room back at the hotel, it looked completely different from usual; large tables with crisp white cloths straddled what was normally the dance-floor. Shutters were pulled across the bar, and Pierre was noticeable by his absence.

By the time everyone arrived there were over 100 people. The band members, supporters, respective Mayor and councillors of Midtown and Lorient, were all handed a glass of Champagne as they entered the room, catering staff on hand, and classical music being played over the speakers. Most of the players' hearts sank when they realised that this would represent the tone of the entire evening. Finger- food and glasses of wine being rationed out by nervous catering staff, civilised conversations being enjoyed by social climbers, and the Lady Mayoress of Lorient keeping a matriarchal eye on the proceedings, giving clipped instructions in English, to the trainees she was mentoring, many of whom had taken the job as a means of improving their language skills. As the Mayoress was chatting to Councillor Ellis about the relative merits of planting hardy perennials in peaty soil, she noticed one of her girls walking out of the kitchen and passing a plate of vaul-au-vents to her colleague.

"No, no, no Colette", the Mayoress shouted over, "through the serving-hatch!" she pointed at the large hatch linking the kitchen with the function room.

The girl curtseyed nervously and disappeared back through the kitchen door.

Over the other side of the room, Eric stood next to Leighton Davis and Terry Horner.

"This is a barrel of laughs innit" Eric mumbled, nursing the last few drops in his glass.

"Where's that girl with the wine then?" asked Leighton, also holding an empty glass.

"I know, she's like the Scarlet Pimpernel", added Terry, before adding, "if you're allowed to say that in this country."

The three of them burst out laughing.

"So anyway…" the Mayoress continued her conversation with Councillor Ellis, "the think about fuchsias is…" she paused as the same girl as before once again carried a tray of food out of the kitchen and handed it to one of the others. "No Colette, through the serving hatch! Like I said before!"

Again the girl smiled weakly at her before running back into the kitchen.

"How long have we got to stay here Haz?" Iestin enquired of Harry who himself was not only bored with the atmosphere, the conversation, the food and the drink, but also slightly disgusted by the fact that they were playing orchestral music all evening.

"Gawd knows", he muttered, "let's give it another half hour then see how the land lies."

"Fair play", Iestin replied. A nearby Mary overheard, and wondered if Tom would embrace an evening of fine wine and intelligent conversation, but had to admit that even she was getting a bit fed up at this particular moment.

"No, No, No Colette!" the booming gravelly voice of Lorient's Mayoress was once again heard echoing around the room, "Through the serving hatch!"

James, Roger, Toby and Emily chatted about the first week, what a laugh it had been, and how much they were looking forward to the remaining seven days.

Eric and the basses meanwhile were formulating a plan. They'd noticed a box containing at least ten bottles of wine tucked under one of the tables, which looked like it had been forgotten about. They reasoned that if it had in fact been forgotten about, then it was meant for them all along, and no-one would mind if they liberated it. So, over the course of the next twenty minutes, each of the basses would visit the gents a couple of times, expertly walking past the relevant table, palming a bottle of wine from the box, running upstairs and putting it in Eric's hotel room, to be enjoyed later on by the select few that would be invited to "the party".

"What are you doing girl?", the impatient Mayoress once again boomed, as a pair of black-trouser-clad legs could be seen dangling out of the serving-hatch as the hapless Colette tried to climb through while balancing a tray of finger-food which clattered to the floor in response to the sudden outburst from the Mayoress.

"Right", said Harry to Iestin, Megan and Mary, "I don't know about you, but I'm off now. Who's up for checking-out that bar on the corner with the tables outside?"

"Now you're talking", replied Iestin, who all but ran out of the function room, closely followed by Megan. Mary finished her glass of wine, made her excuses to those standing nearby, and along with Harry made their way towards the exit. Harry turned around briefly to nod to Eric and Steve, and knew it was now time to leave when he caught a glimpse of a grinning Owain Owain himself now emerging out of the serving hatch and encouraging Norman Lightfoot to do the same.

An hour later, the majority of the band had vacated the reception. Some were exploring nearby bars, others had decided to call it a night, and "the party" had now started in Eric's room. The basses were all there, as was James, Roger, Rachel and Daniel Parry, Lawrence and Ieuan, even Carl and Alex Davis had managed to score an invite, although not so much due to Carl's glittering personality as Alex's glittering miniscule cocktail dress. As the music was cranked up, the contraband wine was distributed, and two of the basses had their heads out of the 4th floor window each with cigarette in mouth, proceedings were suddenly interrupted by a loud and purposeful knock on the door.

"Quick, kill the music", Eric hissed, "everyone shut up. Who the hell is that now?"

"Well its no-one we know", said Terry, "they haven't used the right knock", he referred to an age-old knocking-rhythm made known to everyone who'd attended these "parties" over the years.

"What if they've rumbled the missing wine?" said Steve, "I said we shouldn't take it".

"No you didn't" said Eric, "you were the bloody first one upstairs with a bottle".

"Alright, alright", said James, "look, someone had better answer it. Whoever it is, we'll sort it out somehow".

"Good lad", said Eric, "well, it's my room, so I'll do the honours."

With that, he slowly walked towards the door. No-one dared breathe as Eric slowly turned the handle, half expecting to see the Mayoress, possibly the hotel manager, possibly even the local Gendarmerie. As he pulled the door open, the last person in the world he expected to see was standing there, glaring at him intently.

"Good Lord", said Eric, "It's Ron!"

"Yes" replied the furious Mr Titley, "It's Ron alright. And you lot are for the high-jump. Leaving me in that bar having encouraged me to get wrecked!"

"Hang on", said Eric, "we all thought you'd got on the boat, now be fair Ron, play the game."

"Yeah well, once Harry hears what happened, you'll all be playing the game, in fact that's all you lot will probably be playing in Midtown!" Ron announced, obviously relishing the opportunity to vent his spleen at those he held accountable for his little adventure last Saturday.

"Yes Ron" Eric calmly responded, smiling as if suddenly realising something important, "that's all very well, but I'm guessing the lovely Ophelia doesn't know all the details of you and your friend Delilah, does she? I don't suppose she'd be very impressed to hear you had another woman draped all over you."

"Now just you wait a minute", Ron replied icily, "what other woman are you talking about?"

"Well, that Delilah piece you were singing Tom Jones songs to", said Eric, "you know who I mean."

Ron's reply was sharp, to the point, and caused everyone else in Eric's bedroom to hastily stifle a laugh, "That was no woman!"

To Eric, this little gem of information was like manna from Heaven, "So, you're saying it was a, how can I put it, cock in a frock? Well that's not going to look very good is it? So here's how it's going to go Ron. You don't say anything to Harry, and we don't say anything to Ophelia, or anyone else. You had to go back to Midtown because of what ever reason you must've told your missus. Sorted."

Ron continued seething, "Well, just you lot watch it. You're on thin ice with all this. I mean, OK it was out of character for me to get that drunk and sing Tom Jones, but it's hardly normal behaviour to blackmail the Band Secretary either is it?"

Eric put his arm around Ron's shoulder, happy that the situation was now concluded, and whispered, "It's not unusual mate, it's not unusual".

Ron had shared the same flight that his wife had planned to take all along. He'd obviously come up with some excuse for not deciding to join the band for the first week of the trip, and was heard over the next few days muttering various snippets of fiction to the Mayor and Councillor Ellis, mainly centring around "important Band-room related business". The second week of the trip was only to involve three concerts, and everyone was looking forward to relaxing as much as possible. Both parties in the collusion knew that the truth would never come out. Ron knew he would come off worse if his little peccadillo were to reach his wife's ears, or those of the Midtown Officials; Eric and the basses knew that Harry would feel massively disappointed and let-down if he found out alcohol had affected a Midtown Band event to that extent. Everyone involved knew that it would be sacrilegious for anyone to breathe a word after their agreement had been made; it was a code of honour that no bandsman would violate.

Everyone slept easy knowing this. The band continued to impress at their concerts over the next week. The nightly disco remained a highlight, and James remained cagey about his day with Charlotte back at Ferme d'Église, much to Roger's annoyance. All he knew was that James had a spring in his step from Monday onwards. Ron caught up for lost time consolidating his position of respect and importance with the French and Welsh officials, and all the boys in the band avidly awaited Alex Davis's arrival each morning at breakfast, to see if her choice of clothes could possibly be more revealing than the day before. It was only on Friday night that explanations were called for, following James, Toby and Delmie's arrival back at the hotel for dinner, with cut lips, bruised eyes and a bleeding nose.

"What the Dickens have you lot been playing at", Harry had shouted.

"Well, we were out with Emily, getting some stuff for the journey back tomorrow, and these three lads started taking the mickey out of her, being pregnant and that. Don't worry though; I think one of them is minus a few teeth now!" James explained.

"Right", said Harry, shaking his head, "so you three boys thought it was a good reason to steam in for a ruck did you?

Why not just tell them to get stuffed. In French if you like!"

"Yeah dad, well don't tell us, tell Emily", James said, "it was her that smashed one of them in the face, and kicked one of the others in the 'nads. It weren't us; they just decided they'd have a go at us back."

"OK", said Harry, still shaking his head as he saw Emily walk into the dining room, repeatedly opening and closing the fist she'd obviously used. "They probably thought they had more chance against you three!"

He avoided eye-contact with his daughter but was secretly pleased she'd given them a smack. They had no right to say those things to his little girl, and he still wished he could tell her how he was feeling.

Tonight was the final night in the hotel, they would be leaving during early hours of Saturday morning, and there was to be a farewell event commencing after dinner, in the hotel function room. Everyone in the band was looking forward to celebrating what had been an absolutely superb trip, and at eight o'clock, the room was once again full of players, supporters, families and dignitaries ready to have a good time. There were to be a few formalities first, mainly involving a speech which Ron had prepared. But before this, Eric Trefelyn made his way to the dance-floor, turned and stood facing the assembled crowd. Everyone suddenly stopped chatting and a silence fell, as Steve Pepper loudly knocked on one of the table tops with his knuckle as a signal that a speech was about to commence.

"Ladies and gentlemen", Eric began, "a lot of us in the band thought it only fair to acknowledge, and show our appreciation for someone, without whom these last two weeks would not have been half as good as they were."

Ron started to puff-up proudly, preparing to make his way to where Eric stood holding a gift-wrapped object.

"So, if I could call upon our friend to join me here and accept a small token of our appreciation, ladies and gentleman please join me in a round of applause for...Pierre the barman". A massive cheer, possibly the biggest of the trip resounded around the function room as the surprised barman walked out to where Eric was. His expression was one of delight and shock. He had enjoyed serving the Welsh group as much as they had enjoyed being served by him. They had always made time to chat to him, include him in jokes, and wait patiently during times he'd been rushed off his feet. He shook Eric's hand and accepted the gift which the band had all contributed to; a silver tankard with the name "Pierre" engraved.

"I would very much like to thank my friends from Wales for this wonderful gift", he began, "and I have truly enjoyed myself, and hope to see you again in the future". Another cheer went up. He continued, "But I do have one question I would like to ask. Why do you call me Pierre? My name is John-Louis!"

Everyone laughed out loud at the incredulous mistake, and all eyes turned to Steve Pepper who had, almost as a throwaway comment, christened the barman "Pierre" on the first night, and it had somehow stuck. A very red-faced Steve walked up to John-Louis, shook his hand and apologised.

"Hey, it's OK", laughed John-Louis, "I thought it must be, how do you say, a Welsh thing!" Once again everyone laughed and applauded his good humour.

Ron Titley now made his way to the dance-floor, and produced a clip-board from who knows where? He cleared his throat, turned slightly towards the group of Lorient town officials just to the left, and began;

"Ladies and gentlemen, it now falls to me to say a few words in recognition of our esteemed hosts. Since we stood side by side at the battle of Hastings, has our country embraced all that is French..."

Harry looked at the floor and shook his head. It was going to be a long night.

"Everything that this splendid country is famous for, from the humble yet delicious *fry* to the romantic and mysterious *letter* has found a place near our hearts. Even your marvellous *polish* will be forever revered in our society. And even though we don't believe in eating horses, frogs, or indeed snails, we respect your decision to. Because, after all, as the French say, vive la difference! So, I'd like to invite everyone to raise a glass and join me as I say to our French cousins..." he glanced down at a note which Delmie had given him, containing a translation of "thank you for your hospitality, you are most welcome in Wales" before triumphantly concluding "Je voudrez avoir costume nettoyes a sec!"

He held his glass aloft, encouraging everyone to cheer. Everyone concurred, more out of relief for the brevity of Ron's speech than for its content. The French people there simply looked confused, but cheered anyway, again glad that it was over rather than in recognition of the closing message which in fact translated as "I would like to have a suit dry-cleaned". Delmie, who had provided the translation, was at the back of the room, tears of laughter rolling down his face.

The journey home was relaxed and pleasant. Everyone's injuries had all but healed. Steve's face, bruised during his skirmish on the ferry, was now looking better. Lloyd Wenby was also more or less over the fact he'd been hanging out of the coach's boot at 70mph, Eric's lip was a lot less swollen, as were James, Toby and Delmie's.

For the second time that year, the two coaches found themselves at Hercule Buckmaster Services. However this time, the coaches travelled as a couple, rather than separately. An earlier start meant that less of the ferry-crossing home was overnight, and even though the whole journey lasted from 4am until 11pm, the time seemed to pass quickly. People on both coaches were lost in their own thoughts. Ron and Ophelia had decided to fly back, they both thought it best. The Midtown Mayor and councillors were pleased at how things had gone for them, the highlight of which being an invitation from the Mayor of Lorient that Midtown Band return next year as part of Lorient Culture Week. Iestin and Megan were partied-out, and content to return to Cefngoed revelling in the fact they'd had a good time. Harry couldn't have hoped for a better tour, his band had played better than ever and had conducted themselves with decorum at all times, however as the UK loomed ever closer, thoughts of the Bandroom once again filled his mind, and the battle that still had to be fought. Mary was thinking about Tom, again. She was also wondering how long it would be before Harry and Emily managed to sort things out. For Emily, the sight of the British coastline twinkling once again on the horizon as she stood out on deck represented the beginning of a new and scary chapter in her life. She'd regarded the France trip as a kind of oasis between the first and second half of her pregnancy. Whenever she'd thought about the future, there was always the France trip as a reassuring buffer. The buffer had now gone; the oasis was now behind her. Toby, not realising that Emily seriously valued their friendship but did not want any other relationship than that, had all but decided to propose to Emily when he thought the time was right. For James, the trip had been a turning point. His wander-lust had been re-ignited, his ambitions galvanised, and he had managed to forge some connections and potential employment opportunities in France. He felt that now more than ever the world was his oyster. He would just need to decide what to do in the meantime. He knew he had work lined up next week, but was getting fed up of driving. He knew he would have to discuss his possible leaving with his parents and was apprehensive about their reactions, particularly Harry's. He also didn't want to leave when his sister was in the situation she was. She would need as much support as he could give her. As the announcement on the ferry indicated they would be docking in 30 minutes, and passengers needed to return to their coaches, everyone took a moment to reflect upon the euphoria of the last two weeks, and what returning to the UK meant to them in their own way. All were agreed on one thing however; the holiday was over.

Chapter 10

Carnival of the Animals (Camille Saint-Saens)

It was predicted to be the hottest day of the year so far, and Emily was struggling to find reasons to get out of bed. As she lay there looking around the room, wondering how she could have ended up in such a mess, her gaze fell upon the panda-bear on the shelf and she remembered the day her dad gave it to her. How simple and uncomplicated life was then, and how long ago it all seemed. Emily had always drawn her strength from her parents, and her brother. She was the kind of person who found the unknown exciting, but sought security from the constants in her life. There had always been Harry and Mary, there had always been James, and there had always been the band. Right now she felt that all of these were somehow out of reach. Mary was trying to put on a brave face and kept saying things like "everything will be alright" without really explaining how, Harry was seemingly refusing to acknowledge both Emily and the pregnancy and was acting as though it was a situation conceived solely to annoy him and let him down, James was simply James, cheerful as ever but ensconced in his own dream-filled and seemingly directionless world, and even the band now seemed like a club of which Emily was no longer a member, perched on the peripheries with her mother, watching rather than participating. A fifth wheel. The panda looked back at her, not critically, not judgementally, just lovingly as he always had. All Emily wanted was for her dad to knock on her door, walk in with a cup of tea, and tell her she was still his little girl. The irony that she'd spent most of her teens wishing her parents would treat her like an adult was not lost on her.

Downstairs, Mary sat watching Saturday morning television. James was lying on the settee and Harry had gone into town to collect his copy of The British Bandsman. Both Mary and James had now accepted that Emily was spending more and more time in her room, particularly since Harry, despite an uneasy truce in France, had pretty-much now stopped talking to her following the announcement of her pregnancy, and subsequently her increased non-attendance in band. The combination of which had obviously gone down like a sausage roll at a Jewish wedding.

The atmosphere in the house had been frosty to say the least. Mary knew that Emily had been a "daddy's girl" since she was little. When Harry was working nights at the factory, Mary had spent endless hours with a young Emily who just wouldn't sleep and insisted on playing, and running around the house at three in the morning. Mary had walked up and down the house, doing laps and laps of the lounge, wishing for and dreading day break. When it came, it was a relief that the night was over but it also meant that she had missed another night's sleep. Harry would come home, and Mary, who had to get ready for work, would hand Emily to Harry. "You look after her" she'd say and leave them to it, only to return five minutes later to see Harry and Emily tucked up in bed together, both snoring away. Emily couldn't remember of course, she was only two at the time, but if she could have remembered she would have felt the warmth of her daddy's body and the confidence of his hands as he held her which made her feel safe and warm and like she was the most precious thing in the world.

Mary vowed to have a long chat with Emily and Harry to try and find a way to get past the current tension and find some way forward. She glanced over at the settee.

"Alright James?" Mary said. She never called him Jim.

James just answered lazily. "Yeah."

"Has Emily said anything to you lately about it all?"

James knew full-well what his mother was talking about, but chose not get involved in it all at that particular moment. He wasn't in the best of moods, was nursing the remains of a hangover, and was not looking forward to the rest of the day.

"Well, she's still sick of courgettes" he replied, affording Mary a brief glance as Top Of The Pops Two continued on the television. His comment was part of a lingering reference to Emily's decision, about a year ago, that she was turning vegetarian. She had watched a documentary on battery-farming and had proclaimed that all meat eating was evil. This was a shock to "meat-and-two-veg Mary" who had subsequently struggled at meal times and often relied on courgettes as some kind of meat substitute. The first month of Emily's conversion had seen her have courgettes with everything and this was now a stock family joke to the point where Harry had once brought everyone ice cream with a courgette sticking out of Emily's bowl. Still, at least Mary and Harry had accepted it; Emily and James' Nan just hadn't understood it at all.

"Wish that's all it was", Mary chirped back at James, now also finding her thoughts turning to the late Gwladys, due either to a Freudian connection with courgettes, or some inexplicable mother-son telepathy.

James and Emily had decided to go and stay with their Nan just after Emily's shock veggie declaration. They had borrowed their Dad's car and drove the two hours down to Cefngoed. When they arrived, Nan welcomed them in and the following conversation had ensued:

"Now then, do you two want cooked dinner or chips?" This was the traditional greeting from Nan and meant either full cooked dinner or something with chips: sausage, egg, bacon, beans or everything all together. Gwladys had never had a lot of money, but was determined that anyone visiting would always have more cups of tea, biscuits, or even meals, than they could shake a stick at. It was a heartfelt working-class demonstration of affection and hospitality, and no visitor was ever going to leave her house on an empty stomach. Each dinner was also accompanied by half a loaf of sliced bread with a centimetre of butter smeared over the top, something that James and Emily would always giggle about when they spoke of Gwladys.

"Now, if you don't want any of that I've got a lovely bit of corned beef pie left over!" she'd said.

"Oh, no thanks Nan, I'm vegetarian now" Emily had explained. There was a stunned silence and a look of confusion on Nan's face.

"What do you mean?" Gwladys had asked suspiciously.

"I don't eat meat anymore" Emily continued.

Nan had looked bewildered. James started to smile on seeing his Nan trying to comprehend this completely alien concept of not eating meat.

"What, can't you even have a bit of corned beef pie then?" she'd asked.

"Nope".

Nan had started walking off into the kitchen, dazed but wanting to make the best of the situation, "Oh well, not to worry, we've got plenty of bananas in".

James and Emily had laughed out loud. Another gem from Nan.

"There you go Em. She's got plenty of bananas, you'll be alright"

It was comments like this that had made Gwladys who she was, particularly to James and Emily. They loved their Nan for being the kindest woman they'd ever known, but still existing in a world where vegetarians were "not normal", black people were "fine once you get to know them" and where gay men were referred to as "he's good to his mother". As for lesbians, forget it. Nan didn't understand or acknowledge that part of society and when

James and Emily explained, she just giggled and said they were "making it up".

Freudian, or telepathic, James and Mary's reflections on the dear departed Gwladys were concluded by a slam of the front-door as Harry returned, cheerfully whistling The Galloping Major, and clutching his magazine.

"It's boiling out!" he said as he walked into the front-room, "couldn't have been a better day for it, eh Jim?"

James rolled his eyes. Harry was talking about Abertowyn carnival; the most gruelling engagement in Midtown Silver Band's summer schedule, a march from one end of Abertowyn to the other, in the blistering heat, followed by fanfares for the Carnival Queens afterwards. If James had been able to do anything else that afternoon, he would have.

Harry noted James nonchalance, and added "Well, that'll teach you to go on the lash till 1am won't it!"

"Yeah, sorry dad. Sorry it was one of my mate's birthday and we decided to have a few beers and a curry." James answered sarcastically. He really wasn't in the mood for Harry's "band comes first" comments today, partially due to his hangover, but also the fact he'd driven all the way to Abertowyn yesterday to make a few deliveries as part of his temporary job that was fast becoming an inadvertent long-term career.

"Lovely, lovely", Harry answered, "anyway, just remember that as long as the Bandroom is in danger every penny we can make from these carnivals and fetes is more important than ever, and we've got to be at the Bandroom by 1130, so better get ready soon. What about you, you coming today?"

"I don't think so love", Mary replied, "Emily's been sick twice, and it's a long way on the coach, especially in this heat".

"Why don't you drive over there? You haven't driven since you passed your test about twenty years ago", suggested James.

There was a sharp-intake of breath from Harry, who fired a glare at James. James instantly regretted the question.

Mary looked hurt "It was only ten years ago and you know it. I just don't like driving that's all"

"Why did you pass your test then? Just to cover me and Emily in ice cream?" James again laughed as he said this.

"That wasn't my fault it was your dad's", said Mary defensively, remembering the ne'r mentioned period of her life when she'd asked Harry to teach her to drive.

"Why?" Harry had asked on that historic morning ten and a half years ago.

"So I can go places when I want" she had said. But independence was to be a long way off. Harry had taught her only when he wasn't doing something with the band, which meant that Mary had a sporadic programme of lessons with Harry, who outside of banding had less patience than Harold Shipman, often forgetting what had and hadn't been taught. One bright summer evening Mary had shouted at Harry and persuaded him to take her out in the car, and he had relented. To keep young Emily and young James happy as they sat in the back, they had been given an ice cream cone each with a flake in it as a treat. They had been told to hold the cones with both hands and proceeded to lick their way through a heap of ice cream as big as their heads. Under Harry's instruction, they'd driven to an industrial estate where he decided it was time for Mary to attempt reversing.

"Right, now, press the clutch and select reverse on the gear stick" he'd instructed. Mary did as she was told.

"Good. Now gently release the clutch and when you feel the car respond and the engine change tone gently press the accelerator"

Mary didn't have a clue what Harry was talking about. She'd released the clutch quickly and hit the accelerator. The car lurched backward and careered in reverse across the road.

"Watch your tempo! Too fast, too fast!" Harry had shouted. Mary had panicked and just started crying and steering wildly. The car had hit the kerb, bumped up it violently, gone halfway up the bank and come to a sudden stop as Harry reached his leg across and slammed on the brakes.

Mary, who was crying and shaking, had looked at Harry who looked back at her. They had both then looked at James and Emily who were sitting on the back seat, in matching cardigans, covered in ice cream and with ice cream cones sticking out of the middle of their faces like scarecrows' noses.

"Well, I'm not driving to Abertowyn carnival, and that's the end of it" Mary now emphasised to Harry and James. Harry and James sighed with relief.

"And anyway, who's this bloke? He knows how to finish a piece of music properly!", Harry's conversation instinctively reverted to music, as he noticed the television now showing the end of We Are The Champions by Queen, live at Wembley. James and Mary grinned, each bemused at the self-comparison between Harry, and of all people,

Freddie Mercury. Upstairs, Emily was still in her room just looking at her cornet case in the corner of the room, wishing she could talk to her dad, wishing she was going to Abertowyn with everyone else, and wiping away a tear falling down her cheek.

The sun, reflecting on the sea, spot-lit Abertowyn as the band coach sailed into town, greeted by the salty sea air, an endless line of guest-houses, amusement arcades and cafes, and scores of peak-season holiday-makers swarming like ants along both sides of the promenade. Abertowyn was 50 miles from Midtown, a journey which took around an hour and 20 minutes by coach, a journey, which on this occasion was a quieter, more sedate affair than usual. The combination of exceptionally hot weather, the thought of the task in hand, and the fact that many of the band would rather have been sitting in their garden with a cold beer, made for a more irritable, awareness-heightened, somewhat short-tempered collection of people who had remained plugged into iPods, or engrossed in books or magazines for the duration of the trip. Even the coach's sunroof, noticeably lacking in trousers, seemed to display an air of general indifference bordering on malaise. The holiday atmosphere did little to excite the band as the coach drove through town, however the groups of people sitting at tables outside the pubs and bars did generate a certain envy amongst some of the players, followed by the inevitable reality of Harry's rule about not drinking before an engagement. Harry was lost in thought as he sat in his seat near the front. Pregnant daughters, sons on the verge of desertion, Bandrooms about to be flattened, forthcoming National Finals, all whirring round and round Harry's mind like the carousel he could see on the other side of the road. The coach left the promenade, following the signposts and marshals guiding the parade participants into the fields on the outskirts of Abertowyn, between the town and the caravan sites. And finally, the coach turned off the road, slowed down and came to rest, ushered into a waiting space in the middle of what seemed like a strange dream-like village full of space-shuttles, castles, ships, cheerleaders and majorettes.

As the coach's engines wound-down and began a well-deserved siesta, the grumbles from the passengers were audible and numerous.

"Bloody hell it's hot" Steve Pepper said, mopping his brow with a tissue.

A call came from the back of the bus, "Hey Harry, any chance we can march without jackets today?"

Before Harry could answer, Ron Titley stood up and turned around to address the bus, "As official band Secretary…" the whole bus groaned, "…it is incumbent upon me to inform you all that decisions on band attire at said event will need to be a committee decision. If the majority of the band would like to remove any items of clothing…"

Cheers came from the back of the bus, the first cheers of the day, followed by a half-hearted rendition of The Stripper from Leighton, which swiftly petered-out when it became obvious no-one else was joining in.

Ron continued "….then an approach should be made to myself or in my absence the Deputy Secretary and this motion will be taken to committee for a vote. Only in the case of a majority decision from the committee will the motion be carried."

Roger called from somewhere in the middle of the bus. "I'd like to pass a motion, where's the toilet?" Eruptions of laughter from around the bus just served to make Ron roll his eyes with displeasure.

"Alright then Ron, I would like to approach you to ask if we can remove our jackets for the march, in this instance, as it is bloody boiling", Roger called again.

The band bus was now a melee of laughs and applause. James suddenly thought it may not be such a bad day after all.

"Very well, I will convene an emergency committee meeting to discuss said motion". Ron looked around the bus and gestured to Delmie, who was Chair of the committee and to Harry in his capacity as Musical Director, and, that was it. Due to illness and prior engagement the rest of the committee were missing.

"Right, the motion has been forwarded that…" Ron was interrupted.

"Yes, they can take their jackets off for the march" Harry said, concluding the discussion with disguised impatience.

"I agree" said Delmie.

Ron looked at them both. "Very well" he stood up and addressed the bus again.

"The committee have decided that the motion should be carried….." the rest of Ron's words were lost as the band cheered and began an impromptu chorus of We Are the Champions. James grinned, remembering Harry's comment earlier during Top Of The Pops Two.

Ron sat down and considered re-evaluating his position as band Secretary if he was not going to be taken seriously; he contrived to approach the committee with regard to the band's respect for committee members. He took out a small notebook and pencil and wrote the minutes for the emergency meeting that had just taken place and made a note to circulate them to committee members who were not present at the time.

Terry was talking to Leighton as the band started to get changed into uniform on the bus. "All I'm saying is, the carnival doesn't start for another hour, let's just say we are going for a walk, and then get a few jars in en route, as it were."

Leighton was pulling his trousers up, "And all I'm saying is, you know how Harry feels about drinking before playing, if he finds out, he'll kill us."

"But how's he going to find out?" Terry asked doing his tie up.

The band started filing off the bus leaving those players behind who were searching their bags for a pair of missing black socks and amid the usual questions; "Whose coat is this jacket?", and, "Whose shoes are these trainers?" Only Toby Stephens was uncharacteristically quiet as he stepped off the coach. On this occasion he had no cause to call anyone a "nobhead".

The players mingled together in the hot summer air, amongst the collection of carnival floats, and participants in various home made costumes, walked around. Harry was still on the bus buttoning up his shirt when he saw someone familiar out of the window. A boy in a space suit was sitting on the edge of a trailer, decorated like a moon base. He was looking at Harry who once again could have sworn it was the same boy he saw at the cemetery in Cefngoed at his mum's funeral. As he watched the boy, convinced that the familiarity he felt was imaginary, he remembered hiding under the blankets of his bed as a boy; torch in hand, reading The Eagle comic book and dreaming of being Dan Dare, pilot of the future. He would drift into sleep, picturing himself returning to Cefngoed as a man, as a hero, having completed yet another death defying space mission, saving the planet again and pushing through the cheering crowds into his Mum and Dad's front garden. He couldn't ever, even in his dream, stop his Mum from giving her traditional greeting, "What do you want for tea love, cooked dinner or chips?"

The boy stood up on the edge of the trailer, kept looking at Harry and pointed to the sky. Harry stood transfixed. A giant papier-mâché dragon's head suddenly appeared in front of him, followed by the rest of a Chinese dragon, flowing past the window. When it had passed the boy had either gone, or was now joined by other space children on the float and Harry could not see him anymore.

"Come on butty, let's have a wander into town before the march", Eric's voice broke Harry's thoughts.

"Yeah alright" he said and as he left the bus, he couldn't help laughing to himself and jumping off the last step on to the imaginary moon surface below;

"Another successful landing for Harry Jones, pilot of the future" he thought.

Terry and Leighton were now in town, and on their second pints. A few of the other players had joined them, including James who, along with a couple of his mates he'd dragged along, was drinking a glass of cider;

"Ah, nothing like a pint of cider on a summer's day" he said as he gulped another mouthful down, vowing to fully test the whole "hair of the dog" theory.

Rachel Parry walked in and spied them all in the corner sitting at a table. She grinned, walked to the bar and ordered half a lager. The pub was jam-packed, music was playing, and the sounds of Abertowyn flowed in through the open windows; seagulls, traffic, the crashing waves, all mixed together with the barrel-organ of the fairground on the beach, and the electronic beeps and snippets of melody from slot machines in the various arcades along the promenade.

"Hey! Hey! Rachel!" called an increasingly jolly Leighton Davis.

"Yes, I'm coming now", shouted Rachel, pointing at the bar to indicate she was waiting for her drink. She paid, pushed her way through the various groups of people standing in the pub chatting, and eventually arrived at the corner table.

"You'll know this", said Terry Horner as Rachel sat down, "what does LOL stand for? You know, in texting and that."

"Tell him Rach!" interrupted Leighton, "it's LOTS OF LOVE innit. Everybody knows that."

"Actually, it's LAUGHS OUT LOUD", Rachel corrected him. Everyone sitting around the table cheered. Rachel looked bemused.

"Told you!" said James, laughing his head off.

"Oh gawd, that explains it then", said Leighton. "No wonder Molly in The Cock is giving me funny looks"
The others looked confused. "Why, what happened?" asked Rachel, on behalf of everyone.

"Well, you know her mother died a couple of weeks ago", said Leighton, "well when I heard, I sent Molly a text saying '*I heard about your mother. LOL*'"

James, Rachel, Terry and James' two friends ironically couldn't help laughing out loud.

"Oh you didn't, did you?" spluttered Rachel still laughing.

"Yeah, what a pillock", said Terry, laughing and rolling his eyes.

"Oi", retorted Leighton, "if we're talking about dropping clangers you can't really talk can you Horner!"

Terry looked sheepish and tried to change the subject, "Yeah, well we'd better get back soon hadn't we."

This only fuelled everyone's curiosity.

"No, come on Terry", said Rachel, "what clangers have you dropped recently?"

"Well it doesn't matter now does it", said Terry.

Leighton decided to labour the point, now delighted by Terry's obvious increasing embarrassment, and started banging the table and chanting, "Terry, Terry, Terry", inevitably joined by everyone else.

Terry relented. "Well, you remember the Tesco Bomber…"

"Yes", said James, "they never got anyone for that did they?"

"No, they didn't", replied Terry, "and good job really, cause it was me."

Leighton Davis, who obviously knew this already, now had tears of laughter in his eyes. Everyone, not only in Midtown, but in most of the county, had heard of the Tesco Bomber. It had made front page news in the local press almost a year ago when the entire Tesco store on the outskirts of Midtown had to be evacuated after a particularly rancid stink-bomb had been deployed inside.

"Why would you do that though?" asked James, not quite knowing whether to laugh or not, "I mean, firstly why would you have a stink bomb, and secondly what's the point of letting it off in Tescos?"

Terry was now bright red; Leighton had his head in his arms on the table, and was shaking with laughter.

"It..." began Leighton, before Terry had a chance to respond "...it...wasn't a stink bomb!"

Everyone was now totally confused by this odd story and the hilarity it was obviously causing Leighton.

"Well, it was the week everyone had that bug that was going round", said Terry. "You remember?"

Suddenly it dawned on Rachel. "Hang on, hang on...so you're saying you farted in the Frozen Peas aisle, and they had to evacuate the whole store?"

James was now crying with laughter, as was Leighton Davis, soon to be joined by Rachel and everyone else within earshot. Not only because of what happened, but because nearly everyone in Mid Wales had believed it to be the act of some misguided teenager, or extremely amateur terrorist, while all the time it was Terry Horner and his amazing musical arse. As everyone was realising the consequences of this event, the fact it had made the local press and BBC Wales, another wave of laughter cascaded through the Abertowyn pub.

Terry just sat there, resigned to the fact his secret was out, and simply replied "No, no, no…", as if about to deny it, but continued "…it wasn't in Frozen Peas it was Sauces and Relishes." Everyone fell about.

But it was Rachel who managed to engender the biggest laugh of the session.

"Well, if we're 'fessing-up to things, I can top both of you", she began.

"Do tell", encouraged James, now pretty much enjoying the dregs of his second pint.

"Well..." continued Rachel, as if reluctant to share this with the group, "in Ron Titley's car, on the way to Gilfach Village Fete last year, I dared to *speak* when he had a band CD on!"

A round of applause resulted and everyone cracked up laughing.

"One for the road?" suggested Leighton fatefully. Another cheer rippled through the pub, followed by one of James' friends surreally enquiring "Do turtles fart?"

Back on the carnival field, the parade was now formed and ready to embark on its annual journey across Abertowyn. Harry was pacing back and forth next to the coach, wondering where the rest of his players were, subconsciously tapping his watch, but quietly confident they'd be there in the next few minutes.

Leighton who was now three pints worse for ware, on an empty stomach, before 1pm on the hottest day of the year, was on his way back to the field, accompanied by an equally inebriated Terry, James and Rachel, all doing a much better job of hiding it than Leighton was. Despite being twenty years older than Rachel, despite having been in the band for most of his life, and despite being a scaffolder and used to the swearing and shouting on a building site, Leighton was still a little scared of what Harry would say if he knew they'd been drinking before a march.

Terry had the same worries, desperately trying to adopt a respectable gait as they made their way towards the rest of the band. Terry was forty eight years old and probably forty eight inches around his gut, which hung over his belt like a deflating space hopper. He was a big drinking man, to which his pitted red nose testified, but even he would soon be feeling the effects of the amount and speed of alcohol consumption today.

As the four final members took their places, Midtown Band was ready to go, formed into the section lines of a marching band, with the trombones at the front, cornets at the back and a big bass drum strapped to Ieuan's front;
"I know how my wife feels now, these straps are killing me" he said as the weight of the drum pulled into his shoulders. A shout came from somewhere in the lines;
"Why, her chest isn't that big!" laughter rippled around the band.
The sun was beating down now as the rest of the carnival procession got in line behind them, ready to leave the field and head into Abertowyn.
James turned around to Rachel, rubbing his stomach;
"Are you feeling alright Rach? I think that cider was a bad pint".

Terry was stood between Steve and Leighton as he held onto his bass, in fact he was clinging to it as if somehow it would help him stand up straight, "perhaps that last drink was one too many", he thought.

Harry called out from his position with the horns;

"First march, Slaidburn. OK Ieaun, when you're ready"

The bass drum banged out the opening beats as Ieaun shouted;

"By the left, quick march!"

And the band struck up. Everyone in the field suddenly felt the excitement of carnival day and of the procession to come. Everyone that is, apart from Terry, who, as the band started to move off, stood stock-still, as if rooted to the spot.

Leighton and Steve who were standing either side, noticed just before the row of euphoniums and baritones clattered into him, grabbed each arm and dragged him into step.

Over the noise of the music Steve shouted to Leighton;

"What's wrong with him?"

Leighton kept blowing and shrugged his shoulders pretending he didn't know. They both let him go as they left the sports field and turned towards the town. They could see the lines of cheering people up ahead and again only just noticed as Terry started to stumble forward into the line of players in front of him, amongst which was an oblivious Harry.

Steve and Leighton grabbed him again;

"Jesus Christ Terry! What's wrong, are you pissed?"

"Keep your voice down!" Leighton half-shouted, half-whispered.

Terry just stumbled along between them, both arms clinging to his bass, being held up at the elbows by Steve and Leighton either side. The baking sun continued to effortlessly beam down on the band as they were just marching past the first crowds, Steve and Leighton to all intents and purposes carrying a sweating, drunk, twenty-stone man, and his bass as they also struggled to play.

The crowd cheered and waved flags. A water bomb came flying out of the crowd and crashed against the bass drum, showering players all around it;

"Wankers!" Steve shouted.

"Oi!" Harry shouted across angrily "Decorum at all times."

The players who had got sprayed were quite thankful actually as the sun raged and made the music almost too dazzling to read.

James, managing to maintain a pretty convincing demeanour of sobriety to all but the most intent observer, had been trying to ignore the increasingly thick head, increasing temperature and slowly churning stomach that had been creeping up on him since they left the pub. As he marched, he could feel the urge to take deeper breaths. It was a feeling he knew only too well and a cold wave of panic started to envelope him. He continued marching, playing his euphonium, as if in denial, convinced everyone in the band and in the crowds knew what was about to happen. Suddenly, the panic became a cold-sweat, a rush of goose-bumps ensued, and a tingle rocketed through his stomach, up his back and into his mouth.

"Oh no" he thought, desperately hanging onto his last few seconds of dignity, and as they passed the Mayor of Abertowyn and his wife, waving from a balcony, a spray of vomit, comprising 8 pints of last night's lager, Chicken Biriyani and Keema Naan, this morning's cornflakes, and the three pints of cider he'd had half an hour ago, violently left James and hit the ground, splashing his shoes and trousers.

The mayor and his wife stopped mid-wave and looked alarmed.

Without missing a beat, Rachel who was marching directly behind James just widened her stance and marched over it but Daniel Parry on third cornet was not so lucky. As his foot hit the pool of sick, he slipped and hit the road with a splash. And as the putrid concoction of semi-digested food and drink hit his olfactory organs it was just enough to make him lean forward and unashamedly throw-up as well.

The crowd groaned as a stinking, wet Daniel got up and ran back into line, but it was too late. The truck directly behind the band, pulling the Women's Institute float, had slammed on the brakes and sent twelve, fifty-something aged women piling into the wooden and papier-mâché HMS Pinafore they had lovingly constructed. The ship went down. Or rather, it went over the side of the flat bed lorry and crashed to the ground, sending splinters of wood and paper across the road. The crowd screamed. All the trucks behind stopped.

The band however, carried on. Harry, marching two rows ahead was still totally oblivious aside from casually wondering why, rather than their usual enthusiastic applause, the hundreds of onlookers were looking aghast, almost to the point of being pallid. Applause was replaced by confused mutterings from hand-covered mouths. Daniel Parry eventually managed to catch up with the band, got back in line and commenced playing, experiencing a strange sense of purged-relief and looking forward to dinner later on. Terry Horner staggered on continuing to be physically held up by Steve and Leighton. Anti-peristalsis suddenly took grip of James once again as he expelled another batch of chunky fluid as they marched past *Quid's Inn – the Best Value Shop in Abertowyn.* The sun continued smiling down, as if gleaning a strange enjoyment from the day's proceedings. As they approached the end of the promenade they were now on their second rendition of "Castell Coch", blissfully unaware that the parade had stopped half a mile back, blocked by the now abandoned wreck of HMS Pinafore. As they continued marching, in perfect unison, now the only mobile participants in the parade, the rest of the bedraggled and now ruined procession a couple of hundred yards behind them, another water bomb came sailing out of the crowd, and the sound of Harry's voice could just be heard over the music, with a pre-emptive;

"Decorum everyone!"

The onlookers, standing at what was now the other end of Abertowyn, could only wonder what was going on, as the mass-advertised, much-reputed annual carnival seemed to consist of only one act; Midtown Silver Band, with their apparently paraplegic bassist, and amazing vomiting Euphonium-player.

Harry never knew what had gone on, and no-one seemed willing to explain why the band had to wait 20 minutes for the rest of the procession at the end. He could only conclude that it was due, like everything else these days, to "bad organisation, and lack of commitment".

Chapter 11

Music for a Festival (Philip Sparke)

There's something magical about walking through any of London's Royal parks on a mild autumn morning. As the majority of Midtown band strolled through the tree-lined avenues which demarcated the expanses of ever-so-slightly frosty grass, they marvelled at the unlikely marriage of calming greenery with a soundtrack of constant yet unobtrusive background noise reminding them they were in the metropolis. As she walked along, it seemed to Mary Jones that autumn was a season where Mother Nature showcased her own artwork; it was cool but not quite chilly, the sun was blinding yet making no contribution to a warm day. There were no extremes in the autumn, simply colourful and reflective respite from the summer, and an interlude in which to prepare for the oncoming winter months.

The band members and their families were heading from their hotel, across Hyde Park to the Royal Albert Hall. It was the highlight of the year, at least for competing bands; the National Brass Band Finals, in which an extremely creditable 2nd place at the qualifying contest in Swansea had afforded them a chance to compete. Spirits were high. Everyone was excited to be in London, it was an opportunity for band-members to bring their wives, husbands, partners, children, and make a weekend of it.

Ron Titley was already at the Albert Hall. In his capacity of Band Secretary he needed to be present at "the draw", alongside representatives from all the other qualifying bands when the order in which they would each compete was decided. Ron had enjoyed a light continental breakfast at the hotel, adorned his best suit, cufflinks, and Hai Karate aftershave purchased from Midtown market the previous Christmas by his wife Ophelia, and alighted the band coach, accompanied by Harry Jones and Eric Trevelyn. The three die-hard bandsmen, along with all the instruments and uniforms, would be ready and waiting at the Albert Hall in readiness for a possible early draw.

The party of families and bandsmen continued their journey through the park. Several conversations were taking place, ranging from which shops it would be fun to visit, to which band would present the biggest threat to Midtown. The animated atmosphere betrayed thinly disguised nerves. It was a big day. The band needed to deliver.

"The draw will have taken place now", Emily thought out loud, as she walked with James and Lawrence.

"Yup, it's all over now", replied Lawrence, wondering whether they'd be changing into uniforms as soon as they reached the Hall, or have to wait around all day if it was a late draw.

"Hope it's an early one", said James, "be good to have the rest of the day to relax".

"Dad's hoping for a late one I should think", said Emily, knowing all too well Harry's opinions on the various pros and cons of when they might perform. It had been the subject of many a late-night alcohol-fuelled debate over the years. An early draw would set the standard. The adjudicator would then be comparing all the other bands with Midtown, plus the very first band on stage had the advantage of being able to further demonstrate their talents by playing the customary national anthem. However, a later draw usually meant a bigger audience. People making sure they were there for the results. A more exciting ambience, a chance for the band to add Harry's own personality to the performance of a test-piece which the now tiring adjudicator will have heard at least ten times in rapid succession.

The "band widows" and "widowers", were all wondering the same thing as they made idle chit-chat, sun in their eyes, the buzz of the city in their ears, each soaking up the differences between sleepy Midtown in the centre of Wales, and bustling London in the centre of, well, the Universe!

Mary, and Dilys Ap Dafydd, subconsciously caught up with James, Emily and Lawrence. Dilys linked arms with her husband.

For many it was among the few times they'd been to London, if ever. The previous night had been spent exploring the hotel and surrounding areas, enjoying a meal and a few drinks, and generating a holiday-like environment that only comes with a band or club "on tour". Many were surprised that London was quite an open, almost leafy city, encompassing tradition with modernity, shattering their pre-conceptions of grimy, smoky, dimly-lit backstreets infested with pick-pockets, drug-dealers and prostitutes on the verge of being murdered by an unidentified nutcase in a top-hat.

"You'd think your dad would let just one of us bring our phone", Lawrence muttered.

"Well, you know what he's like" James agreed, "ever since the Armistice Day incident he's banned anyone associated with the band from bringing them anywhere!".

As the motley crew of bandsmen and families approached the edge of the park, the majestic Royal Albert Hall stood in front of them, just over the road, looking almost wise and stoic as it consolidated its place, content in its own unencumbered space amongst the terraces of townhouses each with several hundred years of history hewn into its enduring bricks. Bandsmen, like endless battalions were disembarking coaches, renewing old acquaintances, scurrying all about the area. James was sure he could even smell valve-oil in the air, and as he and the rest of the group stood atop the steps leading down to the road, he spied his dad engrossed in conversation with several of the other protagonists in this theatre of banding. Eric walked out of the massive building, spotted his comrades over the road and put both his arms in the air. All of Midtown band, and every one of their supporters suddenly stopped talking, craned their necks forward as far as they would go, and narrowed their eyes in an attempt to view Eric, partially obscured by bandsmen and bright autumn sunlight. Both Eric's hands were aloft, all fingers extended. Suddenly, three fingers on his left hand, and his left thumb, disappeared.

"16th", yelled Emily, "we've been drawn 16th on!" The excited exclamatory nature of her announcement prompted an impromptu cheer amongst the group. No-one quite knew why.

"Right-o" volunteered Lawrence, "let's go over and find out what's occurring"

Ron Titley could be seen strutting around, for no particular reason, suited and booted, hair coiffured to within an inch of its life, smart portfolio of papers tucked under one arm, every inch the Band Secretary, the font, if you will, of all knowledge. The members of Midtown Band saw Ron, but instinctively made their way across the road to where Harry Jones was standing. Family members knew the routine. They would stay well out of the way until the band had been "briefed". All would become clear as to how the rest of the day would unfold.

Eric had now joined Harry, and the 25 other Midtown band members stood amongst the bustling crowd in what was effectively a strangely intimate but completely public band meeting.

"Right boys and girls", Harry began with his traditional opening in these situations, "we're on 16th, that means everyone needs to be backstage, changed and ready to go on by 4'o clock"

"Yes, I can confirm that, 4'o clock", came the high pitched voice of Ron Titley from no particular direction, "or 1600 hours if you prefer". The band sighed.

"So do you want us here at 4 o'clock, or 1600 hours?" somebody enquired. A childish chuckle rippled its way around the band.

"Yes, yes, very droll", replied Ron, "however, 4 o'clock *is* in fact 1600 hours".

"Not if it's 4 in the morning", someone else interjected. Again, titters of laughter manifested themselves. Harry rolled his eyes, aimed more at Ron than the rest of the band.

"Ok, ok..." Harry continued, "We all need to be here, ready to play, at 4 o'clock, that's 1600 hours, in the PM of this afternoon on the day of our Lord God, Jesus, and all the angels, 6th October".

"Plus", interjected Ron again, desperate to assert himself in his official role in some way, shape or form, "I have it on good authority that Llangilfach Band are having trouble with the semi-quavers in the middle section"

"Thank you Ron, thanks for that", continued Harry with a soupcon of sarcasm that 24 band members appreciated, but which was lost on one band secretary, "I think we can all rest a little bit easier knowing that." The band giggled loudly. Similar ad-hoc meetings were taking place all around the car-parks and pavements surrounding the Hall, in the crisp autumn morning, as every band made arrangements following the draw. Harry continued with his briefing, the band listened. Harry always seemed ironically more relaxed on the actual contest days than he did in the rehearsals. It was as if his more paternal side was allowed to break the surface. His strict instructions about not drinking alcohol "at all" before going on stage, making sure they were back here at 4 "come what may", where the coach would be parked with their instruments and uniforms, how they were "ambassadors for Midtown", were emphasised, but now interspersed with smiles and banter. It was Harry's view that as well as playing to the best of their abilities, what was also important was that everyone enjoy the day and immerse themselves in what was the Mecca of brass-banding. The band also knew their role. They knew that months of rehearsals, painstakingly perfecting each nuance of their own particular part, sacrificing social and work events in favour of additional sectional practices, were not going to be wasted for the sake of a few pints today. And with that, the band went their separate ways, each player seeking out their family members and relaying the plan of action.

"Back to the hotel then", Terry piped up as the band milled about, all making individual arrangements about what to do until 4 o'clock.

"Is it?" asked Chris, "I was thinking more of Leicester Square or somewhere".

"Hotel still serving breakfast till 10 though", said Terry, "I might go and have a fry-up now".

"I thought you had some grub earlier", Phil interrupted, "didn't I spot you when I came down the canteen earlier?" Ron Titley shook his head at the way the not un-stylish and cosmopolitan hotel restaurant had been reduced in one fell swoop to a "canteen".

"Yeah, but I'm on 'oliday 'arn I" grinned Terry patting his ample stomach as if preparing it for the onslaught of whatever was on offer back at the hotel.

"God, meet Terry Horner", Lucy Dann, the band's Flugel Horn player piped-up, "the only bloke I know who once stopped for a curry, *on the way* to going out for a curry". The bandsmen within earshot collapsed laughing at Lucy's dry comment, hilarious for two reasons; its delivery and its accuracy.

The throng of brass band players, enthusiasts and supporters was now diminishing as people now knew what was happening. The bands that were drawn to play early were making their way into the Hall or back to their coach to prepare for their performance; those who wanted to listen to the early bands play were heading into the Hall to claim a good seat. Others were studying Underground maps and bus routes, in preparation for a good few hours sight-seeing and shopping.

Mary glanced over at Harry, now looking at his watch and deciding what to do next. She wandered over. "16th then, not a bad draw that".

"No, good draw, good draw, second-to-last band on" replied Harry, "we'll do well with that".

"Right then, you coming for a look around? Thought I'd go and have a look at the Palace and find somewhere to have a cuppa' tea" suggested Mary.

"You're alright love", came the inevitable response, "I thought I'd go and have a listen to Sprowston. They're on first." Mary nodded, unsurprised at the response, wondering whether she was wrong, on such a unique day in the banding year, to even ask Harry to spend some time with her exploring this beautiful city on a fresh, sunny morning, and also considering an inaccuracy about the term "band widow". At split-seconds such as this it was as if something in *her* had died. She was suddenly interrupted.

"You coming with us Mam?" It was Emily's cheery voice. "Me and Lucy are going up Oxford Street for a look". And with that, Harry disappeared into the Albert Hall, most of the female members of the band, along with wives and girlfriends headed to the West End, and all the men, in respective groups decided to have a look around London, making arrangements to rendezvous at the London Eye with Terry Horner after he'd exhausted the hotel restaurant's supply of bacon and egg.

The grandeur of the Royal Albert Hall's auditorium is unknown and unseen in the rather dull cream corridors beneath and behind the stage. Midtown Silver Band contemplated the array of legends that had themselves stood on this very spot, waiting to go on stage over the years, and now took their own turn to endure the inevitable apprehension and anticipation experienced by the previous 15 competing bands that day. It was now half past four. True to their word, the band members had made sure they'd traversed the various highways, byways, bus-routes and Underground lines that would mean they were back at the coach, getting changed, unpacking their instruments and walking through the artists' door of the Hall at four o'clock. The band drawn number 15 was still playing as Midtown paced nervously, blowing warm air silently into their instruments, each immaculately dressed and focussed, gleaming instrument in one hand, copy of the test-piece in the other, covering nerves with a few last jokes and comments, a few of the younger players asking Harry for some last minute advice whilst pointing at their sheet-music. Harry was grinning.

"Forget it" he said, "you know the part. I know how well you can play it. That's why you're in my band, backstage at the Albert Hall. Just play it, just like in practice. Nothing's changed between there and here."

A few of the band had their ears pressed up against the stage door, trying to gauge Band 15's performance.

"Think the bari' cracked the low B!" whispered Ron Titley, who'd made it his business to be nearest the door. The message filtered its way back along the twenty-five band members all anxiously waiting, although by the time it had reached the tenor horns it had somehow become "Prince Harry's sat in Row 3!", which elicited squeals of excitement from Lucy Dann, Megan Edwards and Rachel Parry, resulting in a brief flurry involving clouds of perfume and even more lipstick being applied. More critiques followed;

"Delmie, they messed up the syncopation"

"The horns sound good though…"

"The principal cornet missed that top D…."

All messages whispered down the line and relayed to nervous players.

At the other end of the corridor was a blue, rather grim-looking door marked "Toilet". It slowly creaked open and a silver-haired bandsman slowly lumbered out, eyes moving from left to right as though surveying the area.

"Here comes Eric now! Eric where have you been? We're going on soon", Steve Pepper, Eric's fellow bass player, said anxiously. Eric came squeezing through the corridor holding his bass in front of him looking sheepish and trying to hide a smile.

"Where have you been?" Steve repeated, as everyone shuffled along to accommodate Eric and his bass. Eric's hair was swept back, a paunch and a warm face of deep wrinkles built up from an early life down a coal pit and a longer life of laughter greeted the band. His blue eyes sparkled when he spoke and he was Harry's oldest friend. They had both been in the same band when they were younger in South Wales and when the pits closed down, they had both moved to Midtown in search of employment in the new fabrication and manufacturing factories being set up in this new town:

"I been to the toilet, all that Guinness last night"

"Good idea" said Lucy "I've got time just to pop to the loo quickly" She walked back towards the blue door and opened it, only to take an involuntary step back, coughing spluttering, and covering her nose and mouth, "Oh my god that is just rank". A suppressed chortle relayed its way down the line of bandsmen, "That nearly took the skin off my eyes! What the hell have you been eating Eric?" continued Lucy in a loud whisper, deciding to wait until after they'd played before visiting the toilet.

"Well what took you so long anyway?" asked Steve.

"And come to think of it", added Terry, "what did you do for bog roll? I was going to go in there just now but noticed there wasn't any".

"Oh, I managed", said Eric, "anyway, how are these boys sounding?" he asked, trying to play down the question and change the subject back to the current band on stage.

Harry stood down the corridor, not interested in how the previous band was playing. He was wishing it were somehow possible to capture moments like these. His entire band seconds away from performing on stage at the Royal Albert Hall. Each member, whether bin-man or bank-manager, in good humour, finely groomed, impeccably behaved, instrument shining, and each carrying their copy of this year's test-piece. It was moments like these that Harry lived for. He had done his job, the band had put in the effort, and all that was required now was to close the deal.

"Yeah Eric, what did you use then?" Delmie shouted from somewhere down the line, interrupted by Harry, making his way through the line, which instinctively parted for him like the Red Sea as he approached the stage door. Band 15 was just about to finish, and Harry wanted to take his place, ready to go on.

"Use for what?" he enquired, catching the tail-end of the exchange between Delmie, Eric, Terry and the growing number of interested parties. The colour drained from Eric's face and he made a mental note to strangle that Delmie pillock the next time they were alone.

"For toilet paper", the reply to Harry's question slowly made its way from Delmie's lips and finally shattered Eric's last-ditch futile attempts to gloss over this particular issue.

Harry suddenly became curious, "Yes, I looked in there earlier as well and noticed the distinct lack of paper. Bit annoying actually, what with last night's Guinness and all that." Eric smiled weakly, hoping that events would suddenly take over, and the answer to Harry's inevitable next question would remain forever a mystery. But alas, it wasn't to be. Eric watched helplessly as Harry's lips started forming a "W" and the question came crashing forth, "What did you use then?"

As soon as he'd finished asking the question, the answer suddenly became apparent to Harry. He hadn't been able to put his finger on what exactly was niggling his subconscious, but as he looked at Eric, then at everyone else in the line, the results of a bizarre "spot the difference" game registered with him. Eric was the only person holding his instrument, and nothing else. No sheet music.

Suddenly, the Albert Hall erupted in applause. The nervous tension in the corridor, and in the line of Midtown Band players, reached new heights. Six months of rehearsals, a lifetime of missed nights out and hours of practice seemed to matter now more than ever. All those times in band practice of wishing they were somewhere else came back to haunt some players, who now wished they could have just one more run through the test-piece. The doors opened, Harry remained stood with his back against the right-hand wall of the corridor, Eric stood against the left-hand wall, and the players started filing past them both, walking onto the stage. Each player stole a glance at the crescent of faces, hundreds of them in the audience looking down, before walking up and onto the stage.

The tiered galleries of people, the lights, music stands glistening, mutes on the floor, the upside down giant acoustic mushrooms suspended from the ceiling. A moment in a player's life captured in a snapshot of images and feelings, and yet the whole thing put to one side by the worry of getting those opening bars as good as they knew they could.

All the cornets were on now. The youngest member, Norman Lightfoot, ten years old and playing third cornet, put his cornet case on the floor in front of his seat to rest his feet on as his legs were too short to reach the floor. The whole of the Albert Hall let out an audible, "Aaah". Norman's mum, who had only just managed get to the hall after travelling round the Underground for two hours and becoming involved in an altercation with a slow moving gentlemen from Acton, burst into tears at seeing her

Norman on stage at the Royal Albert Hall. All those nightshifts at the washer factory to afford the repayments on that cornet were suddenly worth it.

All the members of the band were now on stage. All, that is, apart from Harry and Eric, still stood opposite each other by the stage door.

Harry slowed his breathing and looked Eric in the eye as the moment of comprehension came, "Eric, we've been friends for over twenty years. This moment is what we both got into banding for. It's the Royal Albert Hall, the band are all on stage," he pointed up the steps but kept looking at Eric, "Now, tell me the truth. Did you wipe your arse with the test piece?"

Eric knew the game was up. He had run out of time.

"Yes".

Harry's eyes closed, as Eric added.

"But only the first movement".

Harry shook his head, disbelief giving way to laughter in a brief moment with his old friend as they were about to experience what every bandsman dreams of.

"On stage with you then," grinned Harry, "and let's not have any bum notes".

Chapter 12

The Night To Sing (Bramwell Tovey)

As James relaxed and sipped a mug of coffee from the comfort of the armchair in the front-room, he'd more or less decided that setting foot outside on a freezing December evening was pretty much the last thing he wanted to do. But he would anyway. It was the annual carol concert at Beglwys Chapel, always the first engagement in Midtown Silver Band's Christmas schedule, heralding the busiest time of the year. Every night of the next few weeks would either involve a concert, a hospital visit, or simply playing carols in Midtown and the surrounding villages, aided by a series of door-to-door collectors drafted from family, friends and supporters. Harry was ensconced on the settee, oblivious to everything save the sheet-music on his lap which he was frantically editing whilst humming repeated sections of Christmas tunes to himself. Mary and Emily were upstairs, trying to decide whether it was a good idea for Emily to attend the concert as she'd not been feeling too well all day. James was trying to muster up the energy to get out of the warm inviting chair and start getting changed, and he promised himself that as soon as the News finished he'd head upstairs. The television seemed to make the room even cosier, providing a glimpse at what was going on in the world, whilst the closed curtains and flickering gas fire provided a reminder that James was, at least at that moment, not out in it! The News continued, delivering the latest information about an on-going debate centred on whether or not doctors should give under-age girls the contraceptive pill without their parents' knowledge.

"There are plenty of things a girl under the age of 16 should practice", explained the person being interviewed, "and sex is not one of them".

At which point Harry absentmindedly looked up from his work and added "No, the euphonium is one." He continued his feverish amendments, and James grinned to himself. Harry would never change.

Emily lay on her bed, her mum sat on the edge holding her hand.

"Why not just stay here and relax Em? It's only Beglwys, and you know what it's like getting there this time of year"

"Yeah, I know", said Emily, "But I haven't missed a Christmas function, playing or not, for years". Emily had always loved Christmas, and apart from anything else, she couldn't help feeling that her absence tonight, even as a non-player, would just represent another nail in the coffin of her and her dad's relationship.

"Yes, but things are different this year love", Mary stated the obvious, gently patting Emily's bump. "And if you hadn't been feeling so rough today I wouldn't be so worried, but I really think you'd be better off staying in tonight".

"Ok then", Emily finally agreed, "But would you explain to Dad that it's because I'm not feeling well?"

"Why don't you tell him?" Mary suggested, still vainly trying to cement diminishing relations between father and daughter.

Emily shrugged and gave a "what's the point?" look to Mary who was finding the role of mediator ever more difficult, and it didn't help that the two opposing parties were just as stubborn as each other in many ways. The thumping of footsteps on the stairs indicated Harry and James coming up to get changed.

Beglwys was a village, almost 12 miles north of Midtown, nestled in the hills. Very picturesque, but a challenge to even the most experienced of drivers. The only roads in and out were amongst the narrowest and winding in Wales, and the pitch black frosty December evening did nothing to improve things. Harry, Mary and James arrived at the Bandroom roughly at the same time as the other band members. The lights were already on, and instruments were being loaded into cars, as the group of musicians in their biggest coats and thickest scarves prepared to leave town. James got out of the Mondeo leaving Harry and Mary to head off towards Beglwys. One by one, car boots and doors were slammed shut, the Bandroom and car-park were once again engulfed in darkness as the lights were switched off, and the players were on their way out of town.

Even though Beglwys was only 12 miles away, it wasn't a place that was visited unless there was a reason. However pretty it was, there was actually very little there, and the residents comprised a mixture of farmers and retired bank managers. Apart from the Carol Concert, the only other reason anyone in Midtown Band had ever travelled there was the dance that used to take place every Friday night in the now run-down Tiffany's Café, which had been a failed attempt at an American-style diner, that however basic, uninspiring and inconvenient to reach, had provided the only venue for teenagers within a 20-mile radius to have a drink and a boogie. That was, until The Starlight Lounge opened giving Midtown its first nightclub. Everyone in Midtown over the age of 30 had a story or two about "Tiffany's", little more than a farmer grabbing the opportunity to cash-in on one of his old out-buildings, and how The Starlight Lounge would never re-capture those "glory days". The younger element would just regard it as a piece of folklore and could never imagine life in Midtown without "The Lounge". As each car's headlights revealed the next section of dark tree-lined road, the lights of Beglwys eventually came into view beyond the final twisting hill, someone in every car would regale the story of how that bend is known locally as "Horner's Corner", following a motoring mishap almost twenty years ago during which Terry Horner misjudged the bend on his way home from Tiffany's and managed to literally park his Astra in the top of one of the trees on the steep banking below. As a very smart-looking "Welcome to Beglwys" sign greeted each car in turn, the most prominent sight was the brightly lit chapel, right in the centre of the village, and around which the community was based.

There was a small car-park to the side and rear of the chapel, and the band's cars all claimed a space next to the few already there. Harry's Mondeo was parked next to a large expensive looking estate, out of which a group of women were busy transporting plates of mince-pies, and boxes of raffle-prizes into the chapel. Everyone began getting out of the cars and organizing themselves. Coats and scarves were left in cars, instruments were carried out of boots, and the band made their way not into the chapel, but to the low fence on the other side of the car-park which adjoined a very smart-looking bungalow. On the other side of that fence, upholding a tradition that had existed longer than any of the current members had been in the band, Mrs Bromham stood ready to hand over the first plastic cups of mulled wine, and home-made piping hot soup to the waiting bandsmen.

"How does she get it like this?" enquired Steve Pepper as he took his first mouthful of soup. "Yeah, I know. It's blinking splendid 'innit", replied James, "I'm surprised Terry's not first in the queue, he's normally banging on about the soup until at least February"

"We'll he's always last to arrive at Beglwys", recalled Eric, also savouring the soup, "…insists on driving himself, and goes 20 mile an hour for the last mile since his little adventure!" Everyone sniggered.

The frozen grass crunched underfoot as each player took their turn at the fence, wishing Mrs Bromham a merry

Christmas and complimenting her on the "best batch of soup and wine yet". The churchyard glistened under the sparkling lights. Those band members who smoked sparked-up and added their contribution to the mixture of steam from everyone's breath and the warm beverages.

"It's cold tonight mind", Toby Stephens added, "flippin' freezin' actually!"

"Really cold." agreed Delmie. They stamped their feet as they spoke.

"Although, not the coldest", contributed Phil in an almost discussion-opening manner.

"Nah, not the coldest", agreed Delmie, "that would have to be Pontdewi Christmas Parade three years ago." Each player then remembered this event, one consigned to the immortal annuls of Brass Band mythology, where it was so cold that during the parade, one-by-one, each player's instrument actually froze up. Valves had stopped working, slides had ceased sliding until the only two sounds to be heard were Lawrence Ap Daffyd's cymbals, and Ieuan Efans' bass-drum which itself had managed to adopt a less than dramatic tone more comparable with a dustbin-lid being tapped with a length of hose-pipe, due to being covered in ice.

"Well, for me..." began Steve Pepper, "the coldest I've ever been in my life was..."

Five other players joined him in unison and announced "outside the off-licence by the bridge, Christmas Eve 1999". It was a reference Steve made every year.

"You may laugh", continued Steve.

"Alright then", interrupted James.

"But I actually thought four of my fingers were going to drop off during In The Bleak Midwinter!"

Inside the chapel, Harry was busy setting up chairs and music-stands, ably assisted by Mary, Rachel Parry, Norman Lightfoot and Owain Owain's mum.

"Hello Harry!" a high-pitched North Wales twang suddenly cascaded around the hall, as Delbert Williams arrived. Delbert was one of the most high-profile members of Beglwys village community. He was a lay preacher, leader of the Beglwys Singers, main contributor to the Beglwys Amateur Dramatics Society and leader of the village Cub Scouts brigade. At any engagement in the village, he would always make sure he was on the programme doing a solo performance of Pie Jesu or some other aria or hymn. He was actually a very nice person who was genuinely concerned for life in the village but had the potential to be more full of himself than he ought to be, which meant he was the subject of good-hearted humour for the band, exaggerated by his consistent off-key performances delivered in a nasal baritone, a legendary impersonation of which was regularly requested of Eric when the circumstances were propitious. It was Delbert that had organised the village carol concert in which Midtown Band, Midtown Ladies Choir, Delbert himself, and the Beglwys Singers would perform, followed by the drawing of the raffle, and mince pies.

Harry looked at Mary and Rachel who were smiling to themselves, and then turned around, "Hiya Delbert. Alright?"

"Yes, yes, very good, very good"

Despite having been in the chapel three times a week for the last ten years Delbert looked around the place as if seeing it for the first time.

"Dew, good acoustics in here Harry," Harry just nodded and turned back to arranging his music on the conductor's stand.

"Right, I wanted to ask, would you mind moving your last piece until after the raffle?" Delbert had adopted a serious, almost business-like air as he broached this subject with Harry. Harry couldn't care less and really hated this type of conversation with, to all intents and purposes, local busy bodies, but humoured Delbert none the less;

"Yes Delbert, that's fine, it will give the concert a good finale" he said, gesturing theatrically. Mary had to turn away as she saw her husband subtly and expertly making fun of Delbert, and burst out laughing.

"Excellent!" said Delbert, "Le Grande Finale!" he chirruped, and trotted off.

People were now arriving, both on foot and in cars, from Beglwys itself, and the surrounding hamlets and villages. The lane leading to the chapel was alive with couples and families, in all their finery, making their way to the concert. The excitement of an ever-nearing Christmas was accentuated by the frost on the ground, the smell of mulled-wine in the air, and even the haphazardly parked cars in and around the chapel car-park indicating an unusually large congregation, which could only mean a special occasion. Harry had cynically predicted an above-average attendance, and although he was all for bigger audiences he made no secret of the fact that he was disenchanted by those who "were never interested in the band before we started winning things". And it was true. The recent run of contest successes, culminating in Midtown Silver Band's extremely creditable 4th place at the Albert Hall, highly publicised by the local press, and made yet more obvious by the bulging cash-register at the British Legion Social Club during the month following the result, had attracted large audiences at subsequent concerts. Mary liked to think it was due to increased awareness and respect for the band, whereas Harry was convinced that it was more to do with "social climbers and hangers-on". To a certain extent they were both right.

Behind the chapel, more steam was rising into the chilly air as a number of the male members of the band were relieving themselves against the chapel wall.

Ron Titley, last to arrive and slightly annoyed at having to park "miles away", came round the corner and noticed the collection of instruments, neatly placed on the frozen grass. In the darkness he was aware of the line of players but couldn't see what they were doing.

"I wouldn't leave those things out too long, the cold can do funny things to them in my experience!", he bellowed, startling Toby Stephens, who was amongst the men pointing at the wall, so much that he jumped, span round and sprayed Ron's shoes and trouser bottoms with steamy fluid.

Ron jumped back and squealed like a little girl.

"My shoes!"

Toby hurriedly regained control and did his trousers up.

"Oh Ron, I'm really sorry" he said.

The gathered players who had witnessed the incident were stifling their laughter without great success.

"Everyone in, now!" Ron shouted as he walked off to rub his shoes in the frozen grass. The smokers discarded the remains of their cigarettes, plastic cups were thrown into the bin near the entrance, and the players shuffled inside still laughing, Toby made a mental note to stay as far away from Ron as possible for the rest of the night, which wasn't going to be easy as they sat next to each other. And throughout the entire concert, Harry kept twitching his nose and looking suspiciously at Ron, as did Lucy who sat the other side of him, both suspecting he had wet himself.

The concert was generating a good atmosphere. The band was playing better than ever, galvanised by their recent success. The choir were in good voice, as were the audience, relishing the opportunity to belt-out the first carols of the year, even Delbert's offering of Pie Jesu, followed by a rendition of "Mary's Boy Child", who apparently was "born on a-chriss-a-muss a-dayy-ah!" In fact it was only Delbert's ill-advised choice of extended sermon which he'd entitled "A Christmas Epistle" which served to provide the only trough in an evening of peaks. And it was during this stage of the concert that Mary's thoughts began to wander. She was seated with some of the other band wives, and had been listening, clapping and wincing, particularly when Delbert went for that top D flat, at all the right moments but her mind was elsewhere. She was wondering how much of her life was actually taken up sitting in cold chapels and concert halls, or how cold she got rattling a collection tin at unsympathetic passers-by in the High Street at Christmas time, and her thoughts inevitably turned to Tom.

It had been six months since he'd arrived in her department at the Town Hall. No-one quite knew what his job was apart from being some kind of "consultant", which gave him a sense of intrigue. He was around forty years old but looked younger, sat opposite Mary and had a picture of his wife and another one of his wife and two children together on his desk. He brought in a packed lunch every day and, this was something that impressed Mary. He also had the neatest hand-writing she had ever seen, it almost looked like typing. She had grown to know him quite well as she had been assigned to show him around and help him settle in during the early weeks of his employment and she had realised how different he was from Harry.

When two people have been together for a long time, they begin to simply accept the way things are. Mary was fundamentally happy with her life but there was always the desire to tweak some things, just little things, like trying to make Harry not take his wife and family completely for granted.

The more Mary talked with Tom, the more she started making comparisons with Harry:

Tom never missed one of his children's birthdays and always took the day off to be with them, whilst Harry would have think for a few seconds to actually remember when Emily and Jim's birthdays were.

Tom arose every morning at seven o'clock, would go for a three mile run and make sure that the breakfast table was laid for his family before leaving the house, whereas Harry dragged himself out of bed about ten minutes before he had to be in work and normally farted his way to the bathroom to send last night's curry on its way.

For their last anniversary, Tom had taken his wife to London for a surprise weekend where they had taken in a show, eaten lovely meals together and strolled hand-in-hand through Hyde Park. For Mary's last anniversary, Harry had gone to work as normal and her "surprise" was tickets to go and see Cory Band playing "the music of Eric Ball".

Comparisons like these are dangerous. Comparisons like these are always biased towards the person making the list and their state of mind. It is all too easy to see the rosy world of someone else when you are not privy to the whole truth but Mary was starting to convince herself that her life needed to change.

Also, and she had to be careful with this, she was starting to convince herself that Tom was in fact seriously flirting with her. She would catch him sometimes looking at her a bit longer than needed or perhaps he would brush a hand against her arm as they walked together. She mostly just took it for harmless fun but sometimes, when her imagination was left to its own devices, she could make herself blush at the thoughts she was having about him.

As Delbert concluded his sermon, Mary forced herself back to reality. Meanwhile, on stage, the increasingly bored players were fighting to hide their growing restlessness.

"I don't know", Daniel Parry whispered to Norman Lightfoot, "ask Eric."

"Eric," Norman tried to effect a combined whisper and shout as he leant over towards the bass section. "Eric!"

"Yeah?" whispered Eric.

"What's an epistle?" enquired Norman. There was a pause as Eric contemplated.

"It's a drunk Apostle I think", he volunteered. The shoulders of the four bass-players shook as they tried to contain their childish sniggers. Norman accepted the answer, and relayed it to Daniel. Thankfully, Delbert finally announced that the band would now perform their next selection.

Mary clapped as Midtown Silver Band finished their penultimate piece, and as Delbert started to call out the winning raffle tickets, the chapel organist Peggy, the Beglwys Singers, Beglwys Ladies Choir and Midtown Band were all shuffling around getting organised for the combined finishing number, "Onward Christian Soldiers".

Everyone was just about settled when Delbert called the final ticket, "Pink 43".

No-one answered.

"Pink 43?" Delbert's high voice reverberated as he surveyed the audience but was met with shrugged shoulders and silence.

"If no-one comes forward we will have to re-draw. Pink 43 last time".

Peggy suddenly heard the number and called out from her place at the organ "Oooh, that's me". A few giggles went round the chapel and Delbert turned round to address Peggy, "Well come on then Mrs. Lewis, come and get your prize", Delbert tried to hide his impatience, after all, this could put the programme back by several minutes!

Peggy, who was sixty eight and in no sense of the definition thin, heaved herself out of the stool by leaning on the keyboard for leverage. The pipes burst into life with an interesting and dramatic minor dis-chord and an audible moan as though signifying the arrival of an un-convincing Mummy in a 1930's horror film. To the left of the organ an elderly gentleman, regular at Beglwys chapel, known only as "Old Benbow", who had been quite contentedly dozing, was rudely awakened by this un-natural racket, and he sat bolt upright, coughed and shouted "It's in the pantry I think!"

The crowd gave an embarrassed giggle, and Harry just shook his head.

It took Peggy a couple of minutes to waddle over to Delbert, all the time muttering to herself that she had never won anything and what a wonderful surprise it was, especially at Christmas. She was so enamoured with her prize that on being presented with it she displayed it to the applauding audience by holding it above her head as she walked slowly backwards. Unfortunately she was not to see the pulpit as she half backed into it, the other half of her continuing alongside it as she began to lose her footing. She reached out to steady herself by grabbing the corner of the pulpit, which normally would have sufficed to regain her balance. However, this was not the kind of pulpit that had stood the test of time, and which had seen generations of chapel-goers stand before it. No, this was the pulpit that Delbert Williams had "knocked-together" a couple of years ago using some off-cut MDF and a knife from the kitchen drawer, after the original pulpit had surrendered to the woodworm equivalent of the Taliban.

"Oooh", began Peggy as she continued to slowly fall backwards.

"Oooh", she emitted again, this time a little bit louder and a lot more urgent as she could see the actual pulpit, rather than steadying her, tipping back with her like some kind of new Olympic synchronized event. Harry, instantly appraising the situation and concluding its outcome calmly shouted, "Basses, get out of there!"

Eric, Steve, Terry and Leighton grabbed their instruments and left their seats before Peggy's centre of gravity went past the point of no return and her panicked shriek of "Ooh 'eck!" was accompanied by the crash of shattering MDF on parquet-flooring as the pulpit crash-landed into the back row of the band, sending music stands flying and wood splintering across the floor.

The horns and baritones pushed through their stands to get out of the way as the pulpit came to rest and there was silence apart from the last few sheets of music floating to the floor next to the spread-eagled organist.

For a second, the audience sat in stunned silence. Harry also took a moment to absorb the situation. The first thing he noticed was Eric Trefelyn, in an unashamed display of schadenfreude, standing at the edge of the stage doubled-up, tears of laughter rolling down his cheeks. Upon seeing this, Harry himself was forced to suppress the smile that was forming on his lips. The rest of the band was simply, as a group, bemused.

"Is Peggy alright?" someone asked, after what seemed like ages but was actually no more than two seconds.

"Yes, yes, I'm fine", said Peggy, who to be fair was now

also starting to laugh as several members of the audience had come forward to roll her onto her feet.

Delbert stood with his head in his hands.

Harry asked everyone in the band if they were OK. People were shaken up but no physical injuries were announced. Inevitably it fell to him to address the audience.

"Right, well. That was more like Backward Christian Soldiers! Next year apparently she's going to do an encore juggling fire…anyway… I think we should call it a night there. Thanks for coming everyone and Merry Christmas!"

James was in fits of laughter as Harry tuned back round, shaking his head with an amused look on his face.

Ron turned to Lucy, "Are you alright Lucy? That was a bit scary wasn't it!"

"Yes it was Ron", Lucy answered "Just try not to piss yourself again if that's alright."

Ron looked completely confused.

As the final applause died down, the audience were invited to partake of a mince-pie on the way out. Peggy was now sitting on a couple of chairs in the front row, recovering from her ordeal with a glass of medicinal mulled-wine Mrs Bromham had hurriedly popped home to fetch. The treasured prize which had caused her distraction was proudly nestled in her arms. A family shoe shining kit. Happy days.

Chapter 13

Theme And Cooperation (Joseph Horovitz)

Roger finished blowing up the last of the balloons and caught his breath, "Dew" he puffed, "That's all of them". He passed it up to James who was balancing atop a stepladder and sticking the balloons up in the corners of the Bandroom.

"Good job, Rog" he answered taking the balloon, "Looks like that could be your last breath mate".

"Yeah" Roger answered leaning on the wall and breathing deeply, "Think I'll nip out for a fag" and with that, departed.

The Bandroom was adorned with balloons, streamers strung across from wall to wall, tables and chairs arranged with paper tablecloths, half the floor-space cleared for a dance-floor and in the corner a disco, with lights, turntables, massive speakers, and a banner on the front which read "Hot Pepper" in big red lettering. Steve Pepper crouched on the floor behind the disco, flicking his way through a metal box full of records. A buffet was laid out, and reached half-way along one of the Bandroom walls, and at the end, a makeshift bar, presided over by Ron, who harboured a secret desire to be landlord of his own village pub, and run it as it should be run; no music, very little raucous laughter, just intelligent debate over fine ales and wine. He mused on this as Denise stumbled up to the table. Denise had been setting up Bandroom for New Year's Eve since early afternoon, along with a few other helpers who had all decided, to one degree or another to start the party early. She was not drunk, but clearly not sober and Ron was clearly unimpressed.

"Hiya Ron", Denise beamed, "Alright love?"

"Good evening Denise. Thank you for your assistance today" Ron answered in measured tone.

Denise leaned in, "Hey Ron, are you going to give us a blast of Tom tonight?"

Ron winced, remembering his all too public fall from grace.

"Would you like a drink Denise, perhaps a coke or a fruit juice?"

Denise straightened up, instinctively shook some strands of hair off her face, and in the most coherent tone she could manage replied,

"I will have a Malibu and coke please Ron"

"I'm sorry Denise, I don't do cocktails."

"Cock, what? Malibu and coke Ron" Denise was confused.

"I do not agree with cocktails, I believe they represent a downfall in our drinking habits and are the reason that binge-drinking in younger people, climate-change..."

"Alright Ron" Denise did not need or want a lecture, she just wanted a drink.

"I'll have a Malibu please."

Ron, with a sense of triumph poured the drink into a glass and handed it to Denise. She continued, "And, I think I'll have a coke please"

Ron grabbed the bottle of coke.

"Tell you what Ron, just put the coke in this glass, will save you on the washing up."

Ron thought for a second, and then did so.

"Thank you Denise, that is very thoughtful of you."

"No problem Ron, see you later" Denise sashayed onto the dance floor.

Any minute now, the small group of helpers would be joined by a Bandroom full of party-animals. It was going to be a good night. Midtown Band's New Years Eve party always was.

In Midtown High Street, beneath the frosty evening sky and the strings of lights straddling the road, Mary was just arriving at her own night out. Usually, she would have been at the Bandroom since mid-afternoon, arranging the buffet and getting the place ready for the party with the others, but this year she had made a decision to go to her office "do" instead. She liked the people she worked with, but never made any really close friends there. People never really know their colleagues, which is bizarre, as they are the people with whom more time is spent than anyone else, but you never completely know them. However, Mary had a reason to have taken extra time over her make up tonight, spending a little longer than usual in the bath and for buying that top she had denied herself all Christmas; Tom Twyford was going to be there. Mary had decided, almost, that if she was going to regain some happiness, some romance, some sense of her own self-worth she would make good on the flirting and closeness which had developed between her and Tom.

Her sister's cautionary words rang in her mind but she couldn't imagine there was anything to worry about with Tom; just a grasp at some fun and no talk of band.

Emily had driven Mary to where the party was happening, a new Greek restaurant that had opened in the town-centre called 'Pitta The Great'.

"Should be interesting" said Mary as they pulled up outside.

"You look nice Mum, hope he's worth it" Emily joked. Mary flashed a guilty look at Emily, and realising it was a joke, tried a hideously over-the-top attempt at a cover- up;

"Yes! Yes! Let's hope so! I might just come with you actually, shall I do that instead? Yeah, forget this lot, it's only work. Oh look there's Sandra…"

Mary waved out of the car-window to no-one Emily could see.

"…oh no! I've been seen now. Best go in then, will probably be rubbish, what do Greeks eat anyway? Feta cheese isn't it? And apparently they earn a lot. Do you know? OK, bye then, thanks for the lift love."

Mary bundled herself out of the car and quickly ran into the restaurant.

"Hmm" though Emily, "That was weird." She winced as the baby kicked. Her bump was pressed against the steering wheel and the kick not only sent discomfort through her abdomen, it also sent a reaction through her bladder. "Whoops, best get to the band-room" she thought urgently, slammed the gearstick into first and squealed off up the street, passing increasing numbers of Midtown residents as they were all arriving in town for respective New Year celebrations.

By the time Emily arrived, the party was in full swing. The Bandroom was heaving with party goers, dressed in their finery, chatting at tables, scouring the buffet and dancing to Chumbawumba. The lights had been turned down to enhance the disco lights, which flashed red, orange and green like broken traffic lights.

Carl Davis was stood near the door, pint glass in hand, watching his wife dance with anyone and everyone. Lawrence sidled up to him;

"Hello Carl, enjoying the party?"

"It's as expected" Carl was dour in response, "The forced jollity of New Year."

"I know what you mean, but what else would you be doing, if you weren't here?"

"I would be at home, on my own, watching a film." Carl responded.

Lawrence, desperate to salvage at least something from this pointless five minutes of his night, enquired, "Oh yeah? Which film would you watch?"

"Rosemary's Baby, Requiem for a Dream, something like that or maybe I'd finish looking at the colour supplement that came with today's paper. There's a very amusing article in it about bird-tables".

Lawrence regarded Carl warily for a moment and, with no further word, simply walked away.

Harry stood near the disco with Eric and Roger.

"Emily's just arrived mate!" Eric shouted over the music.

Harry had seen Emily come in and although glad to see her, couldn't bring himself to do anything more. "Yeah, I know" he said, more to himself than Eric.

Roger bellowed over the top, "Watch Ron's face now!" he said, beaming like a school boy. The disco suddenly stopped, "This one is for Mr Titley!" Steve announced on the microphone. The opening bars of 'It's Not Unusual' boomed out provoking a cheer followed by laughter. Terry spat out a sausage roll he was eating as he guffawed; and Ron, well Ron actually gave a little smile and rolled his eyes.

Meanwhile, at "Pitta The Great", the last remnants of food were being consumed. Mary had positioned herself next to Tom and the fact they'd spent almost the entire time talking only to each other and pretty much ignoring everyone else had not gone un-noticed. The starter, main course, and dessert came and went. The group of office-workers, all seated at one long table started to re-vamp the seating arrangements as the extroverts left the introverts to their conversation, apart from those introverts who were now on their 5th glass of wine and had migrated, albeit temporarily to the extrovert camp where Sandra's attempt at traditional Greek folk dancing, once kept to the embarrassment of that night, was now immediately visible to a million viewers on Facebook. And as the evening degenerated into more wine, more dancing and louder music, Mary and Tom slipped away. The few that saw them leave raised their eyebrows, the few that didn't were whispered to later, and then raised their eyebrows. There was a considerable amount of eyebrow-raising in "Pitta The Great" that night.

Tom had driven to the restaurant. As far as anyone knew he didn't drink, and as he steered his expensive car into his driveway on Swanick Avenue, Mary felt a tingle of nervous excitement. It seemed like one fluid movement as Tom parked, and was almost instantly opening the passenger door for Mary, who couldn't help wondering if her perception of time was being slightly affected by the gallon of wine she'd downed earlier. As Tom opened his front door and gracefully ushered Mary inside she found the house to be largely as she had imagined. It was, in every sense of the term, middle-class; the wood flooring and Persisk Gabbeh runner in the softly lit hall, which wafted with winter-spice pot-pourri, not a shoe to be seen strewn clumsily against the wall like at home. Tom closed the door and gently placed a hand on Mary's back; "Come on, let's go through to the lounge" he suggested, and she easily complied. The hand on her back felt firm, warm and thrilling.

The lounge was large, with a Hwam Vivaldi wood burner in the fire aperture, fumed oak wood flooring, two Next leather sofas, a low reclaimed-sleeper coffee table and the middle-class trinkets of candles, pebbles and lamps placed expertly around the room. The Christmas decorations were subtle; a delicate string of white stars in the window and a small silver desktop tree on the Laura Ashley dresser. The look of the room was contemporary but homely, minimal without being stark. Clean. Very, clean. Very clean indeed.

Mary wondered aloud after a minute of taking the room in; "Does anyone actually live here?" she enquired, half joking.

Tom brushed past to the Ipod dock and selected Morcheeba's Greatest Hits.

"Ha, yes, of course, it isn't always like this…"

Mary suspected that it was, and that anything out of place would be met with a severe reprimand.

"…I just had a chance to really clean the place up while the others are away."

"The others?" thought Mary. "Strange way to phrase it."

"Please sit down Mary, unless you want to go to another room?" Tom smiled, raising his eyebrows, not once but twice, in a sort of 'if you know what I mean' facial gesture. Then Tom looked at the ceiling and back at Mary. All the time, Tom smiled.

"Perhaps a drink, 'um, first?" Mary said while sitting down and trying to keep as much weight off the sofa as possible so as not to wrinkle it.

"Of course", said Tom. He crept slowly towards Mary, who started to feel, rather than throwing herself into Tom's arms, like recoiling a little. Tom stood a little too close for comfort as Mary was perching on the edge of the sofa, and she had to look straight up at him as the only thing to look at in front of her, was his crotch area. Their positions remained until Mary's neck started to hurt. "Umm, about that drink?" she enquired of the looming Tom, actually wondering whether it was a good idea to have any more drink.

"Of course" said Tom and moved away, allowing a thankful Mary to put her head down and stretch her neck muscles. This wasn't exactly how she had run through this in her mind. This was becoming less "romantic fantasy" and more "strange dream", reminiscent of having gone to the fridge at a late hour and thinking, "that piece of blue cheese looks good, I'll have that on a cracker"; only to have a night of Hitchcock-meets-David Lynch-style visual assaults involving your boss suddenly being your maths teacher at school and a small monkey living in your car who refers to you as Big Dave.

Mary's thoughts went back to the room as she scanned the perfect, Ideal Homes lounge. For the last year, Mary had lazily dreamed of what Tom's house would be like, and this fitted the dream perfectly; exactly; weirdly exactly. It was like she was in a picture, not a room at all, with a feeling like no one lived there at all, or if they did, had eerily departed; Swanick Avenue's Mary Celeste.

"OK" thought Mary, getting a little nervous, "Don't be stupid now, the booze is addling your brain!" She scanned the room quickly for pictures, photographs, anything to prove the existence of people. The dresser had two white photo frames; one had a picture of Tom smiling, the other had, thank God, a picture of the whole family together. Mary let out a breath.

For the last year Mary had built up an expectation, based on the excitement of office flirtation, the charming demeanour and flattery of a handsome stranger in town who found her attractive, the promise of illicit romance; and suddenly, now she was actually here, all she wanted was to be with Harry, listening to a disco with poor quality speakers playing Come On Eileen, and doing a knees-up with the others in the Bandroom.

She was amused by the thought, a little angry with herself for finding herself half-drunk in Tom's lounge, a little embarrassed but most of all relieved to have come to her senses. She smiled to herself then started to worry a little.

She would have to think of an excuse, get out of Tom's house and try and get to the Bandroom before twelve, to be there when the New Year came in, with Harry.

In total contrast to the contrived, yet sedate atmosphere of Tom's lounge, the Bandroom was, at this stage, a throbbing carousal narrated by Dexy's Midnight Runners at maximum volume. The dance floor was brimming as at least fifty wasted revellers, hands around each other's shoulders, all bellowed "Eileen, 'toora 'loora 'rye-aye!" whilst performing an impromptu can-can, led by Alex Davis who had by this time undone the top-two buttons of her blouse and was sporting an old Midtown Band cap that she'd managed to find in the corner, all contributing to a look which if one had to describe, could be summed up in one word; band-o-gram. Carl Davis looked on, still stood at the door, sipped his pint and said to a passing Eric, "Gawd knows how I'm going to get her home, she's absolutely legless".

To which Eric replied, glancing at the length of Alex's skirt and the visibility of her stocking-tops, "I wouldn't say that mate, I wouldn't say that…" before continuing his journey to the bar, only pausing to consider a point that he and the rest of the band had mused upon over the years, "Why the hell is *she* with Carl?", as he moved his way amongst the non-dancers who were all either clapping, banging their tables in time to the music, or simply drinking more.

Back in Swanick Avenue, Mary was beginning to sober-up, still trying to construct a plausible excuse upon which to base her imminent exit from Tom's house. But where was Tom? She suddenly realised that Morcheeba had now played at least a couple of numbers while he'd gone to get these drinks.

It was very quiet in the house; apart from the dinner party ambient dub sounds from the Ipod.

"Tom?" Mary called. No answer. "Everything alright?"

There was a pause.

"Yes!" came an urgent and slightly muffled reply. "I'll be there in a minute."

Mary's feet started tapping; she held her hands together anxiously and hummed the syncopated quavers from 'Journey Into Freedom' to herself. Her eyes again went round the room and fell on a neat stack of magazines on the coffee table. She glanced down and absent-mindedly picked up the top one. But it wasn't a magazine, it was, on closer inspection a corporate brochure, as was every other one in the pile.

It had a shining edifice of a white building on the front, against a perfectly unnatural blue sky with the words *Eine Kleine Floater GmbH* in white lettering where the clouds should be. Mary frowned, "That's the factory," she thought. "The factory they have been fighting against, the factory that will flatten the Bandroom!"

She opened the cover of the prospectus and a sheet of paper fell out. She picked it up. After all, if Tom saw some paper on the floor, he was quite likely to point an accusing finger at Mary, demand to know why his perfect room was now ruined and throw her into the street!

As she picked it up to replace it in the brochure, she could not help having a quick look. What harm could it do?

It was from Eine Kleine Floater GmbH, addressed personally to Tom, and it read:

'We (the client) Eine Kleine Floater GmbH hereby confirm a share capital to you (the investor) Mr Thomas Walter Algernon Twyford, of 49%. This share capital endows you with voting rights and consultation privileges regarding strategic management decision making....."

Mary's eyes grew wider as she read. Her breathing quickened. Her anger and disbelief intensified. All those times she'd confided in Tom, told him her worries for the future of the band, explained the community impact something like this could have; and all the time, he was in it up to his neck. Well, for 49% of his neck anyway. She stupidly started leafing through the pile of brochures and correspondence, she should have just ran out of there but her anger was now driving her curiosity. Her nerves tingled and her feet tapped as she saw the words she had been dreading, on a letter:

'Re: EKF GmbH Planning Strategy_doc.tt1976_Midtown Silver Band Rehearsal Building'

She grabbed the letter with both hands and frantically skimmed across the words until;

"...EKF GmbH extend their thanks to you Mr Twyford for your continued liaison over the planning strategy and agree on your course of action to continue with the application against local objection. We feel that your arguments for job creation and economic growth in the town will far outweigh the, as you put it, 'squawking of a few so called amateur musicians'...."

Mary was furious. "Amateur?" the word bounced off every surface in her mind like a pin-ball about to achieve high-score. "Amateur?"
 She screwed the letter up and threw it across the room, not caring this time that it spoiled the *Homes And Gardens* photo opportunity. How dare he! Of course the players were not paid; very few in the general brass band

population are, but "amateur" said in this way, as a disparaging remark and critique of their talent? This was too much for Mary. She saw how hard those players worked and what they sacrificed, and what it meant to them. She saw how her family had been ruled by this life but now, acutely, saw the passion of Harry. The focus, talent, determination and at the very utmost, professionalism he displayed in his pursuit of excellence within the band. She saw the younger players who had been given opportunities to develop a talent, exposed to a decent and honourable social circle, and she saw happy couples enjoying life, whose relationships had begun in band practice.

Mary would quite happily slap Tom across his smiling face. She had gone from being Madame Bovary to Madame La Guillotine.

As she stood up to leave, the soft ambience of the room was suddenly engulfed in light as the lounge door swung open, and as she prepared to give Tom a piece of her mind and make a sharp exit, her mouth helplessly fell open in disbelief. Tom, backlit by the harsh hall light which, compared with the subtle nuances of the lounge looked like it could have floodlit the Millennium Stadium, stood silhouetted in the doorway.

Mary's eye's strained slightly against the sudden illumination. She took some seconds to focus on the figure and when she did, immediately wished she hadn't.

Tom was clad entirely in a rubber wetsuit, a gasmask covering his head through which she could see his eyes blazing behind the goggles, a large plunger being brandished triumphantly aloft, and a bright orange ball-cock strapped to his mouth by what looked like tight elastic, where the gas-mask's respirator would normally be.

He was breathing heavily, a sadomasochistic Darth Vader; an asthmatic Marquis de Sade. Mary could practically hear his nostrils flaring as he sucked air in through them.

Rather than the rush of sexual excitement Tom had clearly been convinced would happen, Mary's most instinctive reaction was akin to one who had just witnessed a large, somewhat ungainly toad entering the room.

Tom shouted from inside the mask. The words were lost behind rubber and plastic but the eyes blazed.

Mary, still frozen to the spot, shouted as well, out of fear, "I can't hear you!"

Tom's eyes looked confused.

"You've got a gas mask on and a ball-cock strapped to your face you bloody lunatic!" She offered; following up with a point towards the plunger, "And whatever you were thinking of doing with that, you can forget right now. As far as I'm concerned you can shove it up your..." Mary stopped there, realising she needn't give him anymore ideas.

Tom unclasped the elastic from one side of the gas-mask, causing the ball-cock to fall out of his mouth and be left hanging just below his chin. He took a deep breath.

"I thought you would be willing" Tom said, like a wounded child told by his Mum that she didn't want to go down the 'The Black Hole' water slide at Butlin's Minehead.

"You said you were bored, you said you needed something else in your life"

"Yes, but not a frogman!" Mary retorted.

"You're all the same." Tom started to get angry, both out of embarrassment and annoyance; it had taken him ages and half a tub of Vaseline to get all the gear on.

"My wife was the same"

Mary noted the word 'was' with some trepidation.

"What's wrong with introducing some new things into a marriage? What's wrong with trying new things which may bring added pleasure into your life?"

Mary had now stopped being so scared, she felt she could outrun Tom in his current garb and really just wanted out of there. Also, he was beginning to be really quite whiney.

"Well, start slow Tom you know? Maybe a tub of ice-cream, a candle lit bath, a back rub, then work up to the more, um, extreme, um, things."

Tom looked confused again.

"You're holding a plunger man!" Mary stated, getting angry herself now.

"Yes" said Tom, and added possibly his most ill-advised sentence of the evening, "And you are not leaving until we do what we came here to do!"

Mary folded her arms, raised one eyebrow, "Unblock the toilet?"

It wasn't clear to Tom until some time later what had actually happened next. All he was aware of at the time was a sudden eye-watering stinging to his nose and taking a disorientated step forward. However, due to a combination of the gas-mask itself and the tears in his eyes, he couldn't see where he was going, resulting in one of his flippers slipping on the discarded letter Mary had thrown earlier. He lost his footing and lurched forward. Mary, arms still folded could only look on as Tom flailed forward heading for the coffee table. He let out a sort of pained roar as he pitched forth through the air; the bright orange ball-cock, which was now flapping around Tom's head on its elastic tether, whipped round and smashed one of the eyepieces; "Ahhhh! My eye, I'm blind!" he squealed. He hit the coffee table with some force, slid across it like a penguin belly down on the ice, and nose- dived onto the fumed oak floor, the ball-cock whipping around again and striking him on the back of the head with a sound that imitated two snooker-balls colliding. Not so much hoisted by his own petard, as being systematically beaten up by his own costume. Flapping like a flatfish, dumped on the beach and unable to right himself, Mary stepped over him and quietly shut the door behind her, noting that the plunger was nowhere to be seen and the screams had turned to groans accompanying the ambient bass throb. Her last thought as she opened the front door wasn't regret at grabbing Tom's ball-cock pulling it towards her and twanging it squarely into his face as he'd stood in the doorway, but was simply "Flippers? Why the flippers?" As Tom lay recovering on the floor, reflecting on the evening's events his thoughts were dominated by one all-too-painful lesson. One that had been taken on-board by many a South Wales lad for centuries: never, ever....*ever* threaten a Cefngoed girl.

As Mary burst into the band-room, the disco was throbbing with Frankie Valli belting out the lyrics, *"Oh what a night, late December back in sixty three..."* Mary concurred. Although, she suspected, that the song did not originally refer to near defilement with a plunger by a clearly deluded rubber fetishist with a ball-cock in his mouth. Mary had literally run all the way from one end of town to the other. She was very tired, very sweaty and very happy she had made it. Someone shouted, "It's ten seconds to go!" Everyone cheered, the music faded out and a group chant began, Mary looked for Harry and saw him with his arm round Terry Horner, who was ramming some cake in his mouth while spitting as much back out as he participated in the countdown.

"Ten!" they all shouted.

Mary squeezed in next to Harry and put her arm round his waist.

Harry looked at her with a big drunken smile, "Hiya love, good do?"

"Nine!"

Mary smiled. No resentment shown for not being there, no expectation, no demands on her, no rules about what she could and couldn't do like in some marriages, no fuss, no flippers.

"Eight!"

Mary realised that while considering the virtues of a life outside banding, she had not seen the life she had within it; and how good it was. Rather than being "ruled" by band, she had been invited to share in her husband's passion. How could she have not seen it? How many wives never actually see husbands who are out golfing all weekend, or following football teams around the country? Truly loving someone is accepting them for what they are. Mary had misjudged Harry's attitude as indifference. Now she realised it was an attitude that said, 'you get on with your life, and I'll always be here'. It was selfless rather than selfish, as she had once thought.

"Seven!"

"It was rubbish!" she shouted to Harry.

Harry planted a massive kiss on her cheek and then turned and did the same to Terry. "Gerroff!" Terry spat out some icing. Everyone laughed.

"Six!"

"Five!"

James had his arms round Delmie and Toby, clearly a little worse for wear.

"Four!"

"Three!"

Emily sat at a table. Laughing and holding her bump. Harry and Emily were still uneasy with each other, which Mary hated but could only hope that in time he would come round.

"Two!"

"One!"

Perhaps a new year would bring a new start for them all, as it always promises to do.

"Happy New Year!" the cheer went up. Hugs exchanged, kisses longed for and unwanted were given out, grasped at and quickly dealt with in equal measure. Fifteen of the band boys made a bee-line for Alex Davis, and Mary hugged Harry for all she was worth.

"May old acquaintance be forgot...."

Chapter 14

Labour and Love (Percy E. Fletcher)

The Brangwyn Hall in Swansea was like a haven for sound. Somewhere for it to frolic and flourish, somewhere it could be itself. The remnants of the previous band's earth-shattering final chord continued to playfully, yet rapaciously, devour every spare corner and cavity of the packed auditorium as Harry walked on stage, hands behind back, observing his players as they sat in their positions, and made final preparations, not only for a performance that could once again provide a passport to the Albert Hall, but to take home the cup; something that had always eluded them at the Welsh Regional Qualifiers, and an accolade everyone knew Harry coveted.

He glanced at the audience. Not an empty seat in the house. He allowed his eyes to take in the splendid ceiling in the cavernous room, and made his annual silent greeting to the naked natives peeking out at him from behind lush bright green foliage in the paintings of jungle scenes adorning the walls. Nothing had changed. Nothing ever changes. In the moments that Harry stood, awaiting the adjudicator's whistle signalling he was ready to hear and appraise their offering of this year's test-piece, a wave of confused feelings slowly made its way from his head to his stomach where it remained. He was used to a combination of nerves and excitement, but this was something else. Since this morning, it had seemed like the day was destined to be tinged with an air of malaise. Mary and Emily had intended to come along and listen to Midtown's performance, if for no other reason than to distract Emily from the discomfort she was feeling during what was now a very late stage of pregnancy. He had decided to drive them to Swansea, leaving James to travel on the coach with the band. However, when they were around 40 minutes from Swansea, Emily had indicated she wasn't feeling up to it, and Mary suggested that Harry drop them at Iestin and Megan's house in Cefngoed. Harry had made the final leg of the journey to the Brangwyn Hall on his own, allowing him to reflect upon the past twelve months. Last January now seemed like an eternity ago. The bright optimism of the chilly winter sky was replaced with a strangely indifferent mist, supplemented only by fine drizzle, and now Harry struggled to focus on the job in hand as the final few seconds ticked away before he would lead Midtown

Band in potentially their most crucial competitive performance of the year.

The band members sat, looking at Harry, and then looking past him. Each person dealing with the anticipation, the pressure, and the knowledge that the next fifteen minutes would represent the culmination of months of rehearsals, sectional practices, and personal effort at home to perfect tricky passages. No-one wanted to let down their fellow players, let Harry down, or indeed themselves. As they too awaited the whistle, the atmosphere seemed uneasy. Was it their imagination, or was Harry not himself today? His animated passion during rehearsals was usually juxtaposed with the personification of re-assurance during these unbelievably tense moments before a contest performance. Like a wise father, he would always exude an aurora of calm, encouraging expectation, communicated through a subtle grin at the apprehensive cornets who held the responsibility to deliver the critical first bars, and an almost imperceptible wink at those he knew would be the most nervous players. Yet today, as the players looked at him, Harry was looking through them, as though his mind was miles away. Even the clank of Terry Horner's bass hitting the floor as he adjusted his seat, cutting through the silence and knocking a stand over, was insufficient grounds for Harry to fire one of his trademark withering glances at Terry that could cut a man to the bone, and this concerned them even more. But the two most worried players were James and Eric. James could somehow sense that all was not as it should be. He knew his dad too well. Whether it was body language, the look in his dad's eyes, or even some inexplicable empathy, James too was now feeling very uneasy. Eric had been trying for twenty minutes to talk to Harry prior to going on stage, wondering why an announcement had been made requesting that "Harry Jones make his way to the main office in Reception". But Harry had been nowhere to be seen, until he walked on stage.

A shrill blast of a whistle from the adjudicator's "tent" in the middle of the audience suddenly brought everyone's thoughts into focus. The hall was now devoid of all but the quietest ambient noise, and both band and audience existed in a world dominated by tense anticipation. Harry's eyes moved to the score in front of him and back up at the band, with a strange look on his face. The look of a man lost in a daydream. He lifted his baton and the band knew it was time. Each player sat slightly straighter, took a breath, and prepared to play. Harry paused again. He turned round to look at the audience and then back to the band. The adjudicator, sat in his green, cloth covered crucible was waiting to hear how this, the penultimate band, whose identity was known to him only as "No.14", would compare with the previous bands in the competition. The only words he had written so far on the adjudication, "Nice opening note!", were his attempt at a joke in reference to the bang of metal on the stage when the stand had been knocked over. Adjudicators, like referees, were often hated and not renowned for their sense of humour, and in his own way he was trying to show a more positive side to his profession.

As Harry's baton fell, the straightest, roundest, most definite and solid bass note literally filled the hall. There is something very primal about bass, particularly the un-amplified combination of brass-tubing and human skill, which only works if the note is absolutely in tune, unwavering and expertly controlled. And as the hairs on the back of 1000 people's necks involuntarily stood up, and the rest of the band, like some massive church-organ uniformly hit their respective opening note at double-forte volume, accompanied by a rolling crash-cymbal, a surge of adrenalin shot right through everyone in the hall. Harry knew it was on the money. Everyone in the band felt the atmosphere change, all thoughts of fights on ferries, sly drinks before carnivals, practical jokes on Ron Titley, could not have been further from their minds at these moments. They were on stage for one reason only; to play the best they could. Harry had instilled this professionalism in them, and had introduced them to the feeling of being winners. They would always give a performance 100% effort, out of respect for the former, and a hunger for the latter. Every rehearsal for the last ten weeks came flooding back to the players, who could even now almost hear Harry's words "Impact, impact, impact!", as they delivered the opening bars, remembering Harry's sage advice "If we don't grab him during the first few bars we may as well go home!". Replacing the self-congratulatory reflections of his opening remark, one thought now filled the adjudicator's mind; "Hello…*now* I'm listening!"

It was almost three minutes into the piece when Harry leaned towards Mike on principal cornet, "From here you don't need me", he shouted, "Just get them through this Mike".

With Mike still blowing but looking completely confused, Harry ran across the stage to Paul on lead trombone, "Keep the control in the last thirty bars, and don't let them run away with it".

And with that, Harry left the stage pausing only to nod at a very worried looking James and point at his music as if urging him to continue. The nude women continued to peer out of the jungle on the paintings around the hall. The audience whispered to each other and, however confused and bemused, the band played on, with no General in command but with two splendid sergeants that Harry trusted to get them through this.

Harry could hear the band entering the fast final section of the opening movement has he ran through the corridors backstage, searching for the nearest way onto the car-park. Pointed semi-quavers seemed to accompany his footsteps as he ran down the stairs, out into the brisk air of the now dark evening, and over to where his car was. He frantically searched the pockets of his jacket. Nothing.

"Keys! Keys!" he actually shouted out loud at the Mondeo, before locating them in his trousers. "Come on Haz, hold it together."

He jumped into the car, started it up, and screeched towards the exit of the car-park, full of vehicles but devoid of people. As he turned onto the main road and headed towards Cefngoed two lorries flashed their headlights as they passed in the opposite direction.

"Lights. Idiot!" Harry berated himself as he flicked the light-switch and put his foot down.

He didn't particularly believe in premonitions but had felt that the last few days had been building up to something important. He had put it down to contest-nerves. There was a lot riding on this competition. Not only the chance of another crack at the London Finals, but the profile it would once again give to Midtown Band during the continuing struggle to keep the Bandroom. As he now continued driving through the increasing drizzle and darkness, Mary's quiet matter-of-fact words filled his mind. Knowing that Harry wouldn't have his mobile-phone with him in Swansea she had called the Brangwyn Hall and asked if they could make an announcement requesting that he come to the office and phone her. Her message had been brief; "Em's in a lot of pain, Iestin will drive us to Prince Charles hospital and have them check her over". It wasn't so much the content of Mary's words which chilled Harry to the bone; it was more the fact that on this day, of all days, she would think it serious enough to contact him in Swansea.

In the Brangwyn Hall the band continued playing. Their suspicions that all was not well now very much confirmed by Harry's unheard-of absence from the stage. Harry would never the leave the stage, ever. Not unless something was very wrong, yet at that moment, without their leader, their leader was still with them as the messages and lessons from rehearsals were now at the forefront of their thoughts;

"Keep it low Phil"

"Don't over-blow, second cornets"

"Think about your breathing Roger"

Each player heard and listened and the band played on. And this time, they played not to win the contest, but they played for Harry. They had been alerted to Harry's out-of-character mood during last night's practice when he had overheard James telling Roger that he'd got word from Charlotte in France that there was a job for him at Ferme d'eglise if he wanted it, starting in March. James, upon realising Harry was standing behind him, had turned and said, "I dunno dad, it would mean leaving the band, leaving home. It's a lot to think about".

Harry had angrily snapped back at him, "For goodness sake Jim, what are you thinking about the band for when this is something that could change your life?"

Those that had heard this would speak of it always. For James it was both encouraging yet disturbing. He knew his dad wanted the best for him, but he'd never known him to tell anyone not to think about the band!

As he sat on stage, Paul kept the trombones in check and in those last thirty bars, for the first time in three months, they played the syncopated quavers in perfect time. There are times in music when the players and their instruments become part of each other; when notes and harmonies connect in a fusion that splits a listener's very being in two, releasing an intensity that makes them forget themselves and shows them something much bigger. Such a moment had been achieved by the time the last bar arrived. Mike held his hand in the air and let the sound ring out around Swansea just a moment longer than usual. The rapturous applause from the audience, now on their feet, was a double-edged sword. It served to electrify the atmosphere in the auditorium, leaving the players in no-doubt that they had done Harry proud, but it also drowned out the final lingering triumphant chord which Harry had spent so long rehearsing, a chord which tonight made Mike's hand hover before finally signalling the band to stop, wanting to relish the orgy of sounds and frequencies saturating the hall in all but perfect harmony. It was the sound Harry had yearned for Midtown Silver Band to make, and even though he had made it possible, he was not there to hear it. As the adjudicator sipped a cup of coffee from the flask inside his tent, he paused to consider the opening sentence of his concluding paragraph, before writing "We have heard something very special today…"

"Come on, come on", Harry urged the traffic in front of him. He was now passing Cefngoed and heading for the hospital. He remembered the last time he had been desperate to reach this particular destination as he hammered his car onto the A465. Pleading for each mile to go quicker than the last, he shouted at the car and hit the steering wheel, "Come on!"

Following the phone-call, Harry had gone on stage numb. The opening bars had allowed him briefly to be a conductor again. He had intended to get the band through this test piece as best as he could and then he would go to Emily.

But, as he'd been standing there on stage something else had taken over. His soul led the way and he'd suddenly felt the pain of his little girl; the little girl who he had stayed up with all night when she was three with croup, coughing until she cried; the little girl who had ran to him when she fell off her bike, and the little girl who had been waiting for her dad to come back to her. He had felt her pain, the pain as she struggled to survive and to keep her baby alive inside her. For the first time in a very long time, Harry felt something bigger and more important than Midtown Band. He felt and heard his little girl calling him.

Harry skidded into the hospital car park hoping that Emily would have needed nothing more than a check-up, but fearing something else entirely, and after frantically searching for a parking space, just abandoned the car. Again, Harry chose the ambulance bay. The last time he had done that it was to see a life depart and he had missed saying goodbye. This time, he prayed, it would be different, and that pretty soon he would see a life begin. He was now determined that he would not miss it, and would assure Emily he would be a part of it. Bursting through the doors he bolted in through the Reception, slipped, and crashed to the floor. The Reception area was empty, and a solitary nurse stood behind the desk, concluding a telephone-call in a thick Cefngoed accent;

"Alright love, you just make your way to A & E and we'll see if someone can pull it out for you."

Harry, out of breath, wet from the rain, sweating and panicky got back on his feet and ran over to her, slipping and crashing to floor once again, in front of the desk. The nurse let out a little scream as a hand suddenly grasped at the top of the reception desk and Harry heaved himself up,

"Maternity?" he gasped.

"It's down that way, but you can only go in there if you are a parent or carer", the nurse stated, a little nervously.

"I had a call from my wife, my daughter Emily Jones was brought in… I don't know why, some kind of pain…I think she's dying…" Harry looked desperate as his voice cracked; surprising himself with his own feelings and the conclusions they were drawing.

The nurse looked at Harry, thought about the complex directions she'd need to give him, looked at the empty reception area and decided that she would single-handedly win back the reputation of the NHS right now.

"Right, come with me".

Harry didn't remember much of the journey from Reception to Maternity, only that corridors and signs seemed to fly by, doors seemed to "whoosh" open, and the nurse apparently had the strength of a horse as she simultaneously pushed the wheelchair, into which she'd thrust Harry, across the entire length of the ground floor whilst bringing him up to speed on how "next-door" kept parking their caravan across her driveway. Doors continued to fly open in front of them as she swiped her card at each one and pushed Harry through the multitude of corridors at a breakneck pace.

"Out of the way!" she barked at any nurse, orderly or patient in their way. Nurse Myfanwy "Muvvie" Haddock was now on a crusade to get this man to his daughter no matter what the consequences to her job, the fact that she had burst through the last door and given the senior registrar a bloody nose without noticing, and that behind her the hospital was littered with orderlies diving onto trolleys, nurses getting up off the floor and confused old people asking if the war had begun again, was testament to her single-mindedness. As they triumphantly burst into Maternity, Nurse Haddock quickly scanned the ward notes, Room 3, Emily Jones. She turned the wheelchair 45 degrees, and with a grunt accompanied by the squeaking of two soles struggling to gain purchase on the shiny floor, heaved Harry forward, and with a final almighty lunge, tipped the wheelchair up, sending a shocked and panic-stricken Harry hurtling out of it and crashing through the double-doors of Room 3.

"Good luck" she said, grinning and giving Harry the thumbs-up. Harry just had time to say thank you before the doors swung back closed, leaving Nurse Haddock to sigh, rub her hands together, and stride off confidently pushing the now empty wheelchair, satisfied that she'd managed to make the journey in two minutes flat, and trying to ignore the fact she'd abandoned her post and broken most of the hospital rules. She felt proud that she had helped a desperate man find his daughter and as she walked back into reception, she came across the senior registrar, sitting on the floor, with his head back pinching his bloody nose.

"What happened to you?" she asked, "Come on, let's get you cleaned up".

The senior registrar was explaining to Nurse Haddock that he didn't really know what had happened; he had just been smacked in the face by a lunatic running through the hospital. "Well, I hope they catch him", Nurse Haddock said purposefully.

In Room 3, Emily was lying on her hospital bed in agony, wires were attached to her stomach monitoring the baby and a drip was pulling at her arm. Mary was with her, offering soothing words, desperately trying to be strong, but feeling like her own insides were tearing apart. Harry had just a second to take it all in before Emily opened her eyes, unclenched her teeth and sobbed out, "Dad".

Mary turned round to see Harry standing at the door, panting. He had made it. He had done the whole journey in incredible time. He had left the band in Swansea, broken all road laws, broken many of the hospital laws and probably broken some kind of record to get to his family. But he had made it.

"Where have you been?" Mary shouted angrily. Harry threw his arms in the air as his moment of glory deflated in front of him. "The baby Harry, the baby", Harry ran to the other side of the bed and held Emily's arm.

"You all right love?" he asked, the months of strained communication trickling away like water down the plughole.

Mary looked completely dumbfounded, "Well of course she's not all right...what kind of..."

Emily clenched her teeth again and stifled a scream, as her round belly convulsed. The Midwife rushed out of the room shouting;

"She needs to breathe. Try and get her to breathe, slowly and calmly, in and out, while I go and get the doctor."

"You heard the woman Em", a shaking Mary shouted, "Now breath, come on...in...out...in"

But all Emily could do was to try and catch the odd breath between painful sobs.

Suddenly Harry knew exactly what to do.

"Em, Em…forget that in-and-out stuff. Remember those minims in the theme from Ski Sunday?" he began.

Mary looked at him in complete disbelief "What the hell are you going on about *that* for now? She can't breathe man! This isn't the right time or place to be remembering quavers and that!"

Harry, now sitting on the edge of the bed holding Emily's hand, looked up at Mary, over the top of his glasses, and in a tone that combined being totally calm and slightly annoyed, replied.

"Firstly, they're not quavers they're minims. And secondly, we practiced playing them, and correctly breathing between them. So now is *exactly* the right time and place to be remembering them. In fact, if ever there *was* a right time and place, this is it!"

And with that, Harry started humming the theme to Ski Sunday, as sure enough Emily started humming the 2nd Cornet minims and breathing between each one.

Mary, now instantly understanding what Harry was doing, seeing that it was working, and remembering why she totally loved this bloke, started joining in.

The doors suddenly opened again and the midwife came rushing back in. "The doctor's on his…", she was interrupted by the sight of Harry, Mary and Emily all humming the middle section of the Ski Sunday theme, Harry now stood at the front of the bed conducting, and bellowing the jazz-cornet solo.

"Excuse me", she said as she brushed Harry out of the way and studied the printout.

"Doctor's on his way Emily. Who are you?" she looked at Harry.

"I'm the grandad, well of the baby, I'm not Emily's grandad, I'm ..."

"Never mind, I don't need your life story, just put a gown and mask on and you can help push your daughter into theatre." The midwife started carrying out all manner of mechanical procedures on the bed as Harry pulled on the gown Mary handed to him. Harry held Emily's hand and watched as the line on the monitor dipped and an alarm started beeping.

Mary whispered panic in Harry's ear, "She's dying Harry, my little girl is dying".

Harry held Mary by the arms and looked into her tearful eyes. "You can cry later Mary. There are two lives here that need us now, three if you count me, because I can't do this on my own". Harry turned back to the midwife,

"Why are we going to theatre?"

"The baby is breech and its heart rate is dipping, Emily can't handle this pressure, her heart won't take it if we leave this any longer." The midwife finished adjusting Emily who was now lying on her side ready for the epidural. Harry looked at his daughter so tired and in so much pain. He leaned next to her but before he could speak Emily opened her eyes and whispered, "I'm sorry dad, I'm sorry for leaving band and everything, I should have told you why."

Harry shook his head and couldn't believe what Emily had just said. Now, of all moments, she was thinking about band, and then he realised. Emily wasn't thinking about the band, she was thinking of him and trying to make amends for the last months of distance between them brought on by Harry's complete lack of understanding, lack of sympathy and myopic view of what was important to him. He held Emily's hand, Mary held Harry, and for a moment there was peace, and then, in that tableau, Emily's heart stopped.

To Harry and Mary the next minute was a blur of doctors, midwives and nurses as the crash-team burst into the room. The noise was a mass of confused shouts and bleeps, monitors blinking and alarms ringing. In the middle of this maelstrom, Harry and Mary held each other and watched Emily for signs of life.

"Come on Emily, breathe, come on Emily, breathe" Harry sent this thought over and over to his daughter, willing her to come back.

"We have to try and save the baby." the midwife called to the doctor.

"Clear!" shouted the crash team.

"One more try guys and then we have to make the baby our priority." the doctor shouted over the noise.

"Come on Emily, breathe!" Harry thought.

"Come on Emily, breathe!" Mary screamed at her daughter.

"Clear!"

But before the crash team could give Emily the final jolt of electricity from the defibrillator paddles, Emily took a breath.

The heart monitor sprung back into life and suddenly all was calm again.

"Right, get her into theatre now!" The doctor grabbed the trolley and started out of the room. Harry went to follow and just caught a fainting Mary as she collapsed against him. He put her in the chair behind them and ran after Emily.

As they got into theatre, one of the nurses grabbed Harry "Put this over her mouth", he handed Harry a mask with gas coming through it.

"Me? Why me? I can hold her hand, I'm good at holding hands, let me do that."

But the nurse wasn't listening. Harry put the mask over Emily's mouth and nose, and stroked her hair.

Behind the small screen erected on Emily's chest the incisions had been made and the doctor reached into Emily's womb. Harry continued to stroke Emily's hair just as he had when she was a little girl. He felt numb. He couldn't contemplate the thought of life without Emily in it. Everything was starting to close in; the machinery bleeping, the lights, the staff bustling past him as if he were in the way. The sounds were getting more and more distant, fading away into his thoughts.

"Come on man", he thought to himself, "hold it together, hold it together",

Until suddenly a strange sense of peace, like a warm blanket being laid to rest over a shivering child, descended in the theatre. Harry first realised it was all over when he heard a baby cry. At first he wondered where it was coming from and then, as he looked around, a nurse was

handing him a tiny bundle, eyes wide open, skin too big for
its body, scrunched up in a blanket.

Harry held his grandson. For the first time in his life he
didn't think of anything else. For the first time in his life,
he felt he was where he should be.

It was an hour, and several coffees later that Harry, a now
recovered Mary, and a sleeping Emily were all back in
Room 3, baby peacefully lying in a cot next to the bed.
Mary giggled quietly as she looked at Harry sitting, arms
folded, beaming proudly at his daughter and grandson.
Harry saw Mary giggling and he too laughed, before
standing up and walking to the window. He couldn't help
remembering Eric's advice months ago about needing to
step-up and be there for Emily. He wished he had done it
earlier, but would be eternally grateful that he'd been there
in time to support her during the birth. It was a moment he
would always treasure. He also remembered the last time
he was standing in this hospital and wished that his mum
had been able to see her first great-grandchild. Although
not particularly religious, Harry couldn't help looking up at
the night sky when thinking about Gwladys. He stared out
into the dark night, partially illuminated by the brightly lit
car-park below, and saw a family getting into a car. He

hoped all had gone well for them, whatever their reason for being at the hospital. As he watched, he suddenly realised that he'd seen one of the children before.

"It's him", Harry whispered to himself, as he recognised the little boy, who he had first seen on the day of Gwladys's funeral, and who he was certain he'd seen throughout the year. "Who the Dickens is it?" he wondered out loud. This time, the boy didn't appear to be reminding Harry of anything. No cigarette-cards, no astronaut suit, no maps of the world, nothing that put Harry in mind of his pre-band childhood dreams and ambitions. As Harry watched, the boy climbed into the car, briefly pausing to look up at the window. A warm smile spread over his face as he spotted Harry at the upstairs window, and he waved goodbye. As Harry noticed his own hand raised in reciprocation, he wasn't thinking of the past at all, only the future. Harry was never to see that little boy again.

"What are you wittering on about over there?" Mary called to him from her chair, in response to Harry's vocalised thoughts about the little boy. Then she added, "...oi, Bampi...I'm talking to you."

Harry laughed. Mary had also been thinking about the events of the past year, she had been angry with Harry for some of it, but had nothing but respect for the way he'd taken control of the situation earlier in the ward. Her thoughts wandered to Tom Twyford, and she knew he may have had the chat, and the style, but he would never be Harry. Out of the two of them, she was extremely happy with her choice. Harry watched as the car reached the hospital car-park's exit and drove away. In the distance something else caught Harry's eye, just on the dark shadowy horizon. He couldn't be sure but it looked, for a brief second, like a coach with bright coloured lights flashing inside, and a pair of trousers billowing from one of the sun-roofs. He peered through the glass but the only thing that was completely clear to him was his reflection peering back.

A distinctive "whoosh" signalled the doors to Room 3 opening, and as Mary and Harry turned to look, a white-faced James appeared, lying on his stomach atop a hospital bed being pushed by Nurse Haddock, came thundering into the room.

"Told you I'd get you here didn't I!" Nurse Haddock shouted as a wobbly James clambered off the bed. And with a valedictory thumbs-up at them all, she gave an enormous audible heave, pulled the bed back through the doors, and commenced pushing it back to wherever she'd obtained it, while singing "I Am What I Am" at the top of her South Welsh voice.

"Jim!" Harry shouted, "You've got a nephew Butt!"

"Shhh", Mary put her finger over her lips, then pointed at the sleeping mother and baby.

"Jim?" Emily suddenly began stirring. "You alright?" she added dopily.

James rushed over to his sister. "Am I alright? What about you?

"Yeah, not too bad, just a bit groggy", Emily said, "I could murder a coffee though". She sat up.

"Listen Em", Mary began cautiously, "just say if you don't want to talk about it, but I'm just wondering if this is a moment that the father should know about, I mean you don't have to tell us who it is, but I just thought…"

"Don't worry Mam", Emily said, "he's not interested. As soon as he found out I was pregnant, he came up with some excuse not to get in touch again. And if that's what he's like then he doesn't deserve to be a father."

"Is it someone we know then?" asked Mary, concerned that he may cause trouble back in Midtown when he realised Emily was home with his baby.

"No, it was a lad I met when I went on that trip with the media-course last December. He was in college studying French Horn, and I really thought he liked me".

James shook his head angrily, "Didn't wanna know when he found out you were pregnant then? Loser."

Mary added, "Couldn't face his responsibilities. You don't need men like that Em."

Harry's face was a contortion of disbelief and disgust. He could hardly bring his mouth to form the words as he added, "He was…a *French Horn* player?"

James and Emily wheezed with laughter, and Emily suddenly remembered her stitches as they twinged.

"Anyway," Harry grinned, "why don't me and James go and get us all some coffee, and then we'll see what's happening, and when we can go home and that".

Emily grinned at her dad's use of the word "we". Once again in her life she felt that everything was alright when her dad was around. She also intended, at the earliest opportunity, to get back into the band. Not because she knew Harry would be pleased, but because she realised what she'd been missing for the past year, also now finally understanding why Harry had always been so keen to share banding with his children. And following events earlier that day she'd be forever grateful for sectional practices concentrating on breathing!

"He's going to score the winning try for Wales one day he is", Harry glanced over at his grandson.

"Only after he's been to band practice!" Emily added sternly, giving Harry a very earnest look indeed. Harry grinned.

As they walked down the corridor towards the coffee machine, James was explaining how he came to be there. Not knowing why Harry had walked off stage, he had phoned Iestin to see if Mary knew what was happening, and then he'd got Lloyd Wenby to drop him off the band coach outside the hospital on the way back to Midtown. Harry and James both smiled, thinking about their new respective titles "Bampi", and "Uncle". James was going to be the uncle who travelled the world bringing his nephew presents from every country. Harry was going to regale his grandson with tales of stolen bush-babies and how he was friends with Nick Childs. Suddenly, Emily's last comment about band practice reverberated in Harry's mind. How could he have forgotten what day it was?

"Hey," he turned to James, "you were there for the results. How did we get on?"

Upstairs in the geriatric ward, it was unclear what had woken the twenty dozing patients. Some thought it was a dream; others assumed it was a TV or radio blaring in one of the nearby wards. Most agreed on one thing however; the prolonged, ear-piercing ecstatic scream bouncing off the walls of every corridor and ward in the hospital was somewhat reminiscent of a brass band conductor who had just been told that his band had won 1st Prize at the Welsh Regional Qualifier contest.

Al Fine

Lightning Source UK Ltd.
Milton Keynes UK
UKOW041937091112

201974UK00001B/194/P